I And You, And Me And Her

BARRY GRILLS

Books by Barry Grills

Non Fiction:
Snowbird (Quarry Press)
Ironic (Quarry Press)
Falling Into You (Quarry Press)
A New Day Dawns (with Jim Brown) (Quarry Press)
Every Wolf's Howl (Freehand Books)

Fiction:
Roadkill (Fluid Grouse Enterprises)
I And You, And Me And Her (Fluid Grouse Enterprises)

I And You, And Me And Her

Barry Grills

FLUID
GROUSE
enterprises

Library and Archives Canada Cataloguing in Publication

Grills, Barry, 1948-, author

I And You, And Me And Her / Barry Grills

Cover Design and Art: Jennifer Rouse Barbeau

Author Photo: Liz Lott

ISBN:
978-1-7751389-1-4

For Jennie

*It is not finally a matter of skill, of knowledge, of intellect; of good luck or bad; but of choosing and learning to feel—*John Fowles

ONE

SOMETIMES, JAN, I want to tell the world how much I love you. It's harsh and painful and I want to get it out. I want the story, the weight of it, off my chest. The fact the love continues after all this time. I want to stop carrying that around all by myself. Then again, telling the world is one thing. Maybe it's *you* I believe should know. I want to write it down, I guess, as if this will help explain it. And after I've written it down, I want to give it to you as a story. My love for you as a story. What happened to us—what continues to happen—as a story. So that you understand it in the way that *I* understand it.

You and I give new meaning to the concept of star-crossed lovers. Talk about two tiny ships meeting in the middle of the deep, dark night, when we probably should have sailed right by one another, happily lost in the foggy depths of some conventional life where we couldn't touch the way we did.

Too late now for *that*, I guess.

We just go on, you and I, like nothing ever happened. But *everything* happened. For me, at least. *Everything*.

And here we are again, Jan, drawing close to seeing one another once more. As if life considers us its favorite joke. As if there's one more guffaw, one more chuckle to be extorted from the tragic coincidence you and I appear to be.

Or is love itself the chuckle, the guffaw? Do we make too much of love? Do we not see the humor in it because we're too close to the tragedy?

Maybe I should spill it all—the beans, the passion—on my way to answering these questions. Or maybe just to see how it all turns out. Just to understand the story in what has existed between you and me for so long.

Maybe someone will listen to my defense and find some justice in it . . . .

IT'S A LONG DRIVE from Ottawa to Temagami. I estimate it somewhere around four hundred and fifty kilometers. Canada's a big country; Ontario's a big province. And, related to this? Well, sometimes I'm a liar. I'm a liar as big as Ontario.

For instance, I've lied to Judy about how long it's going to take to reach our destination—Judy's a shortest-distance-between-two-points kind of woman. I told her driving from Ottawa to North Bay by way of Algonquin Park and Huntsville in Muskoka would only add twenty minutes to our journey—"a half hour tops," I said—when, in fact, it'll increase the drive by more than an hour. The liar and the *liee*, if you will, share a culpability, where dishonesty is concerned. I fear her wrath. I lie a little to avoid it. Shared culpability. That's marriage. One of its rules, its regulations. Or just preventing my cup of grief from running over. Where grief is concerned, I avoid overflow as much as I can.

I'd prefer never to lie. I don't like it—lying haunts me—even when the lie is relatively harmless. But I came to believe some time ago the world itself is often one big lie; no wonder each one of us gives in to fibbing, not only to save our skins, but to cling to our place in line in the crush of deluded optimists queuing up for their reward at society's mythological bosom.

With respect to me taking the long way through Algonquin Park this morning, Judy shares that culpability I've mentioned. Had I told her the truth about the extra driving time, she would have pressured me into taking the more direct route—Highway 17, Ontario's anemically-numbered leg of Highway 1, the Trans Canada—from Ottawa to North Bay. No argument the rest of the way to Temagami, of course. But Tommy taking the scenic route? I would have lost the debate plain and simple. I love the geography of the Park, the rocks, trees, lakes. Judy, not so much.

So you see what I'm saying about lying? You see what I'm saying about culpability?

I run a minor risk as it is, when I take the short way back home on Monday. If Judy notices how much faster our return is—and she might—she'll mention it. She'll feel at ease mentioning it too, much more than I will when I apologize for my miscalculation, for being so stupid. In the end I'll get out of the dog house by being grateful for the lesson I've learned. Sometimes Judy *likes* me hapless. She's mentioned, by times, she finds it rather charming. She's your sister, Jan. I guess you know her nearly as well as I do.

The trouble is it's worth it to me. No, more than that. Whenever I go through Algonquin Park, I *need* to go through Algonquin Park. I *need* the wilderness. When I imagine running away—from Judy, from my peculiar zeitgeist, from you—I see myself in the Yukon or somewhere near Yellowknife or Hay River. Or much closer to civilization, but not exactly *in* civilization. Algonquin Park maybe. Even Temagami, the area where we are headed. Because I think, if I get to live and work in the bush, my sadness will go away. I will rid myself of that little undercurrent of despair that lives inside my skin because I was so mistaken about what it means to take a gamble on happiness.

My thoughts on these matters preoccupy me, especially when I leave the city. I get too close to my past mistakes. I'm a man who frets. I anticipate events that may or may not happen, then gauge whether or not I will have to do penance for them *if* they happen. It's part of the rhythm of driving at this hour around dawn, just playing with life's various propositions until after we make the turn into Renfrew to connect with Highway 60, to pick up a coffee from Tim Horton's at the point where my seventy-five minute side trip actually begins, when there is no turning back.

No turning back. I like the finality in that phrase. I like the courage it implies. As I drive, I consider the nature of courage for a time, delighting in the concept of bravery behind finally making the plunge, never mind what particular plunge I have or do not have in mind. Courage is honesty. Even little lies are cowardice. Sometimes I dislike myself for seeming to be so frequently a coward.

At the Tim Horton's in Renfrew, Judy asks me to park instead of using the drive-through. "I'll get the coffees," she says. "I have to pee."

"Okay," I reply.

"Do you want anything else?"

"No thanks. Just coffee."

And I watch in the rearview mirror as she slips into today's parking lot dawn on her quest for our fix of caffeine. Judy still has one of those teardrop asses that appeal to guys so much. Some lout with a ball cap, ten years younger than her, actually turns as he passes her to watch her walk into the restaurant. I'll bet she noticed it too. I'll bet she appreciated it. Judy's beauty— I'm so used to it, I take her for granted. I barely see her any more. I barely see her at this moment as the glass, bricks, and modern mortar, plus the grayness of this early hour swallow her up like a mist. I find myself feeling cheated by modern life's inherent lack of adventure. You see, Jan, a side of me would prefer to hunt my coffee down with a club or a lance. Go ahead and laugh; at least I'm being honest. Fast food restaurants are painfully facile where a quest for adventure is concerned.

Still, people are congregating here. The parking lot is filling up. And there are large plumes of exhaust lined up at the drive-through around the side, although it's a relatively mild autumn day.

Judy returns. We depart Tim Horton's. I turn right onto Highway 60. *No turning back.*

I'm a persistent ruminator, I've learned. I chew on my thoughts like a cud—ideas, reflections, imaginings or doubts, rendering them finally into nutritionless pulp. If my thoughts were prayers, I think God would answer them just to shut me up, just to avoid hearing me go over them one more time. They're not prayers, though. No way they're prayers. They're just thoughts I contemplate to avoid more important considerations, to avoid addressing the chronic symptoms of some nearly permanent discomfort, the discomfort of *you*, for example.

There's something else too about endless reflection while I'm driving. To me, travel and geography represent the act of life itself. Braking, turning, accelerating, going back, spinning wheels, avoiding rough neighborhoods, dodging potholes. And more: trying to figure out where the hell I'm going and why, after all this time, I'm still going there. People, me included, tend to think they're immortal. Why else would they treat their lives as merely a war of attrition? Just more cowardice, you see. Of course, I'd never be caught *saying* so.

Now that we're cruising the highway again, I glance at Judy guiltily because I'm never really certain she can't read my mind. But she's found her own world of reflection too, reaching for her Tim Horton's coffee, a muddy double milk and double sugar, as engrossed with her private thoughts as I am with mine. Peripherally, I watch as she sips coffee out of the slash in the lid, noticing—or remembering from some other previous occasion?—the small wad of sugarless gum she sticks on the plastic, which she'll retrieve and re-chew—eschew?—after she consumes her beverage. Eyes on the highway, a cautious driver, I manage to watch too as she replaces the coffee in the cup holder nearby before she resumes filing her nails in silence. I am gently fascinated by the process of Judy's ablutions, even though they are now so familiar.

To me she looks more like a hairdresser at this moment than a nursing administrator. It's not just the nail file she maneuvers skillfully in her hands, but the near perfection of her make-up, her stylish dark hair, colored to fend off the grey, but still long and thick. And I still vaguely admire the lush, slim figure that has so far resisted the thickening most women of forty-six must endure. It strikes me then, in a bemused, faraway fashion, that I should desire this woman more often than I do. But "should" is a geographic term in the uneven, subjunctive landscape of a man's life—another reference to travelling, I guess—the notion I should have gone left when I ended up going right. There's a weedy familiarity sometimes obscuring the blooms in the garden of twenty years of marriage, but familiarity isn't the major issue. No, the major issue, Jan, is *you*. And it's never too early in the morning to allow myself to contemplate what awaits me in Temagami, the person who will be there when I arrive—the most significant reason my marriage seems long and strange to me, like it was supposed to happen to someone else but happened to me by mistake.

I glance at my watch. It's drawing close to eight a.m. We're already zipping over the flat terrain in the Bonchere Valley west of Renfrew, the town falling back in the distance behind us, evaporating back there into the rest of an October morning crouched on its own horizon, halfheartedly glum, not quite willing to be sunny, but not dedicated in any way to remaining stubbornly cloudy.

Judy and I enjoy things in common, an inevitable coherence after two decades of marriage, I suppose. For one thing, neither of us is a morning person. Both of us emerge from our respective states of slumber almost against our will. Not until later, when we are at work, when our morning quota of coffee has been consumed, do we begin to communicate with the world in a way it appreciates. Which is why, this morning, as we make our way towards a distant Temagami, Judy is not yet awake enough to feel oppressed by the silence I fall into whenever I'm behind the wheel. Soon, though, in less than an hour, I'll wager, she'll ask me why I'm not saying anything. She'll say, "*You're* being awfully quiet" or, if she's running low on her already small reservoir of patience, "You're not talking to me, Tommy." And the fact we're not talking will then become my fault. I'll say something about being sorry, mentioning I have things on my mind, before we gradually begin to converse. Then, shortly afterwards, the way married people do, we'll convince ourselves our halting conversation was actually spontaneous all along. Cowardice, I guess. Sometimes marriage itself is cowardly, depending on how much of yourself you feel you've lost and now seems irretrievable, how much of yourself you're too defeated to try to take back. Of course, I'd never be caught *saying* so.

I've explained to Judy in the past about the act of driving, though, and the silence that seems integral to covering vast distances behind the wheel. I've told her that driving, for me, is a solitary preoccupation. It gives a man time to think. In truth, driving for me is an opportunity to *brood*. I can call it reflection; I can call it rumination. But mostly it's the need to *brood*. And, considering where Judy and I are headed, considering *you're* going to be there when we arrive, *brood* is the operative word.

For nearly half of my life I've been keeping one big secret I haven't mentioned to a soul. This secret has evolved into a veil worn over the face of even my most innocuous moments in life, moments of casual explanation, for instance, when I would prefer to be silent. Or moments when I want to feel less sorry for a wide variety of sins I have never even committed, yet feel compelled to apologize for anyway. My secret makes me feel constantly that I'm living only half of my life, the half that is an endless explanation to Judy of what only half of me actually is. That's what we do, I guess, after twenty years of marriage, explain so much about our superficial selves—our likes and dislikes over food, hygiene, what domestic priority must be dealt with or delayed. The deeper half of our human duality, the part with the substance, says nothing, I think, for fear of offending society's sensibilities. That's my life in a nutshell— most of it superficial. I've told Judy so much about me over the past two decades, most of it shallow. But I haven't mentioned anything about the real reason for my need to brood. I haven't mentioned anything about what feels like my *grandest mistake*.

No, in twenty years of marriage, I haven't said a word about being in love with *you*.

"YOU MUST BE TIRED," JUDY SAYS as we wait for the light to change in downtown Eganville.

"Tired?"

"You came in late last night."

"Only eleven." The light turns green and I accelerate through the intersection, heading towards the long slope that will take me out of town. "Eleven's not late," I say.

"It is when you're getting up at five-thirty in the morning to go to Temagami."

"I s'pose."

"I thought you and David would pass on going out this week. In view of Temagami, I mean."

I shrug. "No real harm done. I'm feeling okay right now."

Judy pulls down the sun visor and glances at herself in the mirror positioned there. "Tonight will tell the tale," she says, removing a blemish from the corner of her eye with a now well-groomed fingernail.

"I guess so," I reply.

Then, satisfied by either my response or what she has seen in the mirror, she flips the visor back into place. It closes with a *thunk*.

I'VE KNOWN DAVID CRUICKSHANK longer than I've known Judy. He was the best man at our wedding. We go out most Thursday nights for a couple of drinks, just him and me, to talk, to laugh, to pretend we've actually figured out what's wrong with the world. During the summer, we team up for a week to go wilderness camping. He loves the woods like I do. David's probably my best friend, although I don't actually think about best and worst, where friendships are concerned. It's not the Olympics: it's not about awarding gold, silver or bronze. Where David is concerned, I just hang out with him on a regular basis and feel a better man for it afterwards. I come away from time I've spent with David, feeling faith. If not inspired, I am at least aware that I glimpsed in the distance some vague, but large inspiration about life I'm fairly convinced I need. I can't define this inspiration. But I like to think it's that famous, secret epiphany we all believe we deserve—our romantic fate in life, standing there in tender neon; I mean just enough neon to get our attention—the minute life's mundane elevator doors slide open, presenting us with our once in a lifetime opportunity to seize the moment like we've never seized a moment before.

I've known an epiphany like that, by the way. It makes me rare or fortunate, I guess. I *did* more or less seize the moment. But then, in the end, immediately afterwards, I *didn't*. Now I dream of another opportunity to seize the same moment once again, this time *permanently*.

"So what did you guys talk about?"

"Huh?"

"You and David. Last night. What's new in David's world?"

"Same old, same old," I reply. "He's working on a new book—we talked about how *that's* going. Politics, of course. The newspaper business, of course. The Senators, of course. He wants us to go to a game, Jude, sometime this season."

"Both of us?"

"Of course. He sends his regards, as always. He wanted to know what you've been up to. I mentioned the Temagami business, why we're going there this weekend, the mystery we uncovered."

"What did he think of that?"

"He wants a report when we get back."

"Yeah, I'll bet. Everything's fodder for a novel for David, isn't it?"

"Maybe," I reply. "But he was really quite interested, Jude. He thinks the whole Temagami thing is fascinating. He speculated that your mother was up to something. He says it might even be 'shocking.'"

"Yeah. Right. What did *you* say?"

"I told him I'd have to wait and see."

Judy says nothing to this. Fascinating isn't the word *she* would use to describe her dead mother these days. And as for our destination, no matter what happens over this elongated weekend, no matter what is ultimately decided, Temagami will remain a dirty word long into our respective futures. Judy won't forget. For a couple of months now, Temagami has been pissing her off. Judy doesn't forget the things that piss her off.

Maybe I shouldn't have told her about David's fascination with the mystery. Even after all this time, I'm not always entirely clear on Judy's criteria about what can be talked about and what cannot, where our personal business is concerned. I can still get into trouble by talking too much. It's not that Judy dislikes David or mistrusts his motives in some way. No, her major complaint about David is that he's a decade older than we are. She thinks he's stuck "back there" in time somehow—unkempt, rebellious, a bad influence on me in some way, like he's going to unwittingly push me off the tracks of conventional life, derailing my commitment to towing the company line, inadvertently mentoring me towards a life of deprivation and ruin, sensual, political, altruistic, or some combination of the three.

It hasn't happened in twenty years of marriage, but Judy remains vigilant, ever on her guard. I guess she supposes a man who's charmingly hapless can't help but be mere inches away from faltering on his obligations or recanting his practical convictions to chase some idealistic grail. At the very least, if David is fascinated by "the Temagami business," then I could be *too*. And *that* wouldn't do. These days, the wrench in Judy's life is Temagami. She's going to be out of sorts until Temagami is dealt with once and for all. Of course, I'd never be caught *saying* so.

I REMEMBER YOUR MOTHER'S FUNERAL well, Jan. What affected me most was how empty of emotion it was. Everything took place with impeccable precision—the wake, the funeral, the burial in the Smythe plot. There was an army of black veils and hats. It didn't rain. No one said something they shouldn't have said. No one muffed a line. The ceremony went off without flaw. But no one wept. Your sister didn't weep. You didn't weep. Judy claimed to be in mourning for a couple of weeks afterwards but, except for the occasional crabby period, I didn't see any real evidence of sadness, and she didn't seem to want to talk about her loss. Everyone was convinced Gladys had led a wonderful life. And while she had fallen short of spending eighty years in this world—she was seventy-nine—she died peacefully in her sleep without so much as a symptom of illness. No protracted ailment. No violence. No apparent pain. Her kind of worry-free death seemed appropriate somehow, an elderly woman told me on the first night of the wake. Fixing me with a stern gaze, as if I wore an armband of heresy around the sleeve of my dark blue suit, she maintained Gladys's generosity to various charities during her life was enough to ensure a comfortable death. More or less because this was an argument I couldn't win, I mumbled something about Gladys's peaceful death being richly deserved. But I felt dishonest about it later. And a little mean. Somehow, not just lying, but mocking the truth.

Still, I remained dismayed that Gladys's daughters didn't weep. When our parents die after reaching an appropriate age, do we feel only relief? I wondered. I would like to ask you about death and relief, Jan. I couldn't ask Judy—Judy's a little like her mother when she is asked that kind of question—she makes up what she believes is a conventionally acceptable answer. But I'd like to ask *you* why you didn't cry at your mother's funeral. Because I believe you would answer me truthfully. You might even tell me about your feelings. Maybe answering my question would stimulate you finally to weep. I would want to hold you then. I would feel my need to hold you conniving breathlessly along my skin; sorry, but love always has a little sex in it, even when the tenderness is real. I know, eventually, you would believe in my tenderness. You would know it was the truth. In a state of mourning, perhaps, you and I would come to believe how necessary we are to one another.

THINKING ABOUT FUNERALS and mourning and love, I just keep driving. I've travelled this route a number of times before, to camp in the wilderness in Algonquin Park. I've even camped north of North Bay a couple of times, but I haven't gone as far as Temagami. Still, when it comes to Algonquin, I'm familiar enough with the route; I could almost drive it by rote—down the Queensway from Kanata, around the sprawling bend where Four-Seventeen reinvents itself into Highway 17, the left we've taken into Renfrew, then the right onto Highway 60, continuing through the Bonchere Valley, Eganville, Golden Lake, Barry's Bay, Whitney, and finally Algonquin Park. Yes, this area is my familiar stomping grounds, camping for the week with David or, by times, celebrating a weekend on my own, alone with my thoughts and some vague need to write some kind of restless epistle about the hope attached in a persistent way to how I feel about *you*. I like the wilderness. I sense that it likes *me*. I don't feel I keep you a secret in the woods in quite the same, propitious way I keep you a secret everywhere else. And being less secretive, less cowardly, I become more creative, like there's something important inside of me that should one day show itself, that one day should be *known*.

The wilderness and camping are definitely *not* pastimes Judy and I have in common. To allow her her due, she gave camping a try in the first five years of our marriage—car camping mostly, suburbia in the woods, gravel crunching under the wheels of heavy traffic, semi-inebriated laughter from around someone's campfire, the sound of a crying child wafting through the silence normally escorting midnight in the general direction of dawn, dealing with too many neighbors as confused as we were about the nature of displaced neighborhoods and obligatory tolerance, all of these requirements transported prefab from the suburbs to the woods.

Judy tried *wilderness* camping once as well, but she didn't like it much—a family of raccoons who noisily raided our campsite every other night and her incessant worry about the danger of bears, although I've never had any bears show themselves over the years. And then there was the box out in the woods, the bathroom facility she despised, the way she felt exposed to the world. These and other fears and discomforts eventually dissuaded her from wilderness camping forever.

I blame her decision mostly on the toilet amenities. There are two ways to look at the box when you're sitting out there in the woods, having your morning shit. You can gaze up into the sky and feel an extraordinary sense of freedom, or you can sit there terrified that you're exposed to passersby or bears, missing, for reasons of safety and familiarity—actually longing for, I'm afraid—the subtly-splashed, tinted tiles of your modern suburban bathroom. I tend towards the former, feeling by times a tremendous sense of personal freedom while I'm sitting on the box. Judy tended toward the latter because bowel movements in the great outdoors aren't civilized to her. Fair enough, I said. Since then, she and I have learned to live with our differing views about residing in the cultural vacuum I believe is life in the suburbs and vacationing in the wilderness where I feel so at home. And I don't have to car camp any longer. I don't have to trade my crowded urban suburbia for another one served up in the woods.

Since Judy's admission that she doesn't like camping, we've developed a workable compromise over our vacations. Judy enjoys resorts and beaches. In the winter we go south for a week or two—Mexico, Cuba, Barbados, whatever we can best afford—I don't like Florida, there I draw the line. In summer, we find a lodge somewhere, some hotel nestled at the *edge of* rather than *in* the woods. I get one week in the wilderness of Algonquin Park, usually with David who, after a couple of divorces, has been unencumbered for a number of years by any real need to compromise at vacation time. The week I go camping with David is the one Judy uses to visit friends and family in Toronto.

I suspect, when Judy and I retire—she's six months older than me, and we'll pack in our working careers at relatively the same time—if I still crave the great outdoors, she'll suggest a large recreational vehicle to travel Canada's many long highways in style, carrying all the modern conveniences in a large barge that scrapes its way under the tree branches, our home away from home, cell phone shrieking shrilly, e-mails arriving on time, a DVD player to view the latest hot release. Maybe, by then, I'll like this idea too. Hard to say right now.

Sixty-five years of age, and the retirement that comes with it, is still twenty years away. Judy handles the RRSPs. I leave our retirement in her capable hands. I don't really care right now what we'll be doing then. My one activity connected to retirement planning is the speed with which I mute the investment firm advertisements, on the rare occasions I watch television, resenting, the way I do, their not so subliminal promotion of greed, self-interest and mind-numbing security as human virtues. "David's influence," Judy sniffs when she notices me muting the sound in this way. Maybe so. But, in my opinion, investment firms thrive by creating fear.

Funny, as I drive the remainder of the Bonchere Valley, how this setting can sadden me. Sometimes, as I drive through it, I imagine the valley as the tail of some scenic comet, dragged from place to place by a sightseer's spatial imagination, in a state of perpetual, but hopeless optimism that never truly represented fact. It's as if the anticipated success of the valley, its potential when it was first settled by farmers and merchants, was based essentially on myth. I notice this each time I take this route towards Algonquin Park. And today, it being early October, even the spectacle of changing and falling leaves can't ameliorate a sense of sad and tired resignation this valley inspires in me. Like this valley and I are similar to one another, sharing the same mistakes, the same unrelenting regret.

I suppose even a beautiful memory is just a memory in the end. It's way back there, stuck in history, permanently uncompromised, a scab to be picked at, someone's misdirected hope or lack of judgment. In this sense, I am the Bonchere Valley; the Bonchere Valley is me. Even on a warm autumn day, both of us give off some kind of barely discernible sense of tragedy because, in ways neither of us wish to actually define, we did not become what we were supposed to become. We did not ultimately do what we probably should have done. We failed in many ways, this valley and me, to become all that we could be.

Judy and I expect to be away for the better part of four days and three nights. We've taken Friday and Monday off from our respective jobs at Ottawa Civic Hospital and the Ottawa Citizen, to give us time to examine what awaits us in Temagami, to even enjoy ourselves if the opportunity presents itself, if we can find a solution to the Temagami dilemma in time to decide to relax. In terms of my rusting Maxima, it *is* a long drive—Ottawa all the way to the woods around Temagami. That being the case, it wouldn't be a bad thing to enjoy ourselves a little, making lemonade out of the apparent lemon this unseen lodge near Temagami appears to be.

Especially after the process surrounding a trip like this, the rituals we develop over the years. Judy thinks I'm gifted when it comes to packing a car. So it was this morning that she carried out her share of the numerous bits and pieces of our luggage, the grocery bags of food stuffs and the mounds of bedding because the nights will probably be chilly, and set them on the asphalt by the trunk of the car. While she was checking to see the stove was turned off, nothing was crawling up the shower curtain or the water heater hadn't sprung a leak, I worked my loading magic in our Kanata driveway, laboring away in the darkness, feeling like it was still the middle of the night, squeezing six tons of baggage into ten square feet of car trunk and childless back seat. It's a dubious gift, by the way, being able to pack a car. When the subject of inspired car packing comes up at your average party, it doesn't draw a crowd. I don't see why Judy mentions my packing as often as she does. After all, I have *other* talents. Of course I'd never be caught *saying* so.

"JESUS," JUDY IS SAYING for the umpteenth time. "Temagami, for God's sake."

"I know."

"I mean *what* was she *thinking*, Tommy? What could she possibly have intended?"

"I don't think we'll ever know," I reply with an irony I don't intend.

"Obviously not," Judy snaps, peeved at the apparent slight to her mother and her mother's death.

"Sorry," I say then. "I wasn't trying to be funny."

Mollified by my apology, my wife nonetheless falls silent again.

By then we're approaching Whitney on the eastern edge of Algonquin Park. We're now driving through a moody series of sun showers falling to earth in crabby outbursts. I watch the cycle of these rants. I view a buildup of clouds just above the windshield tint, then watch the approach of the falling rain, which takes so long to arrive the sun breaks through again by the time the drops collide with the glass. Watching these exploding droplets against a sunny backdrop of Algonquin area autumn leaves improves my mood. I stop brooding for a time to enjoy the growing ecstasy I'm beginning to anticipate in the potential of the rest of this day, when we at last reach our destination.

I know what's bugging Judy. She doesn't like it when she doesn't understand what motivates people close to her. Over the years she's narrowed her definition of how people should behave. When they do something unexpected, something outside her definition, it puzzles her deeply, much more so, for instance, than it would mystify *me*. Her dismay over the behavior of your mother in the decade before her death is now so deep, she is resentful that we have to make this trip. Judy doesn't want to accept that Gladys might have been crazier at times than we ever realized. Now dead for more than six months, your mother continues to control, at least briefly, where Judy is going and why she is going there, not to mention how much money could be lost or gained after this early weekend Friday in an otherwise innocent October runs its course. Why, Judy wants to know, would her mother end up owning some rundown lodge somewhere on a lake in the Temagami area? And why, for more than a decade, did she purposely keep the property secret from her children?

I'm not as surprised as Judy is about the mysterious lodge or the secrecy it represents. As far as I'm concerned, your family has always been secretive. A lot of families are, my own as well, I guess, although to a much lesser extent. For many, it's preferable keeping issues undisclosed than confronting them when they rear their ugly heads. If you wear thick-soled enough shoes, you can tread relatively unscathed over the lumpy issues you've swept under the carpet to avoid dealing with them in some way. I believe my family was more direct than the Smythes and in the end everyone knew where everyone stood. We've got nothing left to argue about, thanks to the curative passage of time. So it's strange, in my dealings with your family, how I've adopted *your* family's approach to being secretive, as a means to resist a satisfactory resolution to any troublesome issue. As if *your* family's approach to tribulation has overpowered what I learned dealing with my *own* family. But who's right and who's wrong? Who among us then is actually the outlaw? Is it me or is it them? Have *I* become the stranger or is it you Smythes?

Perhaps it's merely a matter of personalities. I think you need to be obstinate to prefer the complexity of keeping secrets over resolving conflict. As far as I'm concerned, Gladys Pinkster-Smythe was the manipulative mastermind behind her family's habit of keeping important matters and basic human conflicts hidden away in the closet. She faked most of society's conventionally sentimental occasions in a conventionally appropriate way. She was polite rather than caring. She favored platitudes and homilies to any kind of actual honesty. She preferred consideration to empathy, manners to real understanding. Everyone was expected to be well-behaved mostly; whether good behavior was warranted or not rarely entered the equation. In my more honest moments, I never forget I didn't like your mother much. She made certain I didn't fit in well with her concept of her family. After all, perhaps Judy could have done much better in marriage; there were times Gladys made me feel this way.

Now that the old lady is dead, I only have to contemplate her in the context of her daughter's surprise that she would keep secret a lodge she purchased near Temagami. I can keep to myself my conclusion that, at some point, secrecy becomes such a habit the need for secrecy itself develops into the most profound secret of all.

Maybe I don't have the right to be so critical. Maybe I'm just a hypocrite. While it's true I have only one secret, there's no denying it's a fucking lulu. That single secret is you. But I keep it so well concealed, I manage to keep it hidden even from *you*. I *think* so, anyway. I *hope* so, anyway.

JUDY'S BEEN FEELING HER DISMAY about the mysterious, small resort in Temagami for the better part of three months, ever since the reading of the will. Over time, knowing we would have to travel some distance eventually to see the place, Judy's been transforming our destination into a monumental annoyance, just another in life's long list of aggravating excuses for angst that will occasionally block her path in life to the end. Life, for Judy, must be dealt with therapeutically. Judy's studied psychology. Most of life's developments only reinforce her belief in the need for analysis, hers or someone else's, or some combination of the two.

"I mean," she's saying now, as we enter Whitney and prepare to leave again just as quickly, "what are we supposed to *do* with the goddamn thing?"

"The lodge, you mean."

"Yes, the lodge. What do you do with a lodge located somewhere out in the woods in the middle of fucking nowhere?"

"Keep an open mind," I offer, my eyes glued to the explosive windshield display of a new sun shower, my right hand turning the windshield wipers on.

"Well, you heard the lawyer, Tommy. He says it's not in the best shape."

"Do we know how he knows what kind of shape it's in? I mean, when he said it was rough, I wondered how he knew."

"He's a lawyer. It's his business to know."

"Or his business to *sound* like he knows. Who can figure out what a *Toronto* lawyer thinks is rough?"

"Yeah, yeah," says Judy. "Always the critic. Has anyone ever told you you mountain men are snobs?"

THE TROUBLE IS, PREOCCUPIED the way I am in anticipation of *you*, I haven't been very interested during this long Friday morning drive about what kind of shape my mother-in-law's secret resort is in. I've been pleasantly-unpleasantly brooding the way I always do when I am thinking of you. I've been considering once again the cosmic joke inside the question I've asked myself for years: What am I doing with Judy, when I should be with you? And why don't you—the woman I'm convinced I love in a much more complete fashion than I love Judy—realize in some wondrous way that I ask myself this question so often in barbed and bloody vowels, in brutal equivocation? Why can't you recognize it, see it for yourself? Am I so capable at hiding love from you? Or is it that you don't believe love is *everything*, the way, God help my soul, *I* believe it is? Do you even realize *everything* is my personal definition of romantic love, a definition I can't outgrow, no matter how hard I try? Do you have any idea you inspired this definition virtually from the moment I met you? Do you notice all this in me? Does it embarrass you, if you do? Or am I just like Judy's version of my best friend, David Cruickshank, stuck somewhere in the past with a few precious moments in time, unable to limp towards the harsh reality of the present, an inertia inspired by my resistance to the way a dull-witted society transforms love—and everything else it encounters or invents—into another boring myth?

Ah, that's the thing about love, I guess. Failed love, anyway. One wants to redefine it into a larger metaphor for life, comparing it to pentameterless poetry or ambulances with engine failure or gods with a cruel sense of irony, accusing love of being another spiteful little joke of hope and futility from which life seems so often crafted. Sometimes, when thinking about you makes me bleak, I cannot escape the conclusion that most of us are two people in one, us and our shadows, inextricably bound, our three-dimensional selves only slightly favored by the gods, our other selves, our shadow sides, dragged along in our wakes like chains, perpetual, clanking victims of metaphysical perfidy.

"What if the lodge *is* in good shape?" Judy is asking me

now.

She's reaching back to tie her long, dark hair into a ponytail. Somehow, in a way I could never explain, her question seems more devious because she's working with her hair. Like I'm being duped into the commonplace, away from the hidden importance of her query, by the distraction of her ablutions. I suspect I've been gently ambushed before by this method of delicate interrogation; Judy can be cagey.

"I don't know," I say.

"C'mon, Tommy. What if the resort has potential?"

"Well, if there's potential in it, Greg will want to sell it. Right?"

Greg, your husband, our brother-in-law, is in real estate. Somehow, perhaps because I'm a journalist of an extremely liberal stripe, his dedication to his occupation of selling someone *else's* hard work has transformed him into cliché in my mind. I can't help it. I like him at times, I guess, but we don't have much in common. He can talk about bad service in quality restaurants for hours, about his most recent purchase from some big box store somewhere, and about what is or is *not* a good investment seemingly endlessly. Fittingly, his best friend is a stock broker, not a reformed newspaperman turned novelist like *my* best friend. No, *his* best friend is another one of those people who buys and sells someone else's vision. And your husband, in my opinion, is focused on amassing wealth in a way I can never be.

His opportunism, in itself, is not an insurmountable obstacle to our potential friendship, when you consider he's my brother-in-law. I mean, my disapproval isn't entirely *personal*. I try to keep separate from my love for you, his wife, the larger issues at the base of my disapproval. I prefer that my dislike is based on a revulsion I feel over excessive greed and material gain in the larger sense. I am repelled that material self-interest has become the accepted paradigm in our social convention at this particular time in history. Greg's greed, as a perfect example of our times, is what makes it difficult for us to be friends. Because our current cultural period considers self-interest a virtue, Greg has "right" on his side and I dare not say a word in opposition. Any objection I could muster would emerge from my lips as some pathetic, idealistic squeak. No one listens to a rebel these days unless money can be made from it.

That's the thing about living in our society. In the game of cultural ideals, by the end of the ninth inning, it's always society ten, yours truly, Tom McNamara no score. Society comes out of the dugout with all its human components braided together like rope. My own small voice is one-pound test fishing line. In the end, I'm wrong only because I'm tiny, a mere individual. Conventional society is right because its vast majority of *tinies* have adhered in large enough numbers to make it strong and relentless, to give it majority rule.

"Of course we're going to want to sell it."

"Sorry, Judy," I say. "What'd you say?"

"I said, 'Of course we're going to want to sell it.'"

"Yeah. I know."

"You need a new car. Maybe we could pay off our

mortgage. I'm suggesting we could make good use of the money. We'll want to sell the lodge for sure. I just hope it's not so dilapidated we have to *give* it away."

I do not comment, distracted by an unexpected twinge of anticipated excitement. We've entered Algonquin Park now and our arrival at this wilderness explosion of autumn color, combined with a whimsical notion that Gladys' resort will be beautiful and welcoming and we will all want to keep it invigorates me. My imagination taxies down an unexpected runway and soon begins to soar. What if *you* want to keep the resort? What if *you* share my whimsy that a wilderness lodge, owned free and clear, could represent an opportunity to change direction in life? What would happen then? It's an unlikely scenario, I know. But it's enjoyable imagining it, you and me together, rejecting a world that places mere money too near the top of the list of our various human needs. You and me resisting convention together, sharing the courage of our convictions. The *end* of cowardice.

IT WAS THE SMYTHE FAMILY LAWYER who stressed that the lodge in Temagami is owned free and clear. This bonus was discussed a number of times when we gathered to figure out the terms of the inheritance. To me, the news there was no mortgage seemed somehow part of the ignominious quality of the day, like debt has become conventional and mortgage-free resorts reflect some kind of shocking infamy, a rebellion against accepted tastes or mores.

Greg was there that day. We *all* were. "Taxes paid up?" he

asked.

The lawyer, an obese, balding man named Tremblay, with an oily scalp and red, capillaried cheeks, nodded soberly.

"Well, that's something, I guess," Judy muttered.

"Yes," said the lawyer.

Everyone seemed in a state of mild shock that afternoon. Conversation was halting and gruff. For me, the state of shock pervading the room wasn't legitimate—I don't care enough about property and what is to be or not be inherited. I admit only that I *wanted* to care at this moment, but I was forced to realize I was only out in sympathy, for Judy, for Greg, for you.

We were seated that afternoon in various chairs and a love seat in what your mother used to call her sitting room, at the western end of the large house in Rosedale. This place had intimidated me ritually over the many years of my marriage to Judy, but I felt recovered from this intimidation that day, now that someone else would soon own the place. But oh the long, bemused silences that day. Even out only in sympathy, I could feel the oppression in this room: the white stucco walls moving in sinister fashion toward us—I swear it felt this way—everyone trying to deal with the news that the Smythe inheritance would be only a fraction of what some among us had anticipated.

Judy was angry, you'll recall. So was Greg. He kept suggesting that his late mother-in-law had erred grievously over the years when she hadn't come to him for financial advice.

"Mother would never have done that," you said gently. "She was proud."

"Well, she *should* have," snapped Judy.

It was now clear to everyone that the home in Rosedale was deeply mortgaged. Although left in comfortable circumstances by your father years before, a man I had never known, we discovered Gladys Pinkster-Smythe had repeatedly borrowed against the equity of the home to live the kind of lifestyle to which she had become accustomed. A housekeeper and maid, a few favorite charities, extravagant clothing, lavish gardening and renovation projects, all of these preoccupations over the years had eaten up much of the equity in the house. And then there was the resort property she had apparently purchased in northern Ontario, to everyone's shock and dismay.

As I said, I don't think about inheritances much. To people like me, they're more important to those who leave their property behind, less so to the inheritor. I tend to prefer everyone live forever. I even feel enough spite over the issue to imagine delightedly the economic crisis immortality would unleash on humankind: we'd have to share our wealth without requiring its recipients to outlive us in some way. I've never respected human beings who seek to control their families from beyond the grave. Bottom line to me? Let's all just live as long as we can and never mind who gets what when we eventually die.

But Judy and Greg were angry that day when they learned net proceeds from the sale of the house might leave less than half a million dollars—and there were still some outstanding bills.

"None to do with the property in Temagami, though?" Greg asked, needing still more confirmation, restraining himself, already switching focus in fact from the lack of opportunity reflected by this property in Rosedale to the possibilities that might exist in a sale of property in the back woods of Temagami.

"None," replied Tremblay. "Your mother-in-law treated the northern property as a priority. There are no outstanding obligations."

Which is all part of the mystery now over what awaits us when we arrive several hours from now. Not only was ownership of this property a secret, but it never occurred to Gladys, even towards the end of her life, to mortgage it with the same recklessness with which she mortgaged her Toronto home. I wonder about this sometimes, although I wonder privately. What made the property in Temagami so much more important to her than her home in Rosedale? Why was it never mentioned to her children? I like to imagine—because I am prone to these kinds of fancies—that there is another secret to be uncovered which might help it all make sense. I would personally delight in uncovering over the next few days some spicy little network of reasons for Gladys's duplicity. I would love to learn your mother wasn't so righteous after all, that there is a skeleton in her closet that will put things to rights between us now that she is dead.

Of course, I'd never be caught *saying* so.

TRAFFIC IN ALGONQUIN PARK IS LIGHT. The few passing cars

there move along the highway with unusual patience, the kind of polite calm that will evaporate quickly when the autumn color weekend traffic arrives later today. The people up from Toronto will bring with them their ritual need for hurry and maintain its urgency until mid-afternoon Sunday. Judy and I will escape most of this. It's only Friday morning, still relatively early in the day, and we are making good time.

But my stomach has begun to grumble. I feel the need for a break from the driving. "You getting hungry?" I ask.

"What time is it?"

We both glance at our watches. Barely eleven.

"Kind of early for lunch," Judy says.

"I'm starved."

Judy has made tuna salad sandwiches which she assembled last night while I was out with David. Normally I do most of the cooking, most of the meal preparation—I enjoy the art of food while Judy has no interest in it—and normally we would eat out to break up such a long drive. But Judy has been preoccupied with arriving in Temagami as soon as possible after you and Greg get there. Because you live in Toronto, she is convinced you do not have as far to drive. In view of my side trip through Algonquin Park, my harmless self-indulgence, she is unknowingly right.

"Do you want your sandwich now?" she asks me, reaching down towards the floor and the small thermos bag positioned there.

"No, I'd like to stop at a picnic table, Jude. The weather's good now. I wouldn't mind a few minutes break."

It's true. The weather has improved. Somewhere behind us in the middle of the park, the sun showers have fallen behind. A final cloudburst, one more steep grade when it seemed we quite literally drove into a low-lurking cloud, then we came out the other side into sunshine so apparently permanent it seemed never to have rained at all.

"If I'd known we were going to stop, I wouldn't have made sandwiches," Judy says. "I thought we could eat in the car. That was the idea, Tommy."

I sigh. "Okay."

"Then we can stop at that Tim Horton's in Huntsville. A pee break, dessert, if you want."

"Okay. Whatever."

"Do you want your sandwich now?"

I nod. "My stomach's growling," I murmur.

She locates my sandwich and unwraps it, placing it on its plastic "plate" on my right thigh. "Don't be petulant," she remarks gently, when I glance at it there in ill-concealed hostility.

I nod. I eat in a meek, chagrined silence, polishing the food off quickly, balling up the plastic wrap and handing it back to her, all the while driving through Algonquin Park in nearly perfect autumn sunshine that beckons seductively to me. I am possessed by you, Jan, and this setting, and by some childish, sulky disappointment that has begun to ache in my belly.

"Tommy?"

"Yes?"

"You aren't going to like this place, are you?"

"Huh?"

"The lodge. You aren't going to like it, are you?"

"Well, Jeez, Judy, I don't know. How would I know what I'm going to like?"

"It's out in the woods, that's all."

"And?"

"I know how Kanata sometimes makes you crazy. I know how much you like the woods."

Her observation is accurate, of course. I don't like strip malls and shopping malls, fast food restaurants, traffic, cheap, decorative fountains, crowds, ringing cell phones, or minimum wage earners forced to wrap their tongues around, "How may I serve you?" then ending the experience with, "Have a nice day."

"What would you have them say?" Judy's asked me more than once. "What's better than 'have a nice day?'"

"See yuh? Take care? Bye-bye? Thanks? Nice to meet you? Keep the faith?"

Judy just shakes her head at my obstinacy. To her, I am a curmudgeon. To me, I remember that sometimes I just want to be left alone with my own version of myself, unassailed by a society that will ultimately be remembered in history chiefly for the vacuity in its consumerism. I hang around unhappily sometimes on the outskirts of society's bustling town, not quite entering, not quite leaving. Of course, I'd never be caught *saying* so.

"Tommy?"

"Huh?"

"Where do you go, Tommy, when you go away like that?"

"Huh? Whaddyuh mean?"

"Just now. We were talking and then you were gone."

"Sorry, Jude," I say, hastily covering my tracks. "I was thinking the suburbs make me crazy but I don't think it's fair to nail poor Kanata with the entire wrap."

"You're going to like the lodge, though, aren't you? Just to spite me."

Her supposition surprises me. "Judy, for God's sake, what difference does it make what I like? Gladys wasn't *my* mother. What happens to the place is up to you and Jan. Not me. Not Greg. *You* and *Jan*. Maybe I'll like the place and maybe I won't. Either way, it isn't going to matter. I'll support you and Jan and what you decide. End of story."

Chagrined by my outburst, she doesn't say anything for a long moment. Then, "Tommy?"

"Yeah?"

"Even after twenty years. . . ."

"Yeah?"

". . . There are things about you I'll never understand. There are things about you that are pretty fucking weird."

"I know," I admit with what I hope is a placating smile. "All part of the rewards, my sweet. You wouldn't want me to be dull, would you?"

To make amends, no doubt convinced of my innocence, she reaches over and pats me on the thigh. I squeeze her hand a moment. Just keeping the peace, just endorsing her verdict.

"How was your sandwich, Tommy?"

"Excellent," I reply.

Judy calls me Tommy, but you have always called me Tom. I remain convinced I stopped being Tommy twenty years ago, the day *you* first called me Tom. In my mind, Tom is who I've been ever since. I have become, in so many ways, what you inspired me to become such a long time ago. It's just one of the reasons I seem to belong so irrevocably to you.

And I can never be caught *saying* so, not even by accident.

TWO

ONE NIGHT A FEW YEARS AGO, when David Cruickshank and I were out for a drink, he said, "I think most men—and women too, for that matter—forced to tell the truth, would admit they would have preferred their lives to be some kind of romantic adventure. I mean romantic adventure in the larger sense, you know? Something richer, Tom, something less mundane—yes, definitely less mundane. A life that wasn't so immersed in casual preoccupations. 'Don't forget to get bread and milk, Dear.' Or, 'don't you remember your pin number?' We spend a lot of time on shit like that, Tom. Some of it's valid, some of it isn't. We spend too much of our time just keeping the big machine running, just making sure we don't run afoul of some system we had nothing to do with setting up."

"Yeah," I said. "I know."

"What is it Nietzsche said? *What hurts is not that you lied to me, but that I no longer believe you now.* Because the first lie you're told when you're a kid is that your life can be the romantic adventure you grow up wishing it could be. Like I said, romantic in the larger sense—respecting the past, deriving perspective from it, feeling vital and purposeful, focused on individual freedom as a main priority, nothing in the world preventing you from what you need to do or be. Anyway, when you learn that *that's* not true, that you've been misled by homilies and myths, you're then told it's actually better, more realistic, more admirable, definitely more *acceptable* to enjoy the same boring, conventional life everyone else does. Right?"

I nodded.

"My question is this, bearing in mind what Nietzsche said: if the romantic fantasy was a lie, the one I just partially defined, then why the hell should we suddenly believe that its alternative, the mundane, is admirable? You know, being more realistic and more mature is now a worthwhile goal? Why should we believe *that*, when the alternative already proved itself to be a lie? What I'm saying here, Tom, is why should we believe anything life promises us, when life has shown itself to be a liar from the get-go, when it's already demonstrated it can't be trusted, especially when it's perpetuated by a mainstream society reflecting the worst we can be, a warlike, avaricious pack of dullards with the attention spans of gnats? Which, by the way, is what you become when you deny yourself or you're denied your true potential, when you have to keep secret everything you want in life."

"Phew," I said, grinning at his passion. "Who shit on *your*

46

corn flakes this morning?"

"My publisher, now that you mention it. But never mind about that. What I'm saying here is give me the adventure, the fantasy, then I'll believe the rest of it, that the reasonable alternative isn't merely horse shit. Let me try another analogy on you, Tom. You can't go around telling a kid for years that you plan to give him ice cream because ice cream is the *truth*, then give him a leaf of spinach instead of the ice cream because, now that he's grown up, you're espousing that the spinach is the truth. Am I making sense here, Tom?"

"You're a dangerous man," I remarked. "In a weird, let's-have-some-more-fucking-scotch sort of way, you *are* making sense. To me, at least."

He squinted at me a moment. "Shit," he said. "Dangerous isn't so weird. We're *all* dangerous. But not for the reasons we're purported to be. No, we're all dangerous because we're so fucking *repressed*. You know something, Tom? The trick is *knowing* you're dangerous, *acting* like you're dangerous. *Preferring* to be dangerous. That's the ticket, Tom. *Preferring* to be dangerous."

As I often do, I thought about cowardice that night, as David finished his rant, but I didn't say anything. Instead I comforted myself by concluding his point of view was at best only amusing. It was a way for me to keep ducking some secret issues only part of me wanted to address.

And as I mentioned, we were drinking scotch. I decided what he was saying probably reflected the wisdom that lives inside *every* bottle of scotch. Fine to talk about the merits of being dangerous when you're holding the least dangerous alcoholic beverage I know of in your hand. In my experience, scotch hangs out in the middle ground. It's *red wine* that makes you dangerous. Bad boys don't drink scotch, do they? Scotch is too wise. And never mind if the wisdom it inspires runs amok. Faulty wisdom or not, if you head in a dangerous direction, scotch will soon tell you when you're being a fool. Scotch will soon remind you where the exit ramp is, so you can turn back safely before you get into any *real* trouble on the freeway.

No matter. Regardless of the merits or drawbacks of scotch, I couldn't get David's tirade out of my mind afterwards. Something about what he said had struck a chord with me. In fact, by the time David and I had this particular conversation about preferring to be dangerous, I was perhaps a decade and a half into my marriage to Judy. And I realized I'd given up on being dangerous long before. In spite of everything—even my persistent love for you—I had settled into conventionally familiar circumstances with nary a peep of resistance. It seemed a comfortable way to be, this act of meekly giving in. It seemed safer and more ultimately satisfying than arguing incessantly with a cantankerous destiny that—having the support of conventional society—knows it's never wrong. With society's endorsement, fate gives in to the notion that we, life's solitary citizens, don't have nearly as much real choice from day to day as we like to pretend we do.

But it occurred to me that night—after David and I had left the bar to return to our respective homes, as I was going over our conversation in my mind—that I had stopped being dangerous about life at some point *prior* to when I first met Judy. In fact, when I met Judy, I already preferred *not* to be dangerous. By the time I met Judy, I believed I was grown up entirely. As a grownup, being dangerous seemed downright foolish. Back then, had I looked, I wouldn't even have found the need to be dangerous at the edge of my radar screen. As I remember it now, I think I already believed that being dangerous wasn't worth the pain. Although I was young, I was convinced I already had the scars to prove being dangerous was flirting with various emotional agonies, a kind of potential for masochism that didn't appeal to me. By the time I met Judy, I'd already concluded there's no point in making a statement in life that is only going to give you grief, that runs the risk of being unpleasant. Being dangerous, that is exercising your personal choice, your freedom in life, presents us with a spectrum of risk. By the time we understand the merits of "danger" we've also concluded that we can suffer various punishments connected to the risk. Fearful, we embark on life with little imagination. Yes, we play it safe. Maybe we don't have to eat our spinach, but the ice cream we devour is vanilla all the way. And somewhere along this chosen route, *vanilla* seems to evolve into our version of the truth.

"YOU'RE FROM *THE CITIZEN*," Judy said the night we met.

"Yes," I admitted. "I am." I was in uniform; I carried a camera bag.

She had materialized at my left side, interrupting my contemplation of a painting on the wall in front of me. It was a rendering of families recreating on the Rideau Canal, the world's longest skating rink. In a couple of months time, early in the new year, this painting of skaters and snack bars and flowing scarves would mirror life again as residents of Ottawa did their best to make fun of the misery too often passing for a Canadian January. For now, though, it was only early November and this collection of paintings was on loan to Ottawa Civic Hospital, I've forgotten the reasons why. But I remember the painting of the Canal. It captured for me a scene I was familiar with.

I said as much to the good-looking woman now standing beside me.

She gazed at the picture in silence, weighing my words, I guess. While she was thus engaged, I glanced at her left hand to check on the status of her third finger. As she turned in my direction, she caught me doing so. Of course, I didn't know that then. It wasn't until after our third date that Judy boasted about how I'd been interested in her from the very beginning, that she'd seen my clumsy attempt to discern her marital status. I admitted it. I admitted I was grateful there was no ring on her finger that night, engagement or otherwise.

"I'm Tom McNamara," I said, extending my hand.

"Judy Smythe."

"Terrible night to be out viewing paintings." It was raining on the other side of the entrance doors, heavily at times, and Ottawa drizzles tend to be cold when they fall during the month of November. They come down at a nasty angle, like they actually *intend* to be mean. "You don't *look* like a patient,"

I said, trying to be amusing.

"I work here," she replied. "I'm in nursing."

"Ah," I said. "I see."

"Should I be in pajamas or something?"

"Careful," I replied. "I'm tempted to answer that."

Actually she was wearing a business suit, pinstriped, I remember. I thought she was terribly attractive and I was aware she had a wonderful figure. The suit, while conservative, couldn't hide her feminine qualities. I was grateful for this. While I wasn't actually a pinstriped suit type of person, on Judy I approved of the outfit.

Shortly she joined me as I toured the rest of the paintings on exhibit here. They were displayed on walls around the hospital waiting room and some of the adjoining hallways not far away. We didn't really spend much time examining each painting. When we stopped and remarked on a particular work, we were both aware we were mostly faking it. In a casual way, we were already more interested in each other than in the art providing us with this happy excuse to meet.

"What's your specialty?" I asked her at one point.

"In nursing?"

I smiled. "Yes, in nursing."

She blushed slightly. "Management. Administration. I'm an assistant director of nursing."

I was here to take a photograph of proceedings. In the end, the newspaper ran a picture of Judy gazing at one of the more provocative pieces of art in the exhibit. I knew enough to gently cheesecake it, pinstriped suit or not, else I doubt it would have made it into print. David Cruickshank, who had already taken me under his wing in my two years at the paper, came over to where I labored the next day and gently tsk-tsked as he placed a copy of the published version, folded to the exact page, on the rubble on my desk.

"I hope you got her phone number," he said. "If not, I'm resigning as your mentor and patron saint."

"As a matter of fact I did. We're going out for dinner next Saturday night."

"Good-looking woman, Tom."

"I noticed," I replied.

I MOVED CAUTIOUSLY where seeing Judy was concerned. It wasn't that I perceived any danger in my interest in her, or because *she* was dangerous to me emotionally, but because our relationship possessed a natural calm. It didn't seem *capable* of danger. It developed with consistent ease. I enjoyed this absence of danger. I found it a delight to care about Judy quietly, to be patient through the process that caring actually becomes. In this case, my emotions whispered gently in the early days of our courtship, even though I knew, given an opportunity, they would gradually evolve into the necessary shout love must eventually become. A whisper that is willing to evolve into a serious shout seemed preferable to me to the screams of caring I'd felt previously as a somewhat younger man. In the end, when these short-lived affairs hadn't worked out, I'd grown increasingly cynical about romance. No wonder it was a great relief to me to fall in love with Judy in a gentler, calmer fashion. It made the love seem deeper. I didn't have to ache with feeling all the time. No sleepless nights, no loss of appetite. Was it not a more complete love when angst played no part in it?

This delay in loving Judy seemed to reflect a mature rate of decision-making on my part. Slow bubbling chemistry, I guess. Like my brain was driving my emotional bus, a concept I could be proud of. Safety on the emotional highway. Passions relatively subdued, but the brain cataloging the score in clear, conventional degrees, keeping me informed, advising me on my progress. In a way it was like going back to school. The more of Judy I saw and the more I cared about her, the more it seemed inevitable that I would get some kind of passing grade. I'd had enough of the child's play of intensely passionate love. I wanted something deeper, something solid, an institution, I suppose, in which I could comfortably enlist, fairly certain it would last forever without so much as a moment of regret.

IT WASN'T THAT OUR COURTSHIP was dull or sexually pristine. After our third date, when Judy and I at last made love, we were astonishingly ferocious in our physical attraction to one another. I recall we went at each other like we'd been celibate for years.

Her place—I remember there was a trio of teddy bears on the dresser. We joked about what voyeurs they were, their heavy breathing of dismay as we made love, *our* heavy breathing, the relief, the release in *our* cries of gratification drowning every other caution out. We made love most of the night. I'd brought a couple of condoms, hidden on my person in the usual safe locations—for sanguine reasons of course—but a whole night's lovemaking? Fortunately for us, Judy had some of her own stashed in the small drawer of her night table. We were cautious, a product of our times, children of AIDS, informed and nervous about every sexual peril.

In between periods of nearly ceaseless lovemaking, we talked.

"You know something?" she said at one point. "You're the first only child I've ever really liked."

"I'm honored," I replied. "And why's that?"

"The conventional reasons, I guess. Children without siblings tend towards self-absorption. They can be awfully demanding."

"Maybe they get lonely. You shouldn't dislike the lonely. I mean are you the kind of woman who picks on orphans because they're out there on their own?"

"Of course not," she replied.

I chortled to make certain she knew I was kidding her.

At some point, though, she asked me if I wanted to have children of my own.

"Well, yeah, I guess so," I replied. "What about you?"

"I don't know," she said with a gravity she did not explain.

At this point, whether or not we wanted children represented a purely casual topic. It came up more or less in passing. Yet I detected, and never forgot, the edge in Judy's voice when she replied that night. Her ambivalence about children was clearly more than casual. Unfortunately I didn't give it much credence at the time; it was much too early for us to be seriously discussing the opportunities we might share in being parents. By the time it really mattered—as an issue, as a loss—it was much too late for us. The idea of raising a family merely went away, like a career in another field one doesn't get around to launching.

I HAD ALREADY LEARNED Judy's family was much better off economically than mine. Her father was dead, the victim of a premature heart attack. Her mother lived in Rosedale, she told me. She mentioned she had a younger sister, *you*.

"How much younger?" I asked the first time we discussed my lack of siblings.

"Two years."

"You must be close then."

"Not really. I mean, we get along. But I wouldn't say we were close. Part of it is the distance to Ottawa. She lives in Toronto. We talk on the telephone or when we get together with my mother. But we're not the kind of sisters who share everything. I've heard about sisters like that, although I don't really know any. We live our own lives, I guess. We have different friends, different interests, different aptitudes."

"What does she do?"

"She teaches kindergarten." Her announcement was accompanied by a theatrical roll of her eyes I didn't actually understand at the time. It was apparent I was to conclude there was probably something wanting in your average kindergarten teacher.

We fell silent at this point. Judy had run out of ways and any need to describe her relationship with her sister further. When *something* is only a little more *nothing* than the *something* perhaps it should be, I suppose one merely gets bored trying to explain it, justifying one's failure over a perceived inadequacy. I didn't want her to feel she must defend something that wasn't fundamentally wrong. I know there are no rigid rules about how close a woman must be to her only sister.

Still, I said, "So, in a way, you two are closer to being only children yourselves, more than some are, anyway."

"I wouldn't go *that* far," she replied.

"What's her name?" I asked distractedly, hoping this would dispel her defensiveness.

"Janice."

"Judy and Janice," I said ruminatively, mainly to make it clear I was paying attention.

It was one of the few times during the early phase of our relationship that Judy mentioned you. I soon forgot about you myself. I even mostly forgot your name; living so far away from Judy's family, being so comfortable with where Judy and I were headed, I had no reason to remember it. On the rare occasion she mentioned you, I scarcely heard her remarks. Judy only referred infrequently to you, never mentioning again—as I recall it, anyway—that your name was Janice. It made no difference to me. As you can well imagine, I was focused narrowly on your sister. And fate, I speculate now, was playing a dirty game with me.

I LIKED JUDY A GREAT DEAL when she was naked. I still do, in my way, which is much more subdued, much more diluted by my hazy recollection of *you* in the nude. Still, Judy's been able to keep that voluptuous figure I'm conditioned to appreciate. Often, when I stayed over at her place in the early days, once her initial shyness had departed, I would follow her into the shower just to gaze at her body. Sometimes we'd end up making love in the luxury of the spray. Even if we didn't make love in the shower, I would be content washing her body down with my hands, *just* to appreciate it, just to show her how *much* I appreciated it. Sometimes I would bring her to orgasm in the shower spray, down on my knees, using my tongue to demonstrate how deep were my admiration and love.

In those early days with Judy, I'm convinced, my enjoyment of her nakedness was its own fine and private compulsion. Then, one day afterwards—I no longer remember when exactly—I allowed myself to consider that this appreciation was no longer enjoyed within the purity of its own innocent perception. That is, I allowed myself to wonder if I was merely *conditioned* to appreciate Judy in the nude. It is a perilous fact of life that we sometimes think too much. Once I thought *this* thought, I couldn't get rid of it. The notion of admiring Judy mostly on the basis of social conditioning blackmailed me afterwards, begging from me its ever increasing share of my *fine and private compulsion*. It was like some large, analytical neighborhood had moved into the bedroom of my heart to tell me what I cared about and why, and how little of it belonged to me uniquely. This powerful neighborhood wanted to make certain I realized how much I shared its collective ideal, as if the act of preserving my own perception reflected being too big for my britches.

Over the years of our marriage since then, my blackmailer has eroded much of my savings, where appreciating Judy is concerned. If I had it in my power, if I had it to do again, I wouldn't allow myself to think such a thought the first time I was tempted to. I would not allow so much psychology to steal from me what I felt and appreciated so comfortably on my own. Then again, this may only be guilt. I mean, how do we control our thoughts? Do they not reflect some inner wisdom of feeling we try to bury inside ourselves? Do we not eventually reflect on emotions we have been taking for granted or denying? Do we not at some point realize cognitively that some of our feelings have changed? Is it not the brain that reports this news to us?

You see, by the time I let the blackmailer in, I was in love with *you*. Alas love and its objectives aren't there to make any sense to us. As such, *it*, love itself, rather than a thought that inadvertently leaked into my brain one day, can perhaps be blamed for the erosion of my appreciation of Judy's looks. There's no denying now that I have believed for many years I love two women, albeit in different ways and for different reasons. I have also believed for years that love is wonderful, at least in part, because it *allows* us to love more than one person romantically, without explanation or justification. In this way, love possesses a purity transcending mere morality. As something unstated, as a feeling, it can be pleasantly greedy and selfish, it can live its own majestic life inside what we never admit to anyone but ourselves. Oh sure, it means we skulk through our society like emotional espionage agents. But at least we get to feel what we feel without having to explain it all the time, resisting the need to justify ourselves to our peers, whose primary collective motivation is to rationalize our individual needs as little more than conventional sin. To avoid appearing sinful, I'll sneak around in the darkness like a spy, my soul an important roll of microfilm. But inside I'll know the truth; at least inside I'm an honest man.

I can say all this, of course, because I don't ever expect to have to make a choice where love is concerned. My beliefs about love are less risky, bearing my anticipated inertia in mind. When you get right down to it, love's generosity to me remains little more than a matter of speculation, an ideal, something I can believe in privately while I am pretending to adhere to the creed dictated collectively by everybody *else*.

Nonetheless I loved those first few months when Judy and I were falling in love. They made so much sense to me. I don't think there was any real doubt in either of our minds that we had found the person we would probably remain with for the rest of our lives. So we dated often and made love tirelessly. And we began to talk about the future as something we would peruse together, employing shared goals, ultimately traveling life's geography as permanent partners.

In a way, it's what we've done. In a way, though, because of me and what happened to me, it's a communion I'm not entirely comfortable with. In a secret, unrelenting place inside my capacity for love, Judy lost part of me to evolving expectations and my love for someone else. And sometimes, two decades later, I feel deeply tired about the way I've had to work so hard to make certain no one knows what I actually feel, to ensure that Judy doesn't realize what I once thought was wonderful about her and me has given way so much to what I now believe is wonderful about *you*.

I'D BEEN SEEING JUDY FOR MORE THAN A MONTH before I finally confessed I was obligated to go skiing in March with friends in a place called Westendorf.

"Westendorf? Where the hell is Westendorf?"

"Austria," I explained.

There were five of us from the journalism department at Carleton University going on this trip. We'd earned our degrees together, all of us had been fortunate to land the jobs we wanted with newspapers around Ontario, and we'd decided our mutual success since our graduation three years earlier reflected an excuse for an exotic reunion, namely a chance to ski in the Alps.

I nearly didn't go. Seeing Judy for nearly four months by then, I felt too grown up for a week of skiing in Austria with "the boys." Wasn't it now time, in view of the seriousness of my relationship with Judy, that I let my membership in my friends' bachelors club lapse? On the eve of this trip to Austria, it seemed apparent to me that Judy and I would marry. I sensed she was my romantic fate. I'd booked the trip with Gord, Fred, Brad and George, my buddies from school, before Judy and I even met. It didn't seem appropriate any longer to go, now that I was so preoccupied with the woman I was beginning to believe I might marry.

But Judy wanted me to go. "You need to get this out of your system," she said. "Go celebrate with your friends."

I supposed she was right. I'd never skied in Austria. I might never have the opportunity again. Yet I felt an instinct to renege on my friends and our reunion scheme. As far as I knew, there wasn't anything I needed to do to reconcile my days in Carleton's journalism program.

"Get *what* out of my system?" I asked defensively.

"The school thing. You know. The university days."

"I'm not sure it's still *in* my system. That's my point."

"Well, it's up to you, Tommy. But I want you to know I trust you. I really do," Judy said, her statement not quite the non sequitur it appeared to be.

"I'm glad you trust me, Jude," was what I ended up saying.

As I recall this conversation now, we already *sounded* married. At the time, though, we weren't even engaged. We'd just been dating for a few months, getting to know one another well and making torrid love as often as we could, still enjoying the new, I guess, in what we probably both realized must eventually get comfortably old. And the trip to Austria seemed out of character somehow with where I was happily headed now. I nearly told Judy, on the eve of my departure, that I thought we'd get married eventually. I nearly told her I believed *someone* would propose. Me, her, life itself. It seemed like something I should say before I joined my friends to go to

Europe.

As the old saw goes, though, nearly only counts in horseshoes. I didn't say anything before the skiing trip, not yet feeling an intense enough need to tell Judy my thoughts on partnership. Besides, my brain knew the score. Intellectually I was happy with my circumstances. I thought Judy was very attractive. I thought she was intelligent. She had a job, a career. I thought she was very *nice*. I thought she was great in bed. I thought, if we *did* get married, everything would remain happily in place. After we married, she'd be forever good-looking, intelligent and nice. I thought these were *static* qualities, as static as my appreciation of them, as static as their inherent definition, a definition which wasn't likely—and had no reason—to change. I was very young. I *wanted* to be naive.

After all, I didn't want to change *either*. Whatever Judy appreciated about me romantically would remain unchanged as well, I hoped. Life that just happens, that takes place without a plan? I felt beyond such carelessness now. Not only would Judy remain the same, not only would I remain the same, but *we* would remain the same. I *wanted* to be comfortable with familiarity.

Sure, I overlooked some things about Judy, even way back then. We all do, where the person we love is concerned. In my more honest moments, I thought she was a little self-indulgent sometimes, a little too preoccupied with herself. She was prone to PMS and she expected me to be understanding about her condition no matter what. *I* expected me to be understanding too. I *was* understanding, most of the time at least. It wasn't like her PMS drove her to throw any cats through any windows. I didn't feel her PMS wanted to *murder* me. But there were days of unrelenting, seemingly ceaseless testiness brought on by Judy's condition that were long and painful for me. My understanding over her PMS ultimately boiled down to wanting her bad days to be over as quickly as possible, and denying those not infrequent occasions when I felt she was being a spoiled brat, that her ill temper wasn't PMS at all, merely a demonstration of how to be recalcitrant and mean. I had to work much harder to be understanding after we were married, when her premenstrual furies worsened somewhat and when I remained convinced I'd fallen permanently in love with *someone else*.

We do a lot of forgiving in life. We forgive mountains when airplanes slam into their faces. We forgive fish for not multiplying fast enough. We overlook the blemishes in the people we've decided to love. It's a shame we don't forgive ourselves with the same relative ease and understanding with which we forgive everything and everyone else.

JUDY DROVE ME TO THE AIRPORT the night of my flight to Europe because she wanted to meet my friends. I liked that they thought she was stunning, that they remarked on her gorgeous figure, that she was obviously intelligent, that they thought she was *very nice*. My friends made all these complimentary observations about her after I kissed her goodbye, after I promised to be careful skiing when at last I reached the slopes, when the five of us—four envious bachelors and one ambivalent friend—sat inside our gate, waiting to board our flight for Heathrow, where we would ultimately transfer to Munich. They mentioned how wonderful she was again while we waited in Heathrow, dazed by our need for sleep, when it seemed our flight to Munich would *never* be called. The subject even came up again during the three-hour bus ride from Munich across the border into Austria.

"Yes," I said each time my friends complimented her. "Judy's great. I'm a lucky man."

I knew it and believed it even more, now that my friends agreed with me. It's a lot easier to believe in *anything* when you have a large body of peers to believe in it *with*.

My four friends, my four believers, were all at our wedding more than a year afterwards. Then again, so were *you*.

THREE

BY THE TIME JUDY AND I drive out of Algonquin Park I'm aware of that intensifying feeling I call: *being staked out over a razor blade.* The razor blade's made of velvet, but it's a razor blade nonetheless. I have tried countless times to define this velvet razor sensation in some other, more palatable, more precise way, to capture more clearly the deliciousness of the pain in my thoughts, I suppose. But I fail to improve on the velvet razor description. I feel what I feel, where you are concerned. Cut by joy, slashed by romantic wonder. This is the sensation I must endure when I'm about to see you again. It really *is* a razor blade. It really *is* a *velvet* razor blade.

Consider this, the sweet agony of what—after all this time—is no doubt unrequited love. Never mind if I'm a fool. In fact, never mind the *if;* I *am* a fool. But consider the sensation, the feeling, the pure velvet razor blade agony and delight of how I care for you and how it does not wane. Don't judge me by concluding I am foolish. Take off your armor of judgment, just for a moment or two. Then imagine what the feeling summing up more than twenty years of unrequited love must actually be like. Imagine waiting for something to happen that you know will never happen, waking up each morning, wanting your ritual anticipation—anticipation that something indeed must happen—to finally go away, and then, a moment later, desperately lonely without it, wanting it back again because you *live* to wait for something to happen. Consider this long wait for what you wish for as the emotional imprisonment it actually is. Consider the parole board ruling that too often defines the nature of human life.

Unrequited love. It's a wondrous apprehension, a concoction, a witch's brew of anticipation, disappointment, success, failure, agony, ecstasy, hope, despair—God meeting Lucifer, and the two of them flirting in some cosmic, tacky bar, repressed and insatiable, plus meeting minus, plus *needing* minus—imploding the universe when they no longer can resist their need for one another—all of these ideas a larger, hyperbolic version, I suppose, of what I feel each time I'm going to see you again. Like I'm an outlaw *and* the sheriff. Like I'm going to rob my own innocent bank. It's all some love-fuck stew that never makes much sense to me when I try to think it into words. But the feeling is tragically clear. It's some fuzzy creature with quills, some kindhearted stomach ulcer. It's the in and out of itself, the entrance and the exit, the idea versus the truth, like the wispy, quiet virgin who secretly dreams each night of boinking the entire football team . . . .

. . . Okay, let's everybody calm down. Let's keep our hands on the wheel and our eyes on the road. Deep breaths, McNamara. Let's just slow down the old imagination a little bit. Let's dam up the stream of hyperbole before you drown yourself. You've been here before. All akimbo. All aquiver. Love sucks. It needs deep breaths.

Yes. Deep breaths.

Eventually, deep breathing works. Soon I enter the safety of my personal silence again, the soliloquy of my own emotional womb. I like it here when I'm on my way to seeing you, once I get hold of myself. Nothing's going to happen when I get to the lodge near Temagami. I'll just keep all this emotional chaos to myself, the way I always do, the way I know I must. But you'll be there, and when no one is looking, I'll gaze at you in wonder, trying to figure out how destiny went wrong in my case, how this feeling and you, and the management of my fate, could happen to me—misshappen?—misshapen?—well, I *think* I know what I mean, what it is to be betrayed by circumstance.

I think men and women reach a point in life—I can speak only for men, of course—when some explicit moment of clarity, of mistake, comes into focus for them. We rarely do anything about the conclusion that results when clarity arrives. We don't transform our lives in any significant way. But we gaze for a time at this new picture of what we know about ourselves, all the rationalizations stripped away, all the abject justification removed, our ritual need to compromise our inner selves, our excuses, the self-inflicted, parental cuffs we give ourselves around our ears, all of these self-infidelities of punishment or recrimination set aside for a few precise moments of wondrous translucence. Then we truly see ourselves. We realize what we have done wrong, what, if we had the opportunity, we would go back and change. It's not as compellingly mystical as it sounds. I think it's much simpler than mysticism, and much more important too. I think the self breaks out of its environment long enough to see clearly what we don't like any longer, what we didn't know we didn't like or wouldn't like, in ourselves, in our world, in our many electives, choices we usually leave idle to rust into nothingness, like a field of abandoned farm machinery.

It's disorienting. This moment of clarity is like believing for forty years that you have been a zebra, then suddenly discovering you've been an alligator all along. And no one ever asked you what you really thought you were. We live in a society that doesn't give a damn whether we're a zebra or an alligator, as long as we behave ourselves, as long as, in our behaving, our behavior is mostly human. Society doesn't ask us what we think we really are. In the end, then, somehow we think it's wrong to ask the question of ourselves. No wonder we know so clearly what aspects of our lives feel *wrong*. No wonder, as experts in what is *wrong*, we stumble clumsily backwards into our necessary knowledge of what is actually *right*. Living in the collective of society, we find no one cares what we think is right. In the end, we buy a new deodorant only because we've learned the one we were using all along could be *wrong* for us.

"Tommy? Are you with me?"

"I'm here," I tell Judy, glancing at her in alarm because, indeed, I have all but forgotten she is here with me in the other bucket seat, and because I fear she caught a glimpse of my love struck thoughts and chants a few moments ago. *Tommy can you hear me? Tommy can you see me?* Tom McNamara croaks Roger Daltry.

Someday I will sing every mournful truth of feeling in my life right out loud just to hear the melody and know, once and for all, that I can carry a tune.

"How long to the Huntsville Tim Horton's?"

I glance at my watch. To my surprise, we've already passed through Dwight. Engrossed in my thoughts, I missed the village entirely. "Just a few minutes," I reply, adding, "Thank God!"

"You must be tired," my wife remarks. "This is a long drive. It feels like Greg and Jan will have been sitting there for hours, waiting for us to arrive."

"No," I say, glancing at my watch again and shaking my head. "They're on the road too."

"God, Tommy, I can't believe we're going to all this trouble, traveling this far on speculation."

"At least the rain showers have stopped," I say, for fear I will defend the concept of speculation from Judy's ever more empirical mind.

I suspect Judy of comparing the traveling time—between Ottawa and our destination, and Toronto and our destination— to reinforce her point that she'd like to move to Toronto where she's convinced the bigger money is. I'm now regretting I didn't take Highway 17 directly to North Bay after all. I've made us late and the results are dubious. In fact, my restorative side trip through Algonquin Park has mostly failed. Gobbling down a tuna fish sandwich behind the wheel, while blowing through Mother's Nature's glamorous wilderness like a cruise missile, hasn't been worth what it might ultimately cost me in incurring Judy's wrath for taking the longer route. And you, and you. Not even the colorful beauty of Algonquin Park in autumn can eject *you* from my mind.

"How long until we get there?" Judy's asking.

"Best estimate?"

"Best estimate."

"Huntsville soon. Then up Eleven to North Bay. Not too far after that." I take a nervous breath. "Maybe two, two and a half hours."

"Christ!" hisses Judy.

If she had a buyer for the resort in the back seat of our car, I speculate, she'd sell for half the price right now, just to cut the driving distance down.

"This is Ontario," I lecture in gentle pedantry. "It takes days to cross it."

"I know that, Tommy. Christ!"

"Sorry," I say. "Tim Horton's is coming up." Then I say nothing more.

"I have to pee," Judy tells me after a long, ambivalent pause. "You know it makes me cranky when I have to pee."

I know. I nod. I drive.

MAYBE JUDY'S RIGHT about the mysterious lodge near Temagami. Maybe I'll like the place and suggest the family keep it. Not that anyone will listen to me. It's really none of my business. I'm just the in-law/outlaw guy who knows how to pack the car like it's some kind of calling, who can drive for most of any given day without tiring, as long as he doesn't have to say too much to the woman sitting beside him, the wife who sometimes becomes a little frantic when she discovers he doesn't seem to need to communicate with her.

Suddenly she reaches out and squeezes my right wrist in unexpected encouragement.

I jump.

She laughs.

I feel instantly ashamed of myself for being startled, and because I wish the fingers she touched me with were yours. I nod to acknowledge Judy's gesture. I feel renewed guilt, which, in turn, acknowledges whose touch I would actually prefer at this moment. Strange how the more tempted I am to be honest with myself, the more trained I am to hate myself, to sing the familiar chorus of shame my society has learned to belt out so lustily.

The sun's autumn angle is severe, although it's only mid-afternoon. I pull the visor down to shield myself from the glare. I want to cover my face and my eyes so that the longing in my soul can't be noticed or apprehended. By Judy. By you. By this world. Maybe, in the end, by *me*.

I STAND AT THE LINEUP at the counter in Tim Horton's while

Judy is in the washroom. I know what she wants: coffee and a maple almond danish. I know what she wants *in* her coffee. I only need coffee and I want it as black as my fucking heart. Beyond this and you, and some vague idea of a transactional courage I've been resisting for years, I have no idea *what* I want.

It's busy here for a Friday afternoon. Maybe the sunshine is drawing people out of their claustrophobic neighborhoods Autumn sunshine often inspires people to go somewhere outdoors, I've noticed. The trouble is we don't actually know where to go. So we end up in a fast food restaurant somewhere, lining up, making pointless culinary choices, then gazing out fast food windows into a day that doesn't seem to have any room to include us after all, now that we've rejected it, now that it's clear we didn't know what to do with it. Inside, we step gingerly around signs announcing the floor is slippery because it has just been mopped. On fine days like this, when it appears we've been presented with a choice between quiet and clatter, peace and chaos, ourselves and everyone else, we fall back into the noise because we can't quite remember what the alternative is like.

I don't know. I hate to make this judgment. Sometimes I nearly know myself, other times I do not. But some people must like this world of noise, vacuity and not talking seriously to ourselves. If so, why don't I learn to like it too, just to join the human race? Why can't I learn to get over myself for a change? Or would that be giving in? Would that be embracing safety irrevocably? Would that finally flush down the toilet once and for all my faith in the adventure of life? Would I find something more vapid to believe in that happily filled the resulting void? Would I learn to be attracted by money or security, the numbing enticement of boredom?

Still standing in the drift of people gradually getting closer to the counter, I sense someone staring at me. I turn. Just a plump woman gazing up at the menu signs, biting her lip over the decision she must make. Then I glance down. Her daughter, holding her hand, a pretty little thing in a print dress and gray, baggy leotards, gazes up at me with eyes as big as blueberry donuts. I smile and wink and feel so much better for a moment about just about everything. At my wink, though, the child turns away, tucking herself against the safety of her mother's ample thigh.

"Christ!" Judy whispers in my ear, back from the washroom, glancing at the little girl, but failing to notice her. "What's the holdup? Any slower and they'd be in reverse."

"No panic," I whisper back, feeling an overwhelming urge to protect everyone and everything from Judy's apparent impatience. Especially the little girl who has resumed gazing up at me. Children would have gentled me, I believe. I don't know how I know this, I only know I do. It's something else about me and love I keep entirely to myself. Whom, besides you, would I have ever needed to tell?

JUDY BELIEVES YOU WANTED CHILDREN, Jan, in a way that she did not. It's why you remained a kindergarten teacher instead of advancing through the grades. Judy considers you a private in some educational army, an underachiever, someone who consistently never made the grade. According to Judy, you should have made major by now, teaching Grade Nine or Ten, an officer in the corps, dragging yourself home after a long day of teaching young people who bombarded you with infinitely busy adolescent hormones all day long.

"You see, children in kindergarten never grow up," Judy said. "Like they stay forever four or five years old. That's what appeals to Jan. That's *my* theory, anyway."

I don't remember exactly when Judy made these remarks, except that it was a number of years ago now. I pretended not to pay much attention, protecting Judy from the nastiness I interpreted in her remarks, protecting you from your sister's judgment, and protecting me from another moment in my love, when I wanted to ride to your rescue and slay yet another dragon unleashed from the incubator of this fire-breathing world.

I don't know what makes me feel this way of late, so abysmally alone as a knight, as a protector. Right now, it's the little girl I winked at, I guess, because she makes me think and remember discussions with Judy about the pros and cons of children. Judy and I calmly coming to a *compromise* reflecting her exclusive point of view. And maybe you and Greg. I don't know. We are all childless, all four of us. Is this because two of us married the wrong people, because two of us didn't marry each other? Did two of us decide we didn't need someone to listen to us? Did two of us, you and me, conclude there would never be anyone who truly *wanted* to listen to us? Good questions. I've asked them of myself dozens of times, in some form or other, yet I haven't drawn perceptibly closer to the answers. Nor do I expect to. Maybe I don't want to hear the answers any longer. Maybe I would prefer to forget to ask the questions.

Judy and I manage to find a table where we can sit down to drink our coffee and allow her to eat her danish. But I can feel her hurrying, her impatience to get back on the road. Judy will be better only when we arrive at our destination at last.

Tires squeal from the parking lot outside. Two young men in ball caps, one of them behind the wheel of a rusting Honda Civic, laugh lustily together as they tear, as best they can, *vehicularly challenged*, out of the parking lot.

"Tough times," I remark to Judy. "You'd think it was a Porsche, the way they carry on."

Judy just shakes her head.

"Nothing left now," I add, "but the fantasy, I guess."

"Oh, shut up," says Judy. "Drink your coffee. Stop being a curmudgeon before your time."

Annoyed, I obey. For a long time now, I have had good reason to suspect that Judy no longer enjoys my moments of biting social commentary. In the silence of this moment, I wonder why I bother to enjoy them *myself* if, indeed, I actually do. Of course I'd never be caught *saying* so.

SHORTLY WE'RE BACK ON THE ROAD. It's still easy to get out of Huntsville along the little section of autumn pavement that remains of Highway 60, notwithstanding the new Wal-Mart, its hangers-on and the traffic these attract, stuck out here near

Highway 11 like some pimple on an otherwise clear complexion.

I remark to Judy on the arrival here of this new edifice of commercial enterprise.

"Don't start, Tommy," she says, fearing another of my harangues.

"I wasn't intending to, Jude. But I can't wait to tell David that Huntsville has a *Wally-World*."

Impatiently Judy sighs.

Gratefully I fall silent.

A couple of Augusts ago, while camping in Algonquin Park, David and I drove to Huntsville at what we felt was the crack of dawn, to pick up some steaks at the Metro. We'd had to canoe in from Little Joe Lake, make a small portage, then buck the wind on Canoe Lake. In the grocery store we became embroiled in a human snarl near the meat counter. Fascinated, effectively blocked, and waiting our turn, we listened to a man and woman in their late thirties, obviously from Toronto, nattering endlessly about some high priced cuts of steak. They were having company later that day. The cuts weren't lean enough. They couldn't agree on quantities. They even took time to regret the fact that it might rain, spoiling the entire barbecue anyway. Never mind that it was so sunny outside it almost tore our eyes out of their sockets. They asked young Christopher, their son, what *he* thought, perhaps hoping he could ease them out of their dilemma. Christopher didn't care. He was probably only six. He probably didn't need the stress of trying to help solve an adult anxiety attack. Christopher probably wanted to get the hell out of there. Christopher probably wanted this period of anguish to conclude, or at least postpone itself until something took place of more importance than the marbling in the steaks his parents were manhandling.

At last David pointedly reached around them and grabbed two fine looking t-bones. "Excuse me," he said, more or less as a Canadian afterthought.

The woman glared at him, her sunglasses perched on her head like some entomological tiara.

"Have a nice day," said David, turning away from them, me fleeing along beside him.

"Jesus," he said in my car as I gingerly pulled out of the parking lot—astonishingly busy for such a relatively early hour in the morning—headed back to Algonquin Park. "You know what's going to destroy this planet, Tom?"

"I have a feeling you're going to tell me, my friend."

"Pointless urban angst, that's what's going to destroy this planet."

"Probably," I replied.

We grinned at one another.

"Then again," I added, "Can I trust the opinion of a man who needs a fucking haircut as much as you do?"

"Hell's only angel," David said, as he's pointed out to me a number of times before, settling back in his seat, looking satisfied with himself.

I GLANCE OVER AT JUDY now that we are at last heading north on Highway 11. She's reading the map you dictated to her last week on the telephone, directions outlining the route of the final stage of our journey to Gladys Pinkster-Smythe's secret little resort in the wilderness around Temagami. You phoned someone up there, pleased with the hospitality of the person who provided you with the directions. "What else do people up there have to worry about?" Judy said after she'd hung up earlier this week, after you were gone, after she told me what you'd said about the friendly helpfulness you'd received. "Nothing up there to do *but* be friendly and nice."

I didn't say anything. I wasn't expected to reply. Judy mistrusts friendly strangers. I do not. We don't talk about the contrast in our opinions any longer.

In real terms, I think Judy harangues as much as I do. It's just we feel strongly about dissimilar annoyances or issues. She's in one corner on one soapbox; I'm in the other. In this way, ours has all the earmarks of a conventional marriage.

"We should get an SUV," Judy remarks now without glancing up from the map she transposed from your telephoned directions.

"For the suburbs of Kanata?"

"Well, a minivan, at least."

"To dull, even extinguish my gift for packing a car?"

"Oh, shut up," she says, smiling enough to convey she didn't intend me to take it unkindly.

YOUR MAP, THOUGH, IS A GREAT SUCCESS. Even Judy remarks that your directions haven't missed a beat.

Then, "You don't think Jan and Greg came here on their own, do you? You know, a weekend or two ago? I wouldn't put it past them."

"I doubt it," I reply. "Why would they do *that*? As you've noted yourself, it's a long drive just to exercise some kind of perceived advantage. Besides, without this appointment with us, your sister would never be able to tear Greg away from his work in Toronto."

Judy says nothing to this. We've acknowledged Greg's workaholism a number of times before.

We are now on the final dirt road. According to your map, this road will take us the last few kilometers to our destination. I'm tired, but we've been driving in relatively deep wilderness for the last hour or so and, as usual, I've been feeling the shot of adrenaline the woods inspires in me. And the autumn colors are impressive. They stimulate me. I've commented on their beauty to Judy more than once already. I am a noble savage. In the woods I'm really me. The rest of the time, I tend to feel I am only faking it.

The road is bad, though, potholes, and rocks and tree roots bursting up through the dirt. Steep slopes and sharp bends. Autumn hardwoods or evergreens forming a canopy over the roadway, occasionally scraping along the roof of the car. Along the way, crows and ravens stand confidently on the edge of the road, hardly flinching as the Maxima stumbles by.

"It's beautiful country," I say after steering carefully around a large rock.

"Admire it later. Keep your eyes on the road."

"Aye-aye, Sir."

Playfully, she slaps me on the arm. Her mood has

improved now that the long drive will soon be over.

The resort's main building suddenly bursts out of the woods like it's broken free of a deep dark forest. In fact, it seems virtually to lift off out of the trees, an illusion created by the delicacy with which it has been constructed and now perches in a clearing on a hill. The illusion the lodge is rising is exaggerated as we drive downhill to an overgrown area that may have been used for parking at one time. The illusion of the lodge's elevation and the contrast of our abrupt descent towards the overgrown parking area contribute further to the sensation that the main building is blasting off and will soon rise over our heads, as if on its way to outer space.

"Wow," I remark, impressed by the sight, feeling a little like a child who has just seen the performance of his first childhood party magician.

"Wow what?"

"The way it comes out like that on the hill, all of sudden that way. It's so imposing."

"Optical illusion, Tommy."

"Yeah. But powerful just the same. Do you think this was the intention when they built it?"

Judy doesn't answer me. "At least we know the basement will be dry," she says instead.

It enters my mind, as we pull cautiously into the clearing below, that Gladys's lodge sits on its hill, waiting for us to name it. Sleepy Hollow. Or Pine Nook Lodge. Or View From The Rock Lodge and Housekeeping Cottages.

ONCE I ADMIT THIS NOTION about naming into my mind, it doesn't seem like a crazy idea at all. It's something the tired structure conveys to me clearly, I think. Name me, it says. And, besides, if there was a sign identifying this rustic, old resort back somewhere along the road, I didn't see it. As far as I'm concerned, overgrown or fallen sign, or not, this only proves it wants to be named. And what's wrong with the supposition that I might be the one who's come here this weekend to do precisely that? Until I determine otherwise, I'm going to continue to believe I've come here to name this place. It's just another small responsibility to help bring me back to life.

A few seconds later, abruptly, as I drive the last few yards towards Greg's large SUV, the hospitable sensation of connection, my exhilaration, is displaced by an even more provocative bolt of joy, a connection made all the more powerful because I am so familiar with it.

You.

You walk around the corner of the lodge and wave in our direction as I pull to a stop in front of the lodge. Greg isn't far behind, I notice peripherally. But lost in seeing you, I barely pay him any heed until he places a hand on your shoulder—possessively, I think—perhaps you two made love last night, a speculation I contemplate more or less to abuse myself. Oh, the wondrous agony. For me, this latest of encounters renews bitter sweetness yet again. I feel that velvet razor blade anguish you invariably cut me with. I feel it leering at the vulnerability of my wrists, I feel it seeking out my tortured blood.

Of course, never in a million years, would I ever be caught *saying* so.

FOUR

EXHAUSTED, MY FOUR SKIING FRIENDS and I finally arrived at our destination in Austria. We reached our pension in a daze. The journey, more than two decades ago now, felt as hazy then as I recall it to be now, so many years later: the overnight flight from Ottawa to Heathrow, the long wait for our flight to Munich to be called, spring sunshine in a London shrugging off the gloom of winter, blasting in through the airport windows like God's relentless lantern. Then, finally there was the other flight to Munich, short and long somehow, as if time itself was as tired as we were and didn't know whether to be early or late, slow or fast. The pilot came in to land like there was a rocket on our tail, slamming on the brakes hard enough to create an audible gasp among several of the passengers, as he bounced across the tarmac and brought the plane to a screeching halt.

My four friends were less perturbed by the rocky landing

than I was. I don't like heights. I fly more or less out of necessity. I adhere to a religiously concise proposition where gravity is concerned: if you stay on the ground, you cannot fall out of the sky. Still, I force myself to fly nearly annually, for Judy's sake, south to some beach where she can shrug off the blues of the Canadian winter months. But I'll never be comfortable with the practice of flying. As humans, we choose our acceptable dangers, our methods of flirting with death. Given this choice, flying is not the one I would necessarily select.

Not the point, though. I mention the landing in Munich only to demonstrate that my vacation in the Austrian Alps began with an exaggerated awareness of my delicate mortality. I remember realizing then that life is fragile. I cognitively concluded at some point that week that I will not live forever. My trepidation over the landing—and its apparent relationship with life's inherent risk—seemed a precursory indication of how eventful my vacation in Austria would be. Afterwards I would embrace entirely the notion that there is a synchronicity between our minor brushes with death and certain incidents of choice that tend to accompany them. Aware of my mortality that week in Westendorf, I caught a glimpse of what it means to never stop being; feeling *alive*.

By now, everyone knows one values life more readily when one feels he has cheated death, even in a minor way. The trick, the challenge, the commitment afterwards resides in never forgetting it, in resisting the temptation to become complacent over time, to slide backwards into that state of mere survival most of us find so familiar and safe. These are concepts I did not contemplate until after my friends and I arrived in Westendorf, and then departed again, when our holiday was over. But, plainly, Westendorf was where I first became preoccupied with *living* life as an antidote to unavoidable death. It lives on in me years later because of the importance of love, I suppose. Because of love, and you, and the frightening proposition that a life unlived—or even only partially lived—reflects personal self-betrayal. To me, there is no acceptable excuse for the way I tend to betray myself in life, frittering away precious moments of wonder or joy in a state of half-hearted acceptance that true joy and wonder are only myths, and do not actually exist. You are there, Jan, to remind me that they *do* exist. You are also there, it appears, to underscore their fragile nature, and to remind me that I should continue to resist the conventional temptation to conclude wonder and joy are illusory.

But I'm getting ahead of myself, I guess. I suppose my haste is that endless need to rush into your arms again, the way I did before, like there was nothing in the world with enough strength to prevent the force of our embrace.

For now, that day we landed in Munich, I was glad to be safely on the ground, exhausted but alive. The two or three-hour bus ride across the border into Austria and on to our pension was, itself, uneventful. By the time we reached Westendorf, my friends and I were too tired to even talk to one another. We wanted desperately to sleep. We'd been up more than twenty-four hours by then. And being so exhausted, I had no idea I'd glimpsed a revelation about life and death that would show itself to be a turning point for me, in just a matter of days. Yes, I was too tired to notice that fate was sneaking up on me. Then again, had I been more alert, I'm not sure it would have altered anything. Fate is bigger than any human being, and much larger than our ability to perceive its complex strategies. Fate is a farmer after all; we humans are little more than its terrarium of hapless ants.

STILL, WESTENDORF WAS BEAUTIFUL, even in our sleep-deprived state. My friends and I oohed and aahed out the windows as our bus pulled into the courtyard in front of our pension. It was sunny and perfect that day, the village clogged with prolific spring snow, the temperatures warm during this late March afternoon.

We had fished out our sunglasses from our carry-ons an hour or so ago—it was such a blindingly sunny day. And I think we enjoyed the notion of looking so much like tourists, embracing and simultaneously pushing away this new vacation setting, the way tourists usually do. Like paradise is a good place to visit, but you wouldn't want to live there. Like living in paradise beyond a week or two will reveal its flaws and, in so doing, remind us of *our* flaws and our previous disappointments. Back then, I was like most people I know, committed to believing in as little as possible for fear of some inevitable disappointment. We are especially suspicious of places that look like paradise. Because there's no such place, no such state, and, most of all, no such *person*.

Standing outside, next to the bus, while the driver pulled our luggage out of a cargo bay in the belly of the vehicle, I turned my tired face this way and that towards the village's still windlessness. I turned three hundred and sixty degrees to view appreciatively the gentle splendor of the Alps. I was mesmerized by the calm. There was no traffic. The village was too small and rustic for *traffic*. Across the square from where I stood, I could make out the roof and part of the tail section of a rust-colored Volkswagen Beetle almost entirely buried in snow. Strangely enough, it didn't seem abandoned, the way it would have seemed in Canada under similar circumstances. On the surface of it, it would have probably been violating some parking bylaw in Canada; worse yet, as an abandoned vehicle, it would have been on the wrong side of right and wrong. In Canada, we would have had the Volkswagen towed away. But here in Westendorf it was merely parked to wait out the winter, as if by arrangement. In Westendorf, I decided, it was apparent winter was something good and fine, not something to be overcome as an impediment to commerce, as a breaker of rules, as an obstacle to getting things—our conventional, material imperatives—*done*. In Westendorf, the snowbound Volkswagen didn't seem to be a symbol of approaching anarchy, the way it might have seemed back home.

The Alps—and, by no means have I traveled their entirety—are pretty mountains to me. I've seen the Rockies, of course, on more numerous occasions, despite their great distance from where I live. I see the Alps and the Rockies as mountains of different gender. The Rockies are handsome.

Masculine. Rugged. The Alps are impressive and big, but feminine to me. Flirtatious in a benign way. Coy. Or maybe I bestow these qualities on them because of my own sanguine needs or fancies, employing my sensibilities over panorama only in retrospect. You know what I mean, Jan, the Alps, as beautiful as you are; you, as beautiful as I remember the Alps to be. Like both you and the Alps share a capacity for leaving me, by times, in a state of brilliant breathlessness. You still do this to me, Jan. Years later, you still leave me breathless at the most unexpected of moments. With a turn of your head, with a flick of your hand, with a certain kind of glance. These moments continue to surprise me. Although I look for them, anticipate them, they nonetheless arrive without warning. And I swallow some peculiar something that feels as hard as a walnut in my throat. And I feel that strange concoction of empty fullness that aches through the fibers of my body. It's just love, I know. I can't express it beyond calling it a longing. I can't explain it any better, although this feeling has tormented me for years.

Sometimes I think we should never attempt to describe love in words, at least the power of the feeling that we feel. Not if we're looking for originality, at any rate. To me, the more deeply and persistently love is felt, the more inadequate become the words we would use to describe it. We are forced to fall back, to define love with the only means remaining to us: cliché, hyperbole. I think this is because we don't want to move out of love's enticing feeling long enough to even risk the distance creative thought might require of us. No, we prefer to stay inside the feeling and to hell with finding the means to describe what it is like, the joy we know we feel.

Of course, the link between you and this village in the Alps, well, I'm coming to *my* version of the connection. And you no doubt have a version of your own, if you think about it much at all. This is the ironic aspect about you and me and Westendorf: I have no idea how frequently you remember it in your past, while I recall it virtually every day. But back then, that day, as I stood by the bus, waiting for my luggage to be retrieved from the vehicle's belly, I thought the Alps encircling Westendorf were the prettiest mountains I'd ever seen. And I wonder in retrospect, if even then, I was enjoying a precognitive glimpse of the tremendous circumstance that was about to happen to me. I don't know. Maybe I'm trying to remember too hard. Maybe I'm trying to make too much sense of what is only the perfidy of fate.

The village too was postcard perfect. It was small, its various buildings randomly dotting the landscape inside the fabric border of the mountains surrounding it. Like the village belonged there by birthright. Like Westendorf and its setting were a perfectly harmonious marriage. I could make out a chalet in the distance, on the top of one of the nearest peaks. It, too, seemed placed there to be faithful to the conspicuous union between village and mountain setting. Like it had been on top of this mountain for thousands of years and would remain there for a thousand more. Gazing at this place, I felt both elderly and youthful here, stale and new, vaguely like a problem and its own solution, battered by some maverick electron whizzing around and between my various ill considered incongruities. I guess, mostly, I felt like a demented archaeologist too confused by what he's looking for to even contemplate discovering it.

"How far up do you make that chalet?" I asked my friends, my voice sounding strange to me, as if someone *else* had spoken.

Brad, who always answered a question, who always seemed to know, remarked, "About a mile, I'd say."

No one argued with him. My other friends had joined a throng of skiers who were going over the tags attached to the large stack of luggage on the pavement. Brad, now that he'd answered my question, resumed looking for his bags too.

But I remained mesmerized by the beauty of my setting, almost stupefied by it in my sleep-deprived state. In fact, I felt beyond any need for sleep now. What I *needed* at this moment was to stand here for a good long time, tempted by the astonishing magic I noticed on my horizon everywhere I looked. While my friends had complained to one another on the bus about how much sleep we were going to need, how they couldn't wait to get to their rooms to take a nap before dinner, I felt separate from them now that we had arrived. I refused to believe the instant infatuation I had with Westendorf was inspired by my fatigue. I preferred to feel unexpectedly connected to this place, to feel a powerful sense of *arrival.* This was my *place,* wasn't it? There was some important purpose, beyond a mere vacation, for me to be here, wasn't there?

It was all strange and familiar, both at the same time. The spring snow, granular in the warmth of the sunlight refracting off the peaks, the sun shining down on a village of chalets and pensions that, although postcard perfect, seemed so only because of their apparent disarray. No square blocks of streets and sidewalks here, no shopping malls, no looming big box stores. The homes and shops, the restaurants and cafés and nightclubs seemed to complement one another in a spirit of friendship transcending mere design. Like accidents are *perfections*, not the *imperfections* we believe they are. Like maybe in this world we shouldn't plan so much—our setting, our paths through life, our goals, our arrangements with one another. Maybe we should let much more happen by accident, so that the beauty in the result is less contrived, is permitted to evolve into its more natural self. No doubt this kind of anarchy would invite tragedy sometimes, but ecstasy would be possible too, wouldn't it?

"You coming, Tom?"

I turned, the spell suddenly broken. Fatigue nearly felled me then, as I was pulled dismayed from the inspiration I had discovered residing in this place and inside my private thoughts. I grew dizzy for a second. I didn't even know which one of my friends had called my name. They stood in a grinning cluster in front of the pension entrance, looking back at me, bemused by their own fatigue, but amused by the way I now seemed to be drifting out of orbit. All the other people who had shared the bus with us had vanished. The bus had pulled out onto the street, heading for the village square. My suitcase waited at my feet. I stood by myself, adrift.

"Sorry," I said to my friends.

"You're bagged, man," George remarked. "Time to get some zees."

"But will you look at this place?" I said, managing a clumsy pirouette. "I mean, it's more than I imagined."

My friends nodded or muttered their agreement but it seemed a patient, tolerant acknowledgment only. I was the one, it was clear, who was going to love this place much more deeply than a mere holiday distraction. Fine. So much the better. There are times when a man should be left comfortably alone to sort through the truth revealed by his unique perception.

That was Saturday afternoon. In less than forty-eight hours, on the Monday morning, I would badly tear the ligaments in my hung over right knee. And I remain convinced to this day that it was this careless event that toppled the first in the row of waiting dominoes that would shortly bring you into my world, changing it forever in various dangerous ways, altering its direction in a fashion I could never have anticipated.

MY FRIENDS ASSUMED THE ROLE of Judy's champions during that week in Westendorf. A group of robust men in their mid-twenties can be surprisingly moral once they decide they have someone's best interests at heart. I draw this conclusion clearly more than twenty years after that trip with my friends to the Austrian Alps. Over time I have grown more morally flexible. These days I place morality exclusively in the purview of society. As for what defines my own actions, I prefer to call it ethics, my personal means of defining myself and the quality of my behavior. At the time, though, I was pleased my friends endorsed and protected my relationship with Judy. As the only one among the five of us who was romantically attached in any significant way, it was expected that I would be true to my caring for Judy, that I would have no interest in the bevy of young women we soon discovered had come here that week to ski. I accepted this arrangement without reservation. I was in love and happily connected to Judy Smythe in what I believed was a permanent arrangement. As far as I was concerned, my friends were right to assume that I had no need of anyone else, sexually or otherwise.

I'm out of touch now with my colleagues from Carleton. It happens. Twenty years is plenty of time for young men to mature and drift away from one another as they embark on their own lives. Then again, maybe because they had a minor part to play in what was about to happen to me that week in Westendorf, maybe I unconsciously let them go—as friends, as innocent witnesses—because I didn't want them to know how foolish I would become as I lived the rest of my life. I don't know. Except for David, maybe I've always been faithless. Maybe my heart can't hold onto things as long as I would like it to. Then again, condemning myself as fickle fails to address the apparent endlessness of my unrequited love for *you*. Maybe it's more honest to admit there only exist a few important people in anyone's life, only a few special individuals we find it necessary to hold onto.

Never mind. I still have plenty of time, pending some act of God, to work this out in my mind in a way that ultimately satisfies me. And maybe working it out is the state of attrition I've already mentioned, the attrition that sometimes condemns life to underachievement. Maybe I'll soon learn that life mostly just happens like a wild mustang we can't resist trying to break down into a tired nag. Maybe everything I want to believe in is only myth. Maybe I'm the only person I know who really doesn't have a grasp of *true* reality. Maybe it's time I shrugged off my rather ridiculous ideal surrounding the notion of romantic love.

As for my friends—Brad and Gord, Fred and George—their faces now blur in my memory. I suppose part of this is that they remain perpetually young in my mind. Brad, the one with the answers, the tallest, the handsomest of us, the one who snorted judgmentally when the rest of us mentioned love, who found himself bored as soon as he achieved his most recent conquest. Fred, career-driven and conventional—I'll bet he's the wealthiest of us by now, more at home in the corporate media juggernaut that is the company for which both he and I work, slanting our stories in a way that makes a conservative status quo appear inevitable and good, even to its many hapless, increasing victims. And George? George had no charisma. Sometimes, when the five of us got together, during our university days or even afterwards, if George was late, it would take us a long time to realize he was missing. We all liked George. But he had an uncanny talent for being an afterthought. I suppose I was closest to Gord. Gord was a nice guy. Gord was steady and compassionate. Big and brawny, with a thick mustache all of us envied, Gord cared freely and gently about people and the world. At the time, I was drawn to his caring, his calm patience. But I'm out of touch with Gord too. It's been more than fifteen years since I've talked to or seen any of my friends who accompanied me to Westendorf, the young men who never truly recognized what happened to me there.

I STUDIED A LITTLE GERMAN during my high school days. For just one year. German remains a difficult language for me. Nonetheless, despite its awkwardness on my tongue and the complexity of its vocabulary, my friends from Carleton appointed me official translator for our skiing week in Westendorf. My duties? Mostly I sat at the bar, eavesdropping where I could on the conversation of numerous pretty, young women who, like us, had come here to ski. If I heard German, I informed my friends who then could gauge whether this was an impediment to their approach. It was mostly a game. I wasn't truly necessary to this process of reconnoitering the spoils. My German wasn't good enough. And there were many English-speaking young women from whom my friends could choose. No, this game of linguistic eavesdropping reflected the fact they'd all met Judy and had decided I was committed to a very nice woman who was attractive and admirable. "We," as Fred put it, "are unencumbered by serious romantic arrangement while you are not. And you'd be an idiot to forsake Judy for a fling in Austria." I concurred. I was committed. My friends, unlike me, were here, as most men in their mid-twenties were, to find a woman to spend the week with them. I felt sure enough of my feelings for Judy to resist any similar temptation.

And so, agreeable, knowing I *could* be trusted, I played my eavesdropping game that first evening. After three or four hours sleep and a satisfying dinner in our pension dining room, I sat at the bar in a small club called The Alpen Bar, watching my friends dance with an assortment of attractive women. I believed the unexpected magic I had felt blowing gently down the slopes towards me from the summits of the Austrian Alps had nothing to do with love. If anything, it was merely scenic appreciation. I didn't know I was destined in any way to meet someone like you.

As for The Alpen Bar, we decided the next morning at breakfast that we needed to find another place to have a drink or two in the evenings.

"A disco is only a disco," Brad complained. "I've seen places like The Alpen Bar back home. We need something more . . ." and the word eluded him.

"Authentic?" I suggested.

"Yeah, authentic," he said.

And my other friends concurred.

On our way out to ski that first morning, church bells ringing in the distance from the Catholic church at one edge of the village, I asked Maria, the young woman behind the desk, about a more authentic bar we might enjoy that evening.

"Ah," said Maria with a knowing toss of her head. "The Keller Bar. You should go to the Keller Bar."

That night, we switched to the Keller Bar, where we would gather each evening for the rest of the week. There was an oompahpah band performing each night, not one of its members under seventy years of age. These men fascinated me, not merely because of their timeless musicianship, but they brought a charming verve to their endless nights in the bar, three old-timers who could play Strauss waltzes as well as Johann Strauss himself, I decided in my booze-benumbed exuberance. It amused my friends that I requested so many Strauss waltzes, a waltz for each occasion I was served a *Lowenbrau.*

As for the skiing that first day, I remember the conditions were perfect. Brad skied by me that afternoon, already turning brown in the spring warmth reflected on the snow, wearing only his tee-shirt tucked into his baggy ski pants. He was the only one among us brazen enough to expose himself to the early promise of the March sunshine in this way. While I didn't feel up to stripping down to my tee-shirt, I skied in a light sweater because of the spring like conditions inside the luxury of Westendorf's windlessness.

It was an easy vacation, simply set up, simple to enjoy. Everything was included, we hardly had to think or decide at all. We had dinner at our pension that evening and every evening afterwards—it was included in our package.

But that first day was truly perfect. I loved the setting so much, life felt like it was *enough.* I wasn't looking for *anything* else—no enhancement, no destiny prank, no improvement in my lot. Certainly I wished for no happenstance in Westendorf predestined to change my life. It was to be an idyllic vacation, a skiing package that included everything, travel, three meals per day, my accommodation, even lessons, if I wanted them. The holiday was designed to be uncomplicated. There was no need to injure myself, to put in place the sequence of events that would bring you into my life. So, in a sense, I blame myself. Stupid, really, to assume this kind of responsibility. Life, by its very nature, is too rich in many ways for purposeful analysis. You see, Jan, the things that happen, happen. We have to live with this fact. The things that happen, happen. It's just when and to whom and to what degree. No point in wondering why. Why is a stupid question. In an universe as absurd as this one, "why?" is the only question it will always be pointless to ask.

GERMAN BEER, I DISCOVERED THEN, at least for me, possesses an uncanny ability to ambush me. Prior to Westendorf and in the two decades since, beer has never affected me the same way in Canada. On this night, our second in Austria, sitting at a table with my friends, I consumed six quarts of beer, feeling entirely sober after each one. I even knocked back a shot of schnapps someone ordered for me, without any sense that I was getting drunk. Ten minutes later, though, I was suddenly a wreck—pissed, plastered, toasted and roasted. By the time we closed the place, my friends were deeply amused at how drunk I had inadvertently become. I don't remember much after this fierce state of inebriation descended on me so suddenly. Just glimpses, little snapshots of my hopelessness, me giggling helplessly while my friends dragged me to our pension, the toes of my boots leaving ruts in the wake of my inebriated body, my legs as useful for walking as rubber bands would have been.

Next morning, I woke up to discover I occupied some

strange, new dimension I was not familiar with. It was defined by pain and dizziness. The room was spinning and my bed spun inside it like a solar system inside its own universe. Parched, my head throbbing, I tumbled onto the floor, just to stop the room from orbiting the painful sun my body had become. The headache that immediately followed jumped on me with a terrible ruthlessness, like Thor's hammer or Wiley Coyote's falling anvil. I glanced out the window, holding my forehead in the palm of my right hand, as if my brains might suddenly fall out and splatter on the floor. Outside, the snow was pink, like someone had dyed it with blood. I have never been so devastatingly hung over as I was that second morning in Westendorf.

I told my gleeful, unsympathetic friends at breakfast, after I tiptoed down the stairs—each step a gorge in a hellish, wooden staircase landscape—that I wouldn't be skiing this morning. As good friends will, at times like these, they mocked and tormented me. They convinced me otherwise. My head pounding, the snow still colored pink despite the best efforts of a bright and warming sun, I started down my first gentle slope, trying to reconnect with a physical body that my head was convinced belonged to someone else. I pitched forward. I crashed. It seemed to take a great deal of time for the bolt of pain to break through my hangover to register on my brain. There was, in that first moment, I realized, some poor wretch screaming in agony not far away on the Austrian slopes. Then, acknowledging the pain and the cries, I discovered a second later that that poor wretch was me.

In the aftermath of my accident, my friends took me to a clinic in the village where an elderly and affable doctor assessed the damage to my leg.

"Torn ligaments," he said with apparent familiarity. "You will need pain killers and a bandage."

"A bandage?"

"Yes. With tension. You must wrap your knee."

He gave me directions to the drug store.

So it was that my friends were able to ski for the rest of the week without me while I hobbled around the village of Westendorf, aided by a cane I purchased in a small gift shop not far from our pension. The cane was designed to resemble a mountain climbing pick, obviously primarily a souvenir, but it and the tightly wound tensor bandage, plus some prescription medication, kept the pain of my injury at an endurable level. For me, though, this skiing trip was over. I assured my friends that I would find quiet ways to amuse myself while they continued to recreate on the slopes.

It was a serious injury and my convalescence was long. I wasn't able to permanently remove the bandage until two weeks before Judy and I were married the following September. And even so, I limped for another year. Sometimes, for a few years afterwards, the weather would cause it to act up. The dampness, the humidity, the chill in a day—it didn't seem to matter which. Some days it just wanted to hurt. Some days over the next few years, it seemed a punishment for the way I fell in love with *you*.

The injury and the happenstance that led to it were just

sequential factors, I'm convinced, that set in motion events leading me to you. Maybe I would have met you anyway at some point during that week. But I like to believe fate strings its various pearls in a calculated order, as it makes jewelry of our lives. To demonstrate that there is purpose, a direction endorsing the notion we are open to being alive as much as we can be. Destiny on our side. Destiny existing to help us, if only we recognize what it wishes to *do* for us. Nonsense perhaps. But then who is to say for sure?

Still, I wonder sometimes, if I hadn't injured myself in this way, if all the rest of what happened between you and me might never have taken place at all. And I'm torn when I wonder this. One side of me wants to conclude it would have made more *sense* if the rest of it did not happen. It would have endorsed a more conventional acceptance in me about life and love, if I hadn't met you that week in Westendorf. Perhaps it would have been fairer. To Judy. To you. Perhaps even to *me*.

But then, another side of me cannot imagine the depth of the loss I feel when I imagine missing out on loving you. And, should I have missed out in this way, I'm also forced to wonder if I would have eventually realized that something rich and exotic in my life was lacking. Would the emotional wisdom I now keep secret inside myself still have occurred to me without you to inspire it? Would you still have become the woman I believe I was meant to love? I cannot answer these questions. But, at times, something inside me wants to be let in on destiny's plan. So that I can answer my questions. So I can solve the riddle. So I can understand. So I can find my place in fate's absurdity, and in so doing, come to believe it isn't absurd at all.

FIVE

YOU'VE CUT YOUR HAIR a little shorter since the last time I saw you. I soon admire your new look despite a persistent and delicate resentment I sometimes feel when you transform yourself in my absence. As if, when you change, I lose a little more of you to the onward sweep of time, to the shrinkage of what few moments remain in the potential for our connected futures. When I realize that you continue on in life without me, it feels like the finger of my hope—namely that time will bring us together—has sustained some kind of splinter. I guess I want the sanctity of my memory of you preserved perfectly. Else what is already a tenuous grip on the you I'm allowed to hold safely in my heart will be loosened further.

I can't allow you to recognize any of this possessiveness, of course. And I don't. I won't. Keeping my continued love for you secret—and knowing I must—are essential needs to me, even while I fundamentally believe they're unfair. Repressed emotion is like a giant boil on the inside of my flesh. It hides there in the darkness where it grumbles and festers, refusing to shrink or heal. Sometimes my caring for you is so spectacular in my mind, it feels like a criminal act, a transgression that clearly violates one of the world's taboos. The illegality doesn't reside in what I feel, I know, but there's an undeniably immoral edict about wanting and loving so deeply someone who is, and chose at one time to be, my sister-in-law instead of my wife. It's one thing to be unable to violate the principle in the feeling of love, quite another to challenge the conventional social propriety that surrounds the familial status of the person who is loved.

So here we are, all together again. The ritual hugfest comes next. Approaching our car, you hug your sister. Greg hugs Judy. You move towards me. You embrace me and I embrace you. Shorter than your sister, you reach that point on my upper chest where a man like me recognizes powerfully the fragility of what he is holding in his arms, and grows protective of it. As I embrace you, I smell just a passing heartache of your shampoo, then, in its purest form, the unique, familiar scent that is and has always been *you*. I endure the delicate reminder of what I am not supposed to remember or want about your body. I appreciate a glimpse of your right ear, peeking through some strands of your hair. I detect, just for an instant, your small breasts against my upper belly. Then all of these sensations are ripped away from me, torn out of time as you back away from me and I back away from you, as we politely give each other up. I stand naked and wanting afterwards, foolish because I've been found stealing across the border between two comfortless worlds defined by my notions of *could* or *should*. To me, *could* and *should* are countries in some subjunctive universe, a prison colony world a million light years away from my currently hapless romantic truth.

Greg shakes my hand in a businesslike fashion, the way he always does. "Can you park your car around the side, a little closer to my SUV?" Where people should park their cars is important to Greg. He not only craves an orderly cosmos, he wants to be acknowledged or revered for helping to create it. He told me one evening a few years ago, a little drunk and boastful at the time, that he believes he's cornered a market on an essential efficiency.

"Huh?" I'm murmuring now. I'm still lost in the carnage of your innocuous embrace, in what I can still recall, through the medium of the ache in my flesh, of your gentle touch and feel. I'm trying to remember if you whispered my name as we embraced or if, at this moment, I was caught merely wishing or imagining you did, which is more likely the case.

"I said, 'park your car over by my SUV.'"

I'm thinking how imagination inevitably blurs reality when I first encounter you after an absence of several months. In a larger sense, because of you and the passage of two decades of time, I'm forced to wonder if I will ever know what is actually real.

"Tommy?" This from a vaguely embarrassed Judy, a diplomat from a conventional human country that believes it *knows* what is really real. "Did you hear Greg? Did you hear what he said?"

"Yeah. Yeah. Sorry."

And you glance at me in the spotlight of my apology. I think I notice a tiny smile of compassion trembling along your lips, but in the end I can't be certain.

"Okay," I tell everyone, struggling at this moment to appear amiable.

Inside I feel annoyed. To be honest, I don't believe moving my car where Greg thinks I should put it is going to help the world spin on its axis any more efficiently. Will lives be saved? Will tidal waves be turned back? Will swollen waters recede from vulnerable riverbanks? People with control issues mystify me because they care so deeply about their preoccupation with the inconsequential, with what they can micromanage. I wonder why they do. Are they afraid of these less complex rewards awaiting them in life? Or is it just that they don't know the difference between what is and is not important?

Then again, why should *I* be right? In a way, my own self-doubt makes me a pacifist in the war of ideas or absolutes. My knowing I don't know is a kind of Platonic knowing. Greg's not knowing he doesn't know is a Platonic refusal to know.

But despite my annoyance, with Greg and with the me that differs from him, I hear the sound of my voice busily ingratiating itself. "Sorry," I am saying. "That was a long drive. I'm kind of zoned out, now that I'm out of the car." For good measure, to successfully redeem myself, I form two fists, miming their frozen grip on the steering wheel.

"How long have you guys been waiting for us?" Judy wants

to know.

Your "not long" is overpowered by Greg's "about an hour and a half."

"What time did you leave?" Judy asks.

"Just after nine o'clock. You know Toronto. We waited to avoid the traffic."

"Jesus," Judy says. "We left about seven. And you beat us here. Is Ottawa that much further away?"

I begin to move gently away from the center of this awkward conversation. I feel exposed and embarrassed, not just because I am about to appear foolish for taking the longer route, or because I will once again feel the need to justify myself, but because this topic is so much more important to Judy and Greg than it is to me.

"Ottawa?" Greg is saying. "Ottawa's about the same distance. You must have gone the wrong way."

"Look," I hear you say. "We're all here safely and it's a nice afternoon. What difference does it make?"

Relieved, I glance in your direction but you are preoccupied with your sister.

"Tommy wanted to go through Algonquin Park," Judy explains.

"Yes. I did."

"Well, shit," says Greg. "That would explain it. It's a helluva lot further going that way. You should have just stayed on Highway Seventeen."

"Tommy?"

"Well, look at it this way—it just means going home will be

faster, Jude."

Judy rolls her eyes. There's a gentle flush leaching into her cheeks. Meanwhile, you and your husband gaze at me in contrasting shades of perplexity.

"Sorry, guys," I add. "Obviously it's more out of the way than I thought. I wanted to see the fall colors in Algonquin. I thought twenty minutes more, what the hell? We stopped for a break a couple of times too." When my audience does not respond, I shrug and ask, "Can we stop talking about this now?"

I turn away at this point so that I don't have to deal with everyone's reaction to my last-minute militancy. In the ensuing silence you touch me on the arm. "It's not important, Tom. I don't see where any terrible damage has been done." And for this small token alone, I want to lift you onto my charger and gallop away with you in the general direction of Camelot.

"Speak for yourself," snorts Judy. "*You* didn't have to spend all that extra time in the car."

"Do you need help unpacking?" you ask me.

"We're okay," Judy tells her with an unexpected sternness.

"I'll unload, Greg, then I'll move the car," I murmur.

Hurriedly I unpack, stacking groceries and suitcases and bedding wrapped in hissing garbage bags on the rough wooden steps at the bottom of the lodge's aging veranda I do most of this alone. Judy stands talking to you and Greg, her hands holding you and your husband in place, clutching your forearms, as if she wants to prevent you or even your husband from coming to my rescue. Churlishly I postulate that Judy views my act of unpacking as some penance I must make. Then, at one point, she turns to me and shakes her head in gentle frustration.

"I hope nobody wants to go down the steps," she says.

"It's just for a moment, Jude."

And while I finish unpacking, I wonder why couples reach this point in their relationships where they treat each other like children, looking for little ways to criticize one another, searching for another opportunity to say no without having an actual *reason* to say no. Would you and I have reached this point too, if everything had developed differently twenty years ago, if we had committed to each other instead of to the partners we did?

Strangely enough, though, this penance of unpacking frees me from the awkwardness that has surrounded most of our arrival here. Soon I'm out of the dog house for driving through Algonquin Park, for enjoying the wilderness so much where I annually commune with nature.

While I prepare to park my car in the place by Greg's SUV, the way I've been told, Judy moves inside the lodge with you and Greg. She's smiling now and I'm glad of this. It *was* a long drive and part of me feels sorry for the self-indulgence in my decision to take the longer route. Another part of me is aware Judy and I could never handle driving to a more distant destination. On a drive *that* long, I would probably *brood* her to death.

Around the corner of the lodge, where I can have a moment or two to myself, I lean against the side of the car and admire the deep woods not far away. Some silver birches, white pine, cedar. I'm pleased with a colorful stand of maples, shuffled into the evergreens like a spilled bucket of red paint. And the smell of this mix of trees is sweet, like it's just been pulled out of an oven and left to cool on a window-ledge, evergreen-deciduous pie, a mouthwatering dessert.

I notice a rusty post in the ground ten feet away. Horseshoe pit. I have to search for a few minutes, but I finally find its partner further off to the right. The area is overgrown, but there must be horseshoes stored somewhere inside the lodge. Maybe I can talk the others into a game this weekend, if I find the tools to cut away the weeds growing so prolifically in the sand in the pits.

When I finally walk around to the front of the lodge again, the things Judy and I brought with us have all been moved inside. I realize I'm probably missing Greg's tour of the main building, but I would prefer to have a look on my own anyway, not just to get to know the rooms, and their nooks and crannies, but to see if I can figure out why this place was so important to my mother-in-law. So I stand on the porch by myself and study what I can see of the outdoor portion of Gladys Pinkster-Smythe's hitherto secret resort.

I suspect Greg will soon have figured out the legal extent of the property, if he doesn't know it already, what is owned by Judy and Jan, where it abuts what is likely owned by the Crown. As for me, I can enjoy the luxury of not having to consider this place for legal or resale purposes. I get to take it in on aesthetic grounds only.

I suppose it gets to consider *me* differently too. Certainly, as I stand on the porch now, looking things over, it strikes me that this place is flirting with me. It's batting its aged eyelashes at me, trying to entice me into noticing the beauty it possesses underneath its superficial disrepair. The sense that I am here to name this place remains with me, but now I feel a powerful sensation of familiarity here as well. I say "powerful" because I am not a man who gives any credence to déja vu or reincarnation, or any other metaphysical manifestation relating to past lives or predestination. For me to feel this property is familiar, the sensation *has* to be powerful to break through the various cynical barriers I have constructed around my psyche.

Still, breaking through is exactly what this place does. It *is* familiar here. It's not that I've been here before, it's not *that* kind of familiarity. No, I mean I feel comfortable here. I feel at home, as strange and untoward as this sensation might be. Like a man can find his place even when he has never visited *the place* before.

The property dropping somewhat steeply down to the lake is overgrown with autumn-tired grasses and sometimes brilliantly colored shrubs and sumac sporadically dotting the meadow. I can't tell how long the property has been unused, whether this growth is the result of neglect or was left in place by design. I don't know why, but something suggests the latter.

From my vantage point on the top step of the porch, I can see only two of the cottages that are lined up at different rocky elevations on my right, facing the lake. I counted six cottages when we first arrived, but for all I know there may be more and I decide to take a closer look. I halve the distance between the lodge and a broken down dock jutting a couple of hundred yards away into the lake.

A red squirrel chatters at me from a pine branch over my head to the right. I look up and answer him as best I can, although David Cruickshank is the true mimic of the two of us when we are camping together. The red squirrel gazes at me a moment in silence, then, bored with me, darts along the branch to resume its business elsewhere.

In the end I count eight cottages. Each has been built at a different elevation into the rocks and clearings along a portion of the shore that gradually rises towards a steep cliff approximately two hundred yards away. The cliff falls directly into the lake and a small poplar perches on its summit like a rookie sentry, some of its yellow leaves already stripped away by autumn winds, the remainder waiting patiently for the next stiff breeze to finish *them* off. Then, beyond the cliff summit, a deep woods is evident, growing darker in the distance as it becomes denser. The path heading in this direction is overgrown as well, but I can still make out where it once was well-traveled, and I know, before this weekend is over, I will want to follow it to see where it ultimately leads.

There is another path to my left that heads in the direction of a second patch of woods. This trail too is overgrown until it enters the trees where a heavier canopy of foliage has prevented the weeds from intruding as much. It is clear I have a lot of exploring to do this weekend but, for now, I walk the remaining distance to the dilapidated dock and the rust-splotched aluminum canoe I discover along the way in the long grasses along the shore.

Actually, the dock is more solid than it looked. The upper slats have begun to rot in places but the footings seem solid. And if there has been any significant ice damage over several winters of neglect, it isn't clearly in evidence. Gingerly I tread out onto the dock, stepping carefully over the boards that are cracked and spongy. I find a solid place to stand and, from here, gaze down into the murk at the bottom of the lake. The water is very clear. The lake bottom is a forest of leaves that have fallen here over the years, gone colorless beneath the waters from several accumulated autumns. I can see small branches on the bottom too, waterlogged and still, like fingers, snakes or lengths of cable. Fish, mostly small bass and perch, socialize not far beneath the surface close to the shore, still but for the gentle dance of their fins.

I turn and gaze at the cottages again, assessing casually what might need to be done to them to improve them. At one time they were painted white with a deep red trim, but the paint has peeled badly. The buildings, little more than quaint cabins, seem scarred, defaced by neglect, like they suffer from leprosy. But even *this* neglect feels encouraging to me. I can envision myself sanding and painting the walls, wiping my sweaty brow with a bare and dirty forearm. I even imagine the four of us working here, painting and sanding together, and swatting at insects, all of us partners and friends. Then, inevitably, picking at this fancy like a restless sculptor, I manipulate the cast until only you and I remain in the daydream, laboring as a love-struck couple to save this place. I swallow the wretched lump this fantasy inspires in me, the one catching in my throat, mentally kicking myself in the ass for the endlessly optimistic stupidity you inspire in my imagination.

From the vantage point of this place on the dock, I turn to gaze back at the lodge itself. It too suffers from peeling paint, although to a lesser extent. The windows are relatively small, as was the style half a century or more ago, when this building was probably constructed. The porch exhibits some rough, decaying sections, I've already noticed, but I wouldn't conclude the structure is beyond repair. And everything faces the lake in a spirit of subtle reverence, exactly the way it's supposed to. At one time this place probably seemed like a small paradise to someone: restful, peaceful, tranquil.

I sigh.

Name me, this place urges me again. *Name me, Tom.*

"I will," I murmur out loud, the sound of my voice startling and embarrassing me.

But the embarrassment doesn't last. This resort property is too familiar to me now. And being familiar, it forgives me everything, even the words I forget to keep inside and mutter right out loud.

Without taking my eyes off the main building, I stroll back up the grade, imagining the undergrowth trimmed back around me, a lawn, gardens, pathways of wood shavings perhaps. And, inevitably, I imagine you standing there smiling warmly at me as, in my daydream, I walk in your direction, towards the overdue state of peace and resolution I sometimes crave in my love for you.

THERE IS SO MUCH for me to look at and admire here. It's a pleasure connected easily to this moment of delight in my own company. I am not a shy person but, at the same time, I am not comfortable being constantly gregarious. There are times when people need long moments of being alone to recognize again what they like about themselves. I sometimes think my world is so insistently busy, I rarely have a moment to move off by myself to remember who I am. There are too many phone calls, too many voicemails, too many questions to ask and answer about too many topics and issues that are relatively devoid of personal purpose or importance. My job is defined this way. I write articles that are supposed to convey the earth-shattering implications of, say, political corruption or economic sleight of hand, knowing all the while how old and fatuous these issues actually are. Afterwards, we hardly remember them or their details. And the world spins as it did before they took place. Yet, a good deal of the self living inside each one of us is put aside for long periods of time each day while we concentrate on societal distractions such as these that we don't truly care about.

No wonder I like the wilderness. The distractions are minimal. I have the time and opportunity to make friends with myself once more.

"So what do you think, Tom?" you call as you and your sister step out onto the porch again to catch me approaching the lodge.

Judy answers for me. "He likes it," she says flatly, although

I notice a tight, little grimace of resignation on her face. "I recognize the signs. Look for Tommy to grow more and more pensive and philosophical as the weekend progresses."

"You make it sound like a communicable disease," I complain.

"No, philosophy's good," you say. "There's nothing wrong with philosophy."

"Except it doesn't accomplish much," adds Judy.

We all fall silent to consider the falsehood in *this* remark.

"You missed the tour, honey. We thought you'd got lost already."

"I'll look around inside later, Jude. I was down on the dock. There's a canoe down there. It might be seaworthy. I'll check it out later. It's a nice property. You should go down and have a look for yourselves." Inside I wince. *A nice property?* Now I sound like Greg.

"We thought we would," Judy is saying.

Both of you move down the steps in the opposite direction to me.

As you and Judy pass, you turn to me—I suspect to ask if I want to join you. But you seem to think better of the idea, or perhaps you are thinking about something else entirely, which doesn't include me at all. Whatever the reason, you don't proffer the invitation.

So I sit down on the second step from the bottom and watch both of you make your way down through the tall grasses and unkempt shrubs that lead to the dock and the shoreline.

In a way, you hardly look like sisters. Judy is a half a foot taller than you. She has that tear drop ass. You are shorter and slimmer, smaller breasted. But you have more prominent cheekbones and blue eyes so arresting they often sentence me to a breathlessness I can only define as wonder. Judy has blue eyes too, but they sometimes turn green. To me, they're more ambivalent somehow about being on her face. Your eyes, though, are a deep, uncompromising blue. Their beauty has haunted me for more than two decades. Beyond this, as you move away in the distance, I see only that Judy's hair is longer than yours, that she remains taller, that she walks with a visible swagger you do not affect. It strikes me at this moment that you define femininity to me while Judy wears her femininity like a *weapon* of some sort. Then again, love tends to make these little comparisons; love is very subjective about its judgments. And I wonder: can love, so endlessly subjective and biased, ever be truly trusted to tell the truth?

Still, you are both beautiful women. I suppose, in conventional terms, Judy is capable of turning more heads. But for me there is an exquisite excitement I feel when I glance at you, that Judy cannot inspire. Like the beauty I see in you strikes a mysterious chord deep within me, a chord I cannot grasp beyond the excitement and yearning it unleashes. I sometimes wonder if love has to do with how much we like someone. I assume, after all this time, that I continue to love Judy in my way. But do I *like* her? Certainly not in the way I like *you.* What do I mean by liking? Only this: that your laughter is music to me, that we agree on fundamental, simple things, as far as I can tell. And, when I look at you, you still take my breath away. You have seemed, since the moment we met, without equivocation or qualification, the most beautiful creature I have ever seen. Why this is so, in real terms, I have no idea. It just is and, in the being, does not abate. Some time ago I stopped trying to argue with or rationalize my perception. I decided you were beautiful the first time I laid eyes on you. I continue to think so now—so many years later, long after the cleanup of the wreckage of the accident that resulted when you and I happened to each other.

I breathe deeply and carefully at this moment, more than twenty years later, something I must do by times when I am feeling the rush—no, the explosion—of loving and liking you so much. Still, I gaze at the two of you standing on the dock and I can't help comparing you, especially in this setting. You see, that's it, that's the difference between you two for me. I like it here in this place in the woods along the lake. When Judy stands in the landscape of this place I like, as an artist I feel the need to remove her because I know she doesn't fit. But you, sweet Jan, when I glimpse *you* in the landscape before me, you fit here in so many ways I cannot even explain. I only know you belong in this canvas where, as an artist, I render this place and time into my vision of artistic permanence.

Of course, I'd never be caught *saying* so. The lack of data defining my conclusion would expose me as a fool. I can never say *anything* to *anyone* about *any* of this. I quite literally bleed in silence.

Too bad. There you are on the dock in the distance,

autumn colored leaves a spectacular back drop, you and Judy, you fitting into the picture, Judy in a place where she doesn't belong. And I swallow at the profound verisimilitude in this observation, wondering why it had to be this way and why it cannot be resolved.

I'M STILL SITTING ON THE TOP STEP of the veranda at the front of Gladys Pinkster-Smythe's Temagami area lodge some time later when Greg bursts outside. He doesn't remark about me being in the way, but he veers around me, an iPhone in his hand. He squints into the bright autumn sunshine now sinking towards the horizon to the left of us.

I've been here on the steps quite a long time, examining by times the state of disrepair of the lodge and admiring a large stand of autumn-drenched hardwoods in the distance on the other side of the lake. I've come to believe this lodge owns a curious self-possession I find palpable, a kind of defiance, an attitude of casual iconoclasm I enjoy. Its bay windows, its double doors here at the main entrance give its tattered face a kind of rebellious dignity. If this building was a person, it would bluntly confess it doesn't give a fuck about the various minutiae the rest of the world around it takes so seriously. Which makes it similar to *me*, I suppose, or at least similar to the way I *want* to be.

As for the scenery skirting the lake, I enjoy a section of white spruce to my left, curling along the shoreline towards a wall of rocky shield. This large outcropping of rock levels off gradually giving in to a vivid splash of color from the hardwoods still reflected on the far surface of the lake. Gazing at these sights, I realize how happy I am to be here. I *do* like this place. I like it a *lot*. What would Judy say to a confession such as this? What would Judy say to know that I haven't let her down, that I am deeply attracted to a place she indeed *feared* I would like?

"I'm going to have to drive twenty miles back to make some of my calls," Greg says, intruding on my thoughts. "That's the last point where I could get a signal. Twenty miles back, for Christ's sake." He glances at me. "It'll add to the difficulties of trying to sell this place," he says.

"You think so?"

"Absolutely."

"Don't people come to places like this to *not* use electronic gear?" I suggest.

"Not anymore. Only the occasional dinosaur."

I nod and say nothing. I don't use an iPhone myself, although Judy does. We argue about the device's merits at work sometimes. I am a Luddite, I suppose. I want to remain outside the paradigm underscoring today's cell phone mania, the sense of urgency about trivia that a cell phone tends to create. I don't like being part of a society that, when we come to the end of our era, will likely be remembered for the religiosity of its consumerism and the intensity we brought to each minuscule moment of shopping or electronic banality.

You and Judy come outside to catch much of this exchange between Greg and me. Judy actually winces and I know it's because she suspects what I am thinking. I glance furtively at you, gratified to catch you glancing back at me.

Something subtle is happening here. I can't define it. Me, or you and me, or maybe all of us—except Greg who's gazing once again at his device like it's the leader of an uprising—have suddenly grown faintly embarrassed. Like we've caught sight of the same awkward mirage on the horizon, or we've shared the same glimpse of some troubling precognition. Strangely enough, *I'm* the one who purposely interrupts the moment with the first available innocuous remark, thereby opening the valve and relieving the pressure. Because, if I don't, I'll stand up like an idiot, declare my love for you and bring our familial house of cards down around our tragic heads.

"So whaddyuh think of this place?"

At first no one answers me.

"I mean, so far, you know? Whaddyuh think so far? We'll need a better look around, but you must have some opinions by now."

"Some," you reply, gesturing into the woods. "It smells wonderful, for one thing. I feel like I haven't breathed this way in years."

"Yeah. Amen," I say a little too eagerly.

Judy laughs. "I breathe just fine in the city," she remarks.

"What about you, Greg?" I ask. "Notwithstanding the cell phone interference."

"It's a nice property," he says. "But it's too far out in the middle of nowhere. From Toronto, I mean. Where the tourist market is. The distance from Toronto would bring the value down. And it needs some work. I mean, look at the veranda Inside the lodge is solid enough. But don't be thinking you'll make a killing when you sell this place."

I'm nodding like a fool but I'm not really listening to him. For one thing, it's not up to him and me. Our respective wives own this property. Greg and I are just along for the ride. We're just here to give an opinion if someone asks one of us. But that's not the only reason I'm not listening to Greg. Judy's moved off a little to talk to her sister and I'm more interested in what *they're* saying.

"Can you believe Mother owning this place and never ever mentioning it to us?"

You're nodding thoughtfully but so far you're a good deal less perturbed by all of this than Judy is.

"I mean, shit, Jan, did she lose her mind? Why would she buy a place like this. In fact, *when* would she buy a place like this?"

You glance at me and I gently shrug before I flick my gaze away. I don't know why I shrug. But it seems a safe and gently conspiratorial thing to do at this moment, a way of getting close to you without getting *too* close.

"Tom?" you say. "What about you?"

Judy laughs. "Don't ask Tommy. He probably loves this place."

"You have to admit it's a beautiful setting," I say.

"I think so too."

Your sister swats you on the arm. "You're as bad as *he* is. Too much idealism. It clouds your judgment."

"Jude . . . ."

"None of this surprises me, Tommy. I knew you'd like this

place. I knew, as soon as you got out of the city, you'd like this place."

"What's not to like?" I protest, "It's a sunny day in October. Look across the lake. Look at that stand of hardwoods in the distance. I mean what can you say?"

"Oh, fuck," Judy says. "It doesn't matter. Greg said it best. This place is out in the middle of nowhere. Beautiful or not, it's hardly worth such a long trip up from the city."

"Well, what about the inside?" I want to know. "You guys have seen it."

Greg still holds his cell phone, but it no longer has his undivided attention. "Actually," he says, still the expert in real estate, "the inside isn't bad. Real solid. Craftsmanship when it was first built. Nine bedrooms. Electrical should be upgraded. Drilled well. Plumbing's good. I turned it on. It works. Wood is solid, but not dreary. Generally it's in pretty good shape. Take a look yourself, Tom."

"I intend to," I say. "Not that my opinion will make much difference."

Silence slips among us, grinning at what I've said.

"Anyone getting hungry?" I ask to change the subject.

"I am," you say. "All this fresh air, I guess."

"Greg?"

"I could eat," he says. "You cooking?"

"Yeah. Thought we could barbie some steaks. Maybe on that old colossus out there." I indicate a concrete block structure off to our right, blackened and cracked in the waning autumn sunshine, encroached upon by weeds and shrubs. "I brought some real charcoal and starter fluid."

"Oh, Tommy, it's probably filthy."

I gaze at my wife a moment—yes, barbecues are filthy. "I'll check it out," I manage to say.

Judy is watching me carefully. She holds me back when you and Greg disappear inside. She places the flat of her hand against my chest, a gesture I have always construed to be marginally aggressive, and she glares at me. "That long drive through the park, Tommy."

"Yes?"

"It was selfish and inconsiderate."

"An accident," I say.

My wife gazes at me a moment. "There are no accidents," she says at last.

"I'm sorry it took so long. I meant it to be a pleasant experience."

"Please don't be stupid this weekend."

"Stupid?"

But Judy just sighs and goes inside.

Stupid?

Get over it, I think after she is gone, feeling guilty about my disloyalty, but offended by Judy's words. Gratefully, as I sometimes do, I stand there a time, contemplating what I believe I actually deserve in life. And it occurs to me it's *more.* I deserve *more.* Of course, in a world as doctrinaire as this one, I'd never be caught *saying* so.

SIX

AFTER MY PAINFUL LIGAMENT INJURY on the ski slopes in Westendorf, much of the rest of my vacation there was defined by the physical limitations imposed on me by what I had done to myself. The first day was the worst, of course. My injury was three-fold: not only did I have to endure a throbbing ache in my tightly bandaged knee, but I could not escape the harsh notion that I had brought all this on myself; and the hangover that had precipitated my accident clung to me like a particularly malicious parasite. I was unable to get rid of my throbbing head until the following morning. This left me with the deep torment of my injured knee and the dedicated self-loathing I had adopted as a result of my fall on the slopes. I don't know why, exactly, but I delighted in flagellating myself for failing to stick by my conviction not to ski the morning of the accident. Had I waited—as I had wished to do—for the hangover to subside before donning skis that day, I might have avoided what was a relatively serious injury. Dozens of times, I cursed myself for the extent of my stupidity.

In the aftermath, my friends were generally sympathetic, although they assumed no responsibility for daring me into skiing in my hung-over state in the first place. Nor did my injury interrupt their daily skiing rituals, although they joined me for lunch and then dinner, after their skiing day was through. Usually they found me waiting for them in the downstairs lobby of our pension, the stairs a chore for me during the rest of my stay in Westendorf—there was no elevator in our pension. Taking turns, one on either side of me, my friends were compelled to carry me basket style up four short flights of stairs to the floor where my room was located, because, for the first two days after my crash, I could not bend my knee and manage the steps myself. While I could get *down* the stairs, given enough time and resolve, going upstairs was impossible on my own. And so each day, after breakfast, before lunch, before dinner, and at the end of the day, I was carried up the stairs, my friends tormenting me with shameless dispassion about what they found funny in my humiliating circumstances.

"Don't call me when they admit you to the retirement home," someone would say.

"Maybe you should cut down on the meals, Tom," someone else would remark. "I'm detecting a serious weight gain here."

Or, "How's Judy likely to react when you come home with a gimpy leg? Will this accident represent the end for you and the lovely Judy?"

Or, "You don't suppose torn ligaments spread like gangrene, do you? What happens if the condition works its way to your dick?"

"I'm more worried," retorted another, "that it's headed for his brain."

All of these observations were accompanied by snorting, puffing, and the occasional invective as they carried me up the stairs. Fortunately for all of us, me included, I was able to ascend to my room on my own by Wednesday, although it remained an arduous task for me the remainder of the week.

As for Judy? I too wondered how she would react to what I had done to myself. Privately I felt a minor trepidation about this issue. For one thing, as I tried to conjure her up in my imagination, as a kind of comfort to me during this period of physical pain, I wasn't able to do so very well. She blurred in my mind's eye. Because I couldn't seem to bring her into focus and I couldn't put my recollective arms around her, I wasn't able to muster up the necessary fantasy I needed to imagine her compassion. I wanted very much to miss her, especially in view of what I had done to myself, but I found myself missing *missing* her more than missing *her* per se. I was troubled by this failure and it nagged me nearly constantly. Did I not believe Judy was the right woman for me to marry? Did I not want to spend the rest of my life with her?

As I look back on it now, I was probably a painful mess that first two days after I injured myself on the slopes—the hangover that lasted a full twenty-four hours, the pain and severity of my injured knee, the strange guilt and self-loathing I felt because the injury was clearly my own fault. And finally, a nagging doubt about not missing Judy as much as I wanted to, as well as an ill-defined apprehension that she would be angry about my injury and the over-indulgence that had led to it. All of these factors combined to create a troubling uneasiness I couldn't seem to escape.

I *did* try to make the best of my situation. With the aid of my mountain-climbing pick cane, I hobbled slowly around the village, stubbornly taking in what sights I could. And, in the evenings, I joined my friends at the Keller Bar for a bit of the hair of the dog that had bitten me. But I didn't drink very much. My accident had taught me a permanent lesson about the virtues of moderation.

Exploring Westendorf at the speed of a snail was a rewarding experience for the most part. I still loved the village's beauty. I continued to appreciate the March weather. Each day was sunny and warm, windless and calm. At night the temperature would drop to just below freezing point and the sky would break out in a stunning rash of stars, almost in a kind of delicate, heavenly conceit. The slopes remained sprinkled with colorful skiers each day, many of them oozing gamely over the moguls. In the distance, they looked like tiny players in some ethereal ballet.

I developed rituals accommodating the fragility of my movements. I limped around the village from nine until ten-thirty each morning, then stopped into a small café I'd discovered the first morning. There, stuffing a few schillings into an old jukebox to hear musical hits I recognized from Canada, I enjoyed coffee so strong it clung like tar to the side of the mug. At noon, I joined my friends for lunch at our pension. After they vanished to the slopes, when my pain medication actually seemed to be working, I would struggle upstairs to my room for a nap. After I awoke I went outside again to explore more of the village. This was interrupted by a ritual stop for a cup of tea in another café on the way back to the pension.

By then it was four pm. and I would discover I still had two hours to kill until dinner. I found this period at the end of the afternoon the most difficult each day. Sometimes I read—I usually traveled with a couple of books because I was a relatively voracious reader then—but at other times I was too restless and vaguely troubled. I felt on the verge of something important, although I assumed this was a sanguine state inspired by my boredom. Yet the need for deep reflection persisted. Sometimes I would lie on my bed, my hands behind my head, staring at the stuccoed and heavily beamed ceiling, looking for something cryptically vital there, I guess, some kind of plausible explanation about what life might have in store for me. Somehow I grew strangely ambivalent about my future. Although I couldn't define it clearly, I felt a malaise of dissatisfaction with life, as if my fall on the slopes earlier in the week had injured my complacency as well as my knee. In the end I decided I was merely growing bored. But we weren't leaving until Sunday morning. By the end of Wednesday night it seemed clear I needed some kind of diversion. If I didn't soon embellish my daily routine with something new and interesting,

I would drive myself crazy.

Maria, the young Italian woman who spent all of her Austrian days behind the main desk of our pension, in case someone needed something, was clearly sympathetic to my plight. Each time she spotted me limping through her lobby, the bottom of my cane clicking on the polished wooden floor, she would shake her head sadly to convey her empathy.

"How goes it?" she asked me that Wednesday afternoon, as she often did.

I limped slowly in her direction, then leaned against the counter. "I'm getting bored, Maria," I said.

"Long days when there is no skiing."

"Yes."

"Is it getting better? Your knee is improving?"

"Only a little."

"Do you think you could manage going to the top of the mountain?"

"On the chair lift?"

"Yes, on the chair lift."

"Probably. If I was careful, I suppose I could take the chair lift."

"Then you should go to the top of the mountain."

"I should?"

"Yes. For lunch."

"Okay. For lunch then."

"And for the women in bikinis."

I grinned. "For the women in bikinis?"

"But mostly for lunch." And she laughed good-naturedly.

"Mostly for lunch then. And do you recommend something off the menu?"

"Jaegerschnitzel," she said, rubbing her fingers against her thumb to convey its excellence.

"Okay," I said. "I'll take lunch there tomorrow. Thank you, Maria."

"Enjoy," she remarked as I turned away.

Later I asked Gord if he wanted to join me. "No pressure," I said. "I can go alone. But to be honest, I wouldn't mind the company."

My other friends, I knew, had become increasingly serious about the skill and speed of their skiing. Races for all levels of skier were planned for Friday and Brad, in particular, was preoccupied with the notion that he could take home a first place ribbon. Gord, on the other hand, was interested mostly in the recreational aspects of the sport, one of the reasons I chose to invite him along with me to the top of the mountain.

"Good idea," he said after a moment's thought. "I think I could use part of a day off. It's not like I'm training for the Olympics or something." He raised his voice to address George, Brad and Fred. "Unlike *some* guys I know," he bellowed in their direction.

But they just laughed and waved him off.

"Thanks, Gord," I said. "Maybe I won't go crazy by the end of the week."

"One never knows," my friend remarked obliquely.

I laughed and elbowed him in the ribs. But I soon learned coincidence is a ceaseless lottery. At some time or other most of us win a prize, whether we want the prize or not. Although I didn't know it then, Gord had already made your acquaintance. The prize was moving inexorably in my direction. I just wasn't aware of it yet.

"I'LL GO FIRST," GORD SAID the following morning as we prepared to get on the chair lift for the six-thousand foot climb towards the restaurant at the top of the mountain. "You might need a little help getting out of the chair."

"That's true," I admitted. "Thanks, Gord."

It was mid-morning. The slopes were already teeming with skiers. The line-up to get on the chair lift—while it moved quickly—was long. And, not wearing skis, Gord and I seemed an eccentric infraction in the line-up's purpose. Even carrying my cane, a visible excuse, I was aware of feeling alien here somehow, that my injury had removed me from conventional function, and to travel up the mountain without skis was akin to passive rebellion.

But I was determined to travel to the top of the mountain as a kind of celebration, as a kind of release from prison. I was done with feeling so furious with myself for contributing to my own injury.

Gord went first, easily sliding into the single seat. I limped into position as quickly as I could, as he was borne into the air. Timing was everything in my case. I permitted one empty chair to slip by and then scurried into position to take the next one. I bent slightly to take the swat on the ass the chair would give me, wincing when a bolt of pain exploded from my injured knee. Then I was sitting and it was too late and I was being carried aloft, the chair swinging a little as it settled into its mindless function of going round and round in a large, endless loop.

I recall enjoying the long ascent. Yes, there were two more explosions of pain when I dismounted halfway up and limped towards the lift that would take Gord and me the rest of the way to the top, then again when I dismounted at the summit, but overall the climb was peaceful and aesthetically pleasing, skiers a few meters below me turning and braking on their way down the mountain, the spring snow whispering in silver waves at the edges of their skis, rocky crags breaking up the white slopes and large stands of snow speckled evergreens. All of this possessed its own appeal for me, despite my nervous distance from the ground. And Gord was there ahead of me each time I dismounted, to help me not to lose my balance as I moved away from the chair.

It was nearly noon by the time we reached the top. We stood not far from the mountain's true summit, gazing at the heavy, wooden-beamed chalet and the glistening windows that offered, we could tell, a tremendous view of the valley below and the other nearby peaks carved into the sky all around us. The sun was brilliantly bright and warm, and it exploded against the snow.

"Wow," I said. "Not bad, eh?"

"Not bad at all," agreed Gord, now mesmerized by the women Maria had promised would be sunbathing up here in bikinis.

I had been referring to the setting in a larger sense, I felt, but I didn't say anything when Gord clearly translated my enthusiasm into appreciation for the rows of lounges covered with beautiful, oiled women, lined up on the chalet's large deck. It was *all* beautiful; I wasn't about to quibble over specifics.

Patiently Gord walked with me up a path we noticed behind the restaurant. An arrow revealed this short trail led to the summit of the mountain. There was a steep pitch in the path about halfway up that gave me a few painful moments, but I struggled towards the top of the mountain anyway. It was the first and only time in my life I have reached the summit of a mountain, and I stood there with Gord in wonder for several minutes, scanning the panorama of snow-capped peaks so sharply cut into the fabric of the deep blue sky.

"Jesus," I said at last. "Makes you want to be a mountain climber, doesn't it?"

"Yeah. You're not kidding."

"Do you think you could do that, Gord? Climb mountains?"

He fingered his thick mustache a moment, considering my question. "I'd have to learn the essentials, try it out first. What about you?"

I shook my head. "Sometimes the top step of a step ladder is too much for *me*. You know I get acrophobia, don't you?"

"You're afraid of heights?"

"Yeah."

"You kidding me?"

"No. Deadly serious."

"Shit, man, how do you ski. I mean how do you manage

the chair lifts?"

I shrugged. "I grit my teeth. I like to ski. You have to take the good with the bad, I guess."

"But you can stand here on the summit of this mountain and enjoy the view?"

"Yeah. It's a pretty big plateau. And the view's worth it, I'd say."

"So what do we do after lunch?"

"Whaddyuh mean?"

"The descent, Tom."

I gazed at him a moment, perplexed. Then it dawned on me. Going down on the chair lift, for me, might present a terrifying perspective. "Jesus," I said, suddenly apprehensive. "I hadn't thought about that."

Sadly Gord nodded. "It's going to look like a *long* way down," he said.

WHILE THE RESTAURANT HERE was large, it was jammed with skiers finishing or about to take their lunch. Fortunately skiers tend to eat quickly, guzzle down their beer, then hurry outside to resume skiing again. Gord and I did not have long to wait for a table after we lined up for the now famous chalet jaegerschnitzel. And tables in Austria, I noticed—which I have confirmed a couple of other times since then when I have visited Europe—are not full until every seat is taken. It is culturally acceptable to join perfect strangers if they have an empty seat at their table. It is also culturally acceptable to talk with them, even though they are strangers. So different from back in Canada where a restaurant is full if there is someone at every table. Canadian reserve, I suppose. Or Canadian perspective over space. Perhaps Canada is so large, so big, so sprawling, even our restaurants have seats we feel we can squander.

We enjoyed our jaegerschnitzel; it was as delicious as our friend Maria at our pension had said it would be. And neither one of us dared mention again that the long descent on the chair lift might be frightening for me.

"What about this afternoon?" I asked Gord as we were finishing our meal. "Are you going to ski?"

"Maybe. If we get down on time. I don't know. I'm not taking it as seriously as the other guys."

"Yeah. They're competitive, all right."

Gord nodded.

"Anyway," I said. "I don't want to keep you up here all day. I'm ready to go if you are."

And shortly we left.

I began to feel anxious as soon as we stepped outdoors again into the blinding sunshine. My trepidation felt all the more exaggerated because it was clearly the only flaw inside this perfectly beautiful afternoon.

"Shit," I muttered as we approached the chair lift hut, as the sound of the grinding gears and the shifting of the cable reached our ears. To me, its sound was amplified. I likened it to the noise a snoring dragon must make.

"Are you going to be okay?" my friend asked me.

"I don't know," I said, feeling queasy. "It's not like I have any choice. I can't ski down. It's either the chair lift or spending the rest of my life up here."

Gord reflected on this for a moment or two as we continued to stroll towards the chair lift that would take us down. "Look at it *this* way," he suggested at last. "In real terms, it's no higher than when you're going up. It just looks steeper because you're going down."

"I know." But I could hear the doubt in my voice.

The next few moments are a blur to me now. I dimly recall Gord taking my arm and helping me into a chair ahead of him this time. I dimly remember him saying he would be right behind me on our journey down to the village. I moved gingerly into position. I felt the seat embrace and capture me. I remember rising slowly into space. Mostly, though, I remember realizing that my several minute nightmare had now commenced.

PEOPLE AFRAID OF HEIGHTS know their phobia is unnatural. But this knowledge doesn't help. I told myself a dozen times that day, that what Gord had said was true: that my chair was no higher from the ground going down than it had been going *up*. But repeating this mantra of fact didn't help. In the first few moments of my descent from the top of the mountain, Westendorf below me was so far away and tiny, the entire village looked no larger than my thumbnail. I was agonizingly aware that only a flimsy piece of metal bar and chain prevented me from falling out of the sky to be broken and crushed in the village square below. As irrational as this notion was, I could not escape the plausibility of such a plummet invented by my mind. To survive this trip down the mountain would represent a minor miracle for me.

I suffered crests and troughs of panic all the way down the mountain. I'd never noticed before how a chair lift will swing on the long length of cable above it, like it's held in place by a tiny metal fist of fragile, weakening fingers. Nor had I noted the rumble and bump each time the chair and its length of cable passed under a chair lift tower on its way to its destination. The bracket holding the cable has a tendency to squeak as the chair rocks back and forth. From the beginning, when I left the platform and lunged out into space, the terror of what I was doing struck me with terrible force. I took my hands off the bar in front of me and wrapped them, white-knuckled and horrified, around the stem of the arm holding the chair to the cable. It rocked. It squeaked. When I squinted down on Westendorf about a mile below me, I was compelled to lower my face to my forearms. With my face hidden between my arms, I closed my eyes and tried to figure out how to avoid the inevitability of my death.

At one point, I went a little crazy in my fear. I endured a cruel and ridiculous temptation, during the first ten minutes of my descent, to just get up and dive out of the chair. Falling to my death, it seemed to me now, was inevitable. Why not give up? Why not climb out of the chair and let gravity lead me to my apparently predestined fate? Was this not why I suffered from acrophobia? Didn't acrophobia represent an inevitability of sorts, a fate-ensured certainty that I must fall to my death on the rocks and snow dotting some distant, forbidding mountain? For several minutes, I couldn't escape this idea of predestination in my falling to my death. Would it not then make sense to just throw myself from the chair to get it—my sentence—over with? Wouldn't this backhanded kind of bravery end the suffering I felt in my intense fear and panic? Would I not transform my cowardice in this way into some kind of personal and practical heroism?

But I held on while this fierce sense of death-inevitability gradually receded. By then I had begun making elaborate deals with God. By then I was making promises He no doubt knew I'd never keep, if only He would permit me to survive this chair lift ride down the mountainside. These oaths ranged from the monumental—devoting myself forever to the well-being of mankind—to the banal—never cursing or cussing again, never drinking liquor or casting a judgmental stone at someone I envied or despised. Even *I* knew I would never keep any of these promises, but I now convinced myself that I meant every oath I swore on that long chair lift ride down the mountain. I was briefly born again, briefly saved from my wickedness, as I pleaded for my life, bartering away my bad habits for a newly virtuous life, if only I would be spared. During my endless voyage down the mountain I promised God everything, overlooking that, until this moment, I'd hardly believed in Him at all. In this way, chanting a long, abstract apology for everything I had ever been—so sorry, so sorry for my dysfunction—I made it down the mountainside alive.

Gord rushed up behind me to steady me after I stepped

out of my chair on the last leg of the descent, then tottered nearby in weakness and dizziness, holding onto his arm in desperation, nearly falling in a heap on the well-worn snow. I was giddy that I'd managed to escape death. Not only did my knee, housed securely in its bandage, nearly give out, but my good leg too wanted to collapse in the jubilation of my relief.

"Jesus, man, you're green," Gord said as he guided me away from the endlessly circling chairs.

"I'm scared shitless," I admitted.

He led me across the fifty snowy, rutted yards to Westendorf's main street before he let me go.

I stood there on the edge of the street, swaying woozily, a being from some other world, lost in this new and strange dimension of terra firma.

"Whaddyuh want to do, Tom? You want to go back to the pension? Do you want to go lie down?"

"No," I said. "I'm fine. That café near our pension—can you see I get there safely? I want to have a cup of tea or something. Right now a cup of tea looks extremely good to me. But I just don't know if I can walk there on my own."

"Okay," he said.

But I blathered on, my escape from death exaggerating the delight I now found in the sound of my own voice. "I'd just appreciate you getting me there without me falling on my face. Then you can go skiing."

"Whatever. I'll make sure you get there. Okay?"

"I'll be okay, Gord," I said, gazing intently at him. "I just feel like a fucking idiot. What kind of asshole takes a chair lift to the top of the mountain, it eluding him entirely that he has to get down without skis?"

Gord chuckled a little at my astonishment. His reaction, as much as anything, reminded me of the normalcy I now cherished to affirm my escape from death.

"And I made deals with God up there," I blubbered. "I promised not to curse again as long as I live."

"I'll see you in hell then, I guess," Gord remarked as he strolled slowly along beside me in the direction of the café. "Seems to me that's a promise you've already broken."

I winced. "I have?"

But Gord just chuckled some more.

I still didn't feel very well. My peripheral vision had departed me. It seemed all I could do to focus. I could see only tiny pinpricks of our destination. Everything I glanced towards looked like some tiny dot at the end of my long, dark tunnel. I felt like a ship entirely fogged in. I was even relieved Gord kept referring to me as Tom. Hard-pressed in an interrogation at this moment, I doubted I would be able to remember my name on my own.

Soon, though, I discerned we were approaching the café where, yes, I was going to have a cup of tea. In my daze, I grew vaguely aware that Gord now stopped to talk to someone just outside the door. A woman, I supposed, because I thought I heard her voice. But when I squinted in her direction, I simply couldn't see her. Gord introduced me to her—I learned later they'd met skiing the day before—but I couldn't see her face, not really. It was possible I was blind. And I didn't even hear her name during Gord's introduction. She remained at the end of the long, narrow tunnel I struggled along in the aftermath of my escape from terror. Still too fogged in by the shock of what I'd been through, I allowed Gord to guide me inside the café, while he explained to the woman beside us what had happened to me a few moments before. Even inside, entering the dark wooden gloominess of the little café, I felt like a pebble casually dropped into a deep and narrow well.

Then, rapidly, painlessly, the fog lifted. My peripheral vision returned. I glanced at Gord to thank him again, to acknowledge that I realized he'd ordered tea for me, to reassure him I was now all right. "Wow," I said. "I'm back. Thanks, Gord."

"No problem, Tom," he said, smiling patiently at me.

Then I gazed directly across the table at what I now remembered was a woman sitting there. My eyes gazed at her eyes. I felt a bolt of chemistry I had never known before and have never felt again since. It made no sense. The wonder, the excitement. At that moment, to my dismay—and there is no other truthful way to put it—I apparently fell in love, deeply and completely. The woman sitting there was, of course, a beautiful, breathtaking *you*. For the first time, it was you, sweet Jan. And I realized at that moment, that precisely wonderful and unfortunate moment, in a way I would remember for the rest of my life, that you were the most incredible wonder I had ever seen.

"You've had quite a fright," you said, smiling gently at me.

I nodded, vacantly at first, then with increasing

exuberance, finally with giddy joy. "I'm all right now," I said. "I'm going to be all right now."

And your eyes, your beautiful blue and powerful eyes, escorted me into the vault apparently housing your soul, where, I must confess, I have been imprisoned ever since.

SEVEN

WHEN GREG GETS A LITTLE DRUNK, he somehow becomes beach bum blonder. He takes to calling my wife "Joody, Joody, Joody," like Troy Donahue doing a bad impression of Cary Grant. And although it is late evening now, he continues to carry his phone in his right hand—it still won't work for some reason out here in the sanctuary of the woods—so that, when he gestures, the small device dances through space like some hopelessly inept baton.

We've eaten. We've consumed the better part of three bottles of wine—one red, your choice and mine, and two white, Judy and a very thirsty Greg. We've only partially cleared the table, me again, although I was gratified that you rushed to my rescue until Judy sternly called out: "Just leave it!" Strange, both of us obeyed her without hesitation, used, I guess, to the compelling aspect of Judy's intimidating imperatives. The dregs on our dinner plates now congeal. I shove the plates to one side. I will wash the dishes tomorrow morning, knowing this duty is nothing more than just the way things go. Me, dishes, ritual. I will do the dishes while drinking coffee, as if this domestic obligation can somehow inspire my day with some respectable ideal of productivity.

As I often do on those rare occasions the four of us are together, I've arranged to sit across from you—or fate has helped me in this—so that I can steal a loving glance at you whenever you won't catch me doing so. And, occasionally, when your wondrous blue eyes meet mine, I will be able to pretend you still love me in some way, as you did so many years ago for a brief few days and hours. And when you're turned away, or smiling at someone else, I'll be able to capture with an innocuous glance those perfect cheekbones, unchanged from when I first noticed them so many years ago in a small village café in Austria.

It's dark on the other side of the windows at your back. In fact, darkness showed up rapidly here at Gladys's as yet unnamed northern lodge. I barely had time to finish barbecuing the steaks before twilight dissolved away, replaced by an almost stereotypical starburst northern night. In the quickly arriving darkness, I even tripped up the first step of the stairs, as I was hurrying away from the old stone barbecue to the lodge porch where, we had already discovered, the light bulb was missing. Greg, to his credit, brought some bulbs with him from Toronto. Greg thinks of solutions like these from time to time. I don't envy him for this but sometimes I resent him. So competent and organized and conventionally ambitious. He is one of those people who drives this world I find so outside the definition of who I am. He is someone I can harmlessly blame.

Now, when I am not glancing at you, I peer through the windows into the enchantment I perceive in the wilderness darkness on the other side of the glass. At one point, I suggest we all take a walk, it's such a beautiful night. But Judy begins to tell a story about life where she works and Greg begins to shake his head in drunken, polite, even feigned incredulity at what she's saying, so that my gambit about a late evening stroll garners nothing more than an enigmatic smile from your parted lips, before my suggestion is lost forever. I wonder, by times, where ignored suggestions go. Do they pile up somewhere on the frontier of time and space or do they just dissolve, sucked into some black hole somewhere? Don't ask time and space any questions. Neither time nor space gives a flying fuck. One definition of the human dilemma.

Done appreciating Judy's amusing story, a tale I've already heard, Greg turns his attention to me. "What about you, Tommy?" he says. "What's new in the newspaper wars?"

"Not much. We're continuing to applaud Justin Trudeau's failure to keep any of his election promises or following the adventures of dozens of pseudo celebrities for the edification of our youngest readers. Pretty tedious stuff, to tell you the truth."

Greg snorts. "Every time we see you, you sound more and more burned out. You've got to give the readers what they want."

I open my mouth to embark on the rich inevitability of a debate about the responsibilities of journalism with my brother-in-law.

But Judy's there before I can speak. "And every time we see *you* guys," she says, "I have to tell you Tommy needs a promotion, that he needs to kick-start his career."

I say nothing to this.

"Or a transfer to another city," adds Judy in the silence. "That's more the answer, I think."

"You mean Toronto?" you ask.

"Toronto would be good," your sister replies. "I can see Tommy finding a place at *The Star*. Or maybe, the way newspapers are dying, he could move into advertising."

Everyone but me is nodding, Greg with smug certainty, Judy because she wants us to move to Toronto, you—I'm not sure why—perhaps for no other reason than some ambivalent need to join in with the others. Toronto as utopia, I guess. Still, I resist any notion to pull up stakes and move, even knowing I would get to see you more often there. I would not be the authentic man in Toronto that I really want to be. And, if I was inauthentic, what would be the point in seeing you more often? A man who isn't authentic has no business loving *anyone*. Of course I'd never be caught *saying* so.

"What about you?" you ask your sister. "What would *you* do in Toronto?"

"I'd find something lucrative. I have two decades of credentials."

You flick your gaze to me. It's your eyes that ask me your

question.

"I don't know," I reply. "I don't see Tom McNamara in the way you guys do. My politics are different. My sensibilities. I skate on thin ice where I am in Ottawa as it is."

"Where *do* you see yourself," Greg asks, sounding newly impatient, like some pampered, older brother who believes he should sternly fill in during a patriarchal absence.

I shrug. "I agree that maybe it's time I gave up on journalism, at least in a corporate setting. Do something else, I guess."

"Like what?"

"Christ, Greg, I'm not sure. You know something? We talk about what poor old Tom should be doing every time the four of us get together. I'm beginning to feel like an underachiever, like the weak link in the gang, the guy everyone is waiting to see grow up."

Judy grins. "You see what a sensitive flower he can be?" she says.

"Judy . . . ." This from you, my occasional defender.

"Mid-life crisis," says Greg. "That's all. But we love you anyway, Tommy."

"Thank you," I remark with a smile I've conjured up out of the ashes of my aggravation.

Greg pours more wine, mostly into his own glass.

You glance at me for a moment and, petulantly, I pretend not to notice. Fuck it! I decide with a tragic knot of pain in the pit of my heartsick belly. I'm feeling disapproved of, even by you, and I want to sulk like a child.

Judy's embarked on the lecture we've come to know so well: "Tommy, everyone here loves you. We're on your side. We just hate to see you at a dead end." She turns to you and Greg. "He's turned down half a dozen possible opportunities," she complains.

"Only a couple, Jude."

"More than a couple."

I sigh.

You gaze at your empty wine glass.

Even Greg says nothing.

"To be honest," continues Judy, "and I hope you don't mind me saying so, Tommy, we're all family after all . . ."

". . . Judy, please . . ."

". . . I think you should see someone about this lack of motivation of yours, a professional, a psychiatrist. There's no shame in it. We all go through periods of reticence. It's not uncommon in a man your age."

"Yeah. It's just mid-life crisis," says Greg in case anyone missed his prognosis the first time he uttered it.

I want to paste him. I want to smack him up the side of the head. Mid-life fucking crisis? If you only knew, buddy. If you only knew.

You ask if there's any more red wine.

"Only tomorrow night's bottle or Sunday night's bottle," replies Greg, who keeps track of everything, how many and when, and the cost.

"There's a liquor store in Temagami," I suggest with just a trace of annoyance. "We don't have to be rigid about it. I can go in and buy some more tomorrow."

"Your call, sweetie," your husband tells you.

"No," you say. "I'm okay. But thanks."

"Tommy?"

"I'm fine. Thank you."

"Well," says Judy then about everything in particular, like there's no disputing the umpire's call.

"You know what I think?" I say. "I think we all should go for a walk—it's a beautiful night."

"Jesus," says Judy. "It's October and it's pitch. It'll be freezing out there in the dark. It's why no one answered you the first time."

"We have jackets and a flashlight, don't we?"

"Count me out," says Greg. "Too late for me."

I glance at you but you don't say anything, and I can't read anything in your evasive gaze. I feel the renewed sensation of some tragic sadness clinging to the ledges of my belly. I feel petulant and sulky again. I feel alone on this planet with my own version of romantic love, like I'm now some joke everyone tells in a hushed voice on the other side of the hand covering their mouth, like I'm some cockeyed alien visitor as crazy as a souped up banana.

In the ensuing silence, as it must again, the conversation turns once more to the fate of this hospitable lodge in the middle of what I feel is an exceedingly attractive nowhere in the vicinity of Temagami.

"With a little luck, with the right result to a careful appraisal," Greg is saying, "we might get a few hundred thousand for this place. I've been thinking about it. I mean that's without detailed study. I'll have a more complete look around tomorrow. But, for the right buyer, if we were patient, we might do all right."

"Presuming we want to sell it," you say suddenly, startling all of us.

Greg gazes at you and sighs.

I wonder if you and your husband have argued already about what should be done with this place.

"Isn't this just so typical?" Judy puts in with a bitter snort. "My sister and my husband decide something the whole world knows is hopeless is somehow quaintly attractive, as if it actually has potential. What's the matter with you two? Whatever would we do with this place in the middle of the fucking boonies? It's too far away from anything. No one's going to drive up from Toronto to stay at a place like this. This isn't Muskoka, you know."

I glance at you. You glance at me. I glance down at my dinner plate where the juice of my medium rare steak is turning black in its hapless marriage to the hickory barbecue sauce Greg insisted on slathering all over its flesh during its last moments of productive life, when we stood competing with one another at the large concrete block barbecue now smoldering with a palliative glow in the darkness outside. I sense *you* are looking down too. I don't have to see it to confirm it. I just know it at this moment, as if I've been awarded new wisdom, some whimsical gift of sensory acuity handed out by a benevolent wizard.

"I can't speak for Greg," I say to fill the silence, to break up the vapor trail of awkwardness now staining our social sky, the result of Judy's words, "but the decision doesn't rest with us. Gladys wasn't our mother. Judy, you and Jan probably know best what she might have had in mind."

"I haven't the faintest fucking idea," Judy says with another snort. "When I look at this place, I'm not even sure my mother *had* a mind."

"Judy," you say. "For God's sake. That's a mean thing to say."

"There's a lot we don't know yet," I suggest, hoping my words can ease the tension.

"We're all forgetting the most important point," says Greg, clearly frustrated by our collective ignorance. "If you keep the dammed property, what the hell do you do with it? I mean are you going to move up here out of the city, renovate the place, live in it, turn it into a profitable resort? That doesn't sound very realistic. Everybody has other things they're doing. None of us at this table looks like a potential proprietor of a rundown resort in the middle of nowhere. We all have . . . issues," he concludes.

Issues? Jesus, I decide. Do we all have to sound like someone we've watched on television?

"And," says Greg with a note of finality, "what about the cost of taxes and upkeep?"

No one says anything to Greg's remarks. On one level, he's probably right: this place represents some significant challenges. On another, though, his opinion presumes there's something diseased about this place as a wilderness alternative, as a contrasting lifestyle choice. As if Toronto or Ottawa are healthy, and this quiet wilderness locale is some kind of hapless virus that might sap the life from us. I sit here questioning his intractability. One man's poison is another man's elixir, isn't it? One man's mistake is another man's solution, is it not?

"I heard a loon while we were eating," I announce eventually, just filling the silence, I suppose. But more than this, for reasons I do not fully fathom, I want everyone to know my guard is down and that I'm *proud* it's down. If I'm the one suffering mid-life crisis here, I may as well say whatever I want. Maybe I can play the fool to the hilt, right to the bloody end. Maybe I can assume the role of the lovesick mountain man who embarrasses *everyone*.

Sure enough, cautiously, like my nervous breakdown has at last gotten underway, all of you study me, uncertain what to say about my reference to the loon.

"Hearing the loon made me sad and peaceful both at the same time. Loons mate for life, you know," I add, for even less good reason, warming to my role as family jester.

Judy bursts into laughter. "Tommy, you have to quit drinking wine. It makes you so tragically melancholy."

I feel myself blushing. My bravado bursts like a tortured balloon. I would look up at you to see if I'm as much a fool in your eyes as I appear to be in Greg's and Judy's, but I can't bring myself to do it. I'm afraid I'll catch you agreeing with them. I'm afraid I'll have embarrassed myself in front of you the way I did in front of them, and my humiliation will only deepen. In a way, I suppose, love continually flirts with humiliation. To test our mettle, I guess. I wonder sometimes if love fails because we don't expose ourselves enough to the risk of foolishness it demands of us. I wonder about this often, I know, but, of course, I'd never be caught *saying* so.

We kick the subject of this lodge and its impracticalities around for another half hour or so. No one really changes his or her opinion. The rudimentary issues remain the same: there's no real reason to keep the resort when you and Greg live in Toronto, and Judy and I live in Ottawa, when no one knows how to operate a resort in the first place, especially when it likely needs so many repairs or renovations. I stay out of much of this conversation, still smarting over my wounds, I guess. Besides, I don't think the lodge itself is the real issue here. One of us should find the courage to ask the more important question, the question I believe should be obvious to everyone: does anyone want to change their life and is this resort a viable means of doing so? I won't ask such a question. I don't have the courage. Most of all, being the fool I am would only reduce my query to the very state of foolishness the question would be asked to correct.

But I'm falling in love with this broken down lodge even now, even here after dark, underneath the hapless, brokenhearted illumination of a sputtering electric light dangling above this dining table. It's that walking-backwards-into-knowing-what's-right thing again. Here we are, clichés all of us, stereotypical in our opinions. We're all sitting here knowing what's *wrong*, the way we always do, because what's wrong is easiest to discern. But I wish we'd talk about the rightness I can feel here about Gladys's lodge. Because this place inspires—in me, at least—a sense that it is right. Or have I crossed another bridge on my journey into hopelessness, on my voyage of disappointment? We are all two-sided coins—outlaws on one face, societal adherents on the other—and one side of the coin is knowing clearly what is wrong while the other side of the coin, a million miles away, is knowing precisely what is right. Never mind the time we spend feeling wrong about what we know is right. It's hard being even a sensitive outlaw. Society is right; outlaws are here to be wrong, to offer up the contrast necessary to society's *rightness*. Unless, of course, one demonstrates the courage of his convictions. Which brings me back to authenticity and its humble, aphoristic truth: outlaw or societal adherent, it doesn't matter which, as long as it reflects your personal truth.

Soon, as I conclude the thinking of these thoughts, I notice the topic of this resort has run down like a depleted battery. We sit around the table in a long and stuporous silence. Everyone is tired. It's been a long day of travel and gentle astonishment, of holding our positions and enduring our petty conflicts. Better day tomorrow when we've regained our strength, when we've found the mettle to resume assuming the burden of our endless ambivalence.

"I'm going to bed," I announce more or less to myself. But in the silence of the room, my words sound brusque, even harsh.

I feel you glancing at me. I am tempted to lift my gaze and let it rush into your arms, so something important can pass between us, so that something massive between us can finally find the courage to conclude. But I don't. In the end, I look away. And, of course, with me not looking for it, nothing important happens. Everything remains the same.

"WHAT'S THE MATTER WITH YOU, Tommy?" Judy wants to know a few minutes later, as we prepare for bed.

I'm already under the covers with a book I prop on my upper belly. I tear myself away from its pages to answer her, my finger holding my place. "Whaddyuh mean," I say.

She has shrugged into a cotton nightdress and, ritually, I know, will soon depart for the bathroom. Her hair is already freed of its ponytail but she has make-up to remove, wrinkle cream to apply, and she'll want to brush and floss her teeth. I always go first into the bathroom because I have less to do and won't take as long. Judy's idea. She hates the notion that I would have to wait impatiently for her before I could begin my meager ablutions. Which mystifies me, of course, because I'm not an impatient man. It's *Judy* who's impatient. Sometimes in marriages, I guess, our favorite gift to our partner is a dubious quality we know we possess ourselves. That way, once we share it, once everyone takes ownership of the same characteristic, it's freed of its unattractiveness. If everyone suffers the same disease, it's not a disease after all. It's just an indisputable condition of life. Of course, I'd never be caught *saying* so.

"See what I mean?" Judy is saying.

"Huh?"

"Where did you *go*, Tommy? You went away again. Just now. What I want to know is where the fuck do you *go* when I'm talking to you?"

"Nowhere, Jude. I just don't know what you mean."

"Well, you're being weird. I just asked what was wrong with you."

"Weird? I'm not weird. Nothing's wrong."

"Bullshit."

"Okay. Tell me what you mean."

"I don't know. This place, your affection for it. That stupid long drive through Algonquin Park. Cooking on that big old dirty barbecue. All that stuff isn't like you."

"It isn't?"

Judy sighs. "You're just doing things to spite me."

Having listened to her litany of symptoms of my weirdness, I now study Judy's face, looking for something there that reminds me why I continue to believe I love her in my way. But when I don't find any clues, I remain curiously flat about my failure to discover them. Like it's almost too obvious a failure to warrant my consideration.

"You see what I mean?" Judy is saying.

"I guess so," I reply. "Sorry. But it's all so circumstantial. You have to admit it isn't much to be upset about."

She doesn't really hear me. "And you *like* this place?"

Still holding my book, I set it face down on my lap to answer her question. "Yes, I do. But what you do with this place is up to you and Jan. I keep saying so because it's true."

"I think Jan's waffling."

"Greg'll take care of that, I'm sure."

Judy studies me thoughtfully.

I study her right back, making certain I don't flinch.

"Don't be weird this weekend."

"Or stupid," I add to remind her of her earlier complaint, keeping the annoyance out of my voice.

She grins. "Yeah. Don't be weird or stupid."

"Okay," I say.

"I'll be right back," she tells me, getting up to go to the bathroom.

After she's gone, it occurs to me that my agreeing to avoid weirdness and stupidity for the rest of this weekend—as empty of substance as it was—has probably so cheered Judy she might want to make love when she returns from the bathroom. Winning points sometimes ignites her sexual appetite. Trouble is, I don't truly feel I have been weird or stupid at all today. And my promise to halt these practices is only giving in to her to avoid any further discussion or conflict. In truth, I am offended that Judy's implacable definition of what is weird or stupid behavior has yet again arrested me, then found me guilty. Women, for all their assertions that they are more romantic than men, are more willing to have sex immediately after an argument or a fight than men like me are. I lose my libido when someone has deeply hurt my feelings. I don't want to make love to a woman who has hurt my feelings, until I'm over the pain. Of course, I'd never be caught *saying* so.

With all of this in mind, convinced Judy will feel she's won her point and should celebrate with some kind of fuck, I close my book and turn out my bedside light, rolling over onto my side away from Judy's half of the bed.

When she returns, as she is climbing in beside me, she mentions how tired I seem and I admit this is so. She kisses me on the cheek, chastely, with ritual goodnight acceptance. Then she too rolls over onto her side, reaching out to switch off her light

The resort lamps all work well with Greg's light bulbs screwed into them and, in my mood, I consider this deeply for a while. I reflect that the working electricity is a provocative clue to the resort's general good health. In fact, as I lie there unable to sleep, I decide the electricity in this place is virtually a plea on the part of the rundown structure to have someone like me take ownership of it. Name me, I hear it say. Call me something truthful, give me a name that Jan will like. But I don't know at this moment what this name could be. I haven't figured it out yet. And the twenty years of necessary chasm between you and me is just too wide.

DAVID CRUICKSHANK DOESN'T KNOW what happened between you and me, Jan, so many years ago. I haven't told him. He knows, sweet Jan, that I care about you more deeply than I should. I drank too much scotch one night and confessed, as I recall it, that rather shamefully—I'm sure that's how I put it—shamefully—I am in love with my sister-in-law. I think I said, "a little in love," but I can't recall for sure.

"How did *this* come about?" I remember him asking.

I merely shrugged, conveying my despair.

"Does she know?"

"I don't think so," I replied.

"Are you going to tell her?"

"Why would I do that?"

"Because it's true, I guess."

"Jesus, David," I said. "What kind of reason is that?"

"The best one there is, in my opinion."

"Well, just because something's true doesn't mean it should be told. The world doesn't work that way. What kind of a world would it be if we all went around telling the truth all the time?"

"A more truthful world, my friend. That's what kind of world it would be."

"Yeah. But would it be better?"

"Better than a world where everyone goes around telling lies all the time."

"Wait a minute," I said. "Not telling someone a disruptive truth isn't the same as lying."

"Are you sure about that?" he said. "Or are you just rationalizing?"

"Well, I'm not telling her," I said.

"I'm just saying maybe you should."

"Well, I'm not telling her."

"No. I can see you're not."

"That's right. I'm not telling her."

David only grinned and patted me on the shoulder.

But there it is: I still can't tell him about you and me, and what happened when we first met. He'd steal the plot for one of his novels. Or he'd definitely insist I should tell you how I continue to feel about you. And he'd have a million questions about why you and I decided what we decided way back then. David's a romantic: he wouldn't be able to accept that you and I chose to walk away from an astonishingly immediate and powerful bond of love, not knowing we'd have to live, in ways we couldn't anticipate, with the bitter fruits of our decision, pushed up against one another, over and over again, by a spiteful, even malicious circumstance.

NO WONDER I CAN'T SLEEP. When I allow the devil's advocacy of David Cruickshank inside the lovesick state I feel here in the dark, knowing you are sleeping a door or two down the hall, I realize I'm only conducting the foolish spade work that gardens another sleepless night. So I lie where I am and dare not fidget for fear of waking Judy, who will be unhappy if I do. Not only will she then be awake as well, but she will know that I am having trouble sleeping, and she'll want an explanation. And I don't want to explain my sleeplessness. I'm tired of explaining things. Even this, so modest an explanation, asked seemingly because Judy cares, will be too much for me. It has struck me in recent months how much explaining I do from day to day. The prospect of more justification of myself exhausts me considerably. I'm shrugging off my flexibility, my amicable good nature. I'm tired of trying to be convincing about what I really am. Take it or leave it is what I *want* to say.

Eventually, carefully, I slip out of bed and into my jeans,

sneakers and sweatshirt. I creep out of our bedroom and down the stairs to the dining room. The table where we ate dinner is still illuminated by the lamp dangling overhead, so that the structure looks like some kind of inadequate pool table underneath its rays. The dirty dishes remain. They are as soiled as my troubled soul.

I tiptoe across the room, open the door, which squeaks in protest, and slip outside onto the veranda October's autumn chill crackles delightfully against me and I breathe in deeply the rich scent of the autumn night. It's very dark. There is no moon. But the stars dance like a million frenzied pixies.

I sit down on the top step of the large porch, pleased somehow to hear the wood creak in response in the exotic silence. I sit here wishing for you. I sit here wishing you loved me as completely as I love you. I sit here wishing it would all go away, this endless love I feel, or that something magical would happen to make everything work out perfectly, for me, for you, even for Judy and Greg. My favorite fantasy is no one gets hurt, no one knows any pain, everyone just floats safely along on the current of the profound and obvious wonder everyone can see in the perfection of our love.

Thinking this, I don't turn immediately when I hear a footfall on the steps behind me. I'm afraid to turn around—because I am praying it is you—and I won't be able to hide my disappointment if it is Greg or Judy instead, or God or some werewolf on the prowl, both of them bent on my destruction. The werewolf, anyway. If God is here, perhaps He wants to kill me tenderly by making a fool of me for what I want out of life, exposing the perfection I seek in love and life as a foolish predilection. Maybe the werewolf would be better—me torn limb from limb by love's vanishing, impossible potential.

But it's you. I knew it would be. I am here to be tortured; it's in every step you take, in every breath you breathe.

"Hi, Tom," you whisper from somewhere over my left shoulder. "Can't you sleep either?"

"I'm afraid not," I say, astonished that my voice is so calm and matter-of-fact. I'm so good at sounding flat, such a master of the art of cold nonchalance, it threatens to break my heart. Maybe David is right. Maybe not confessing the truth indeed reflects the telling of a lie.

You sit down on the top step. It's wide enough that you can keep your distance, you don't have to sit too close. I'll bet you're glad you're good at this, keeping your distance, that is. You've been doing so for twenty years, like the custodian of a particularly dangerous criminal, the felon who continues to love you, the man who is hopelessly me, who agreed so long ago to run away from something he desperately wished to keep.

"I don't sleep well either when I travel," you say after you sit down, tucking your arms around your naked knees.

I wonder what you're wearing because I wonder what you're *not* wearing, but a glance in the darkness won't tell me and I don't want to stare. Strange thing about the lofty romance of my caring for you—it always wants to remove your clothes and lick your fragrant skin—it always wants to be joyfully sexual with you. In the conventional world, perhaps my caring would be described as lust. Knowing it is more than lust, knowing it is love makes me proud of myself, even while it makes me lonely. Now there's the ultimate definition of human duality: pride of knowledge and loneliness for knowing it in such a solitary fashion.

"Quite a surprise," you say. "This place, I mean."

"Yes. A pleasant surprise to me, not that it really matters."

"A pleasant surprise . . . ." Your voice trails off, leaving me to wish I could read your mind. For my own selfish reasons, of course.

"A wonderful surprise," I say. "I really like this place. I'm becoming convinced your mother may have known what she's doing."

"But it's not very practical, Tom. It's not a very practical place to own."

"Maybe that's what I like about it. I've had practical up to here," and my hand comes up to rest just below my gasping nostrils.

"Yes. I know."

What do you know, Sweet Jan? That *I've* had practical up to here? Or that you've had practical up to the same here I was talking about? Are we both drowning at this point during our swim through life? And are we waiting, each for the other, to decide who rescues whom?

"I'm all *suburbiaed* out, Jan. I need to do something different."

You don't say anything to my remarks. Discretion is the better part of valor, which is just about the worst fucking homily in our entire societal mantra of aimless, phony excuses.

Thinking this, I feel a strange kind of anger come over me, not at you, but at myself. For being a coward again. Or is it that I'm angry because I believe myself to be always alone in the world? Certainly, by times, I feel much more alone than I really should. Modified George Orwell: *All loners are sadly equal but some are more sadly equal than others.*

"So you think we should keep it?" you say.

"It's not up to me, Jan. It's up to you and Judy."

"I know. But I want to hear your opinion. Do you think we should keep it?"

"I don't know if you and Judy should keep it. I guess what I'm saying, the way I feel these days, if it was mine I'd keep it. This place speaks to me, Jan. I mean, as soon as I saw this place, I felt at home here. When we drove up this afternoon, that first moment we arrived, I sort of fell in love with it."

"Love at first sight, you mean?"

"Yes," I reply tonelessly. But I want to scream, "Like you! Like you!"

"Did you tell Judy?"

"No."

"Because it's not up to you?"

I take a deep breath, careful about what to reveal. "That's part of it, I guess."

You don't reply to this.

Silently I begin to plead with you to somehow understand, to at least *want* to understand. Say anything, I beg. I want to take your shoulders in my hands and gently shake you. Say anything. *Say Anything. Don't leave me stranded out here by myself, lost in space, lost in my own hopelessly hopeful universe. Don't leave me out here wishing you believed in happily ever after, the way I want to believe.*

But you don't say anything.

"What about you?" I ask at last. "I think I know how Judy feels. God, we *all* know how Judy feels. But what about you?"

"Greg thinks we should sell it."

I turn to you. Your head is down. You're staring at your knees. Your knees are bare. Your feet are bare. They must be cold. I want to take them in my hands, warm them, bring each foot up one at a time to warm them against my cheek. "Yeah, I noticed what Greg thinks. But what about you?"

"I don't know. There seems to be more to it than just this place, you know?"

"Absolutely," I say.

"Is that what you mean that it speaks to you? That there's more involved than just this dilapidated resort? That it's the conduit of a turning point in life or something?"

At this moment, ecstatic over your wisdom because it is so similar to mine, if there was music, I would make you dance with me. I'd spin you and twirl you and dance your feet into orbit through the starlit sky. But even now some familiar and relentless sense of truth pushes this notion aside, until I end up concluding once again I'd do all these things mostly because I'm a goddamned fool, mostly because I believe in feelings and opportunities that probably do not exist.

"Is that what you mean, Tom? That this place is connected to turning point?"

"That's *exactly* what I mean," I say, not caring about the sadness I hear in my voice.

We sit there a long time in silence, mulling over what we've discussed. Then, at last, you sigh gently and get up. You stand there, perhaps a foot from me, wearing something warm that reaches to a place just above your knees. Your legs. My palms itch because I want to reach out and touch them. I want to run my hands gently up your thighs. You're wearing a giant man's shirt, I realize at last. I think that's all. Your feet are still bare and cold. I want to run my fingers up your leg and make you feel the magic touch of the wisdom that too few of us are willing to know actually resides in love . . . .

". . . I guess I should go to bed," you say . . . .

. . . If I could find the words, I'd plead my case with you. But I've given up on ever finding the appropriate words. So I don't say anything. I don't reach out to touch your legs to end the stinging need for your flesh I feel in the palms of my hands. I don't move. I don't talk. I feel as if Medusa has passed by a moment ago, and just as an afterthought, turned me forever to stone, so that only my eyes can see the perfect you fate has apparently determined will never belong to me.

You linger a moment longer. "Goodnight, Tom," you say.

"Goodnight, Jan," I reply.

After you go, I sit on the top step of the veranda for another hour, awash in a deep self-loathing and the list of endless wishes spiteful fate keeps telling me can never be.

And all through this period of my self-deprecation, I endure the richly deserved ache of disappointment lapping like sludge against each corner of my secret flesh. This ache doesn't scream, it whimpers. But it finds a home in every pore. It's there because I wanted so much to reach out, to touch you and confess my insistent love for you, yet I knew so clearly I shouldn't or couldn't. So I sit here on the porch for a very long time, awash in my peculiar/unpeculiar ache. I give in to it. To fight it would make me weep. And someone would catch me crying and ask me to explain. And I would feel the need to make up a lie and David Cruickshank would be right: the world demands its truths or else it makes us lie. There is no in-between. Of course, I'd never be caught *saying* so.

EIGHT

THAT AFTERNOON IN THE CAFE in Westendorf, where we remained at our table for nearly three hours, ordering and drinking tea, nibbling on cookies and sweet little cakes, you and I waded through what seemed to me a shockingly visible chemistry. We swam, we treaded water in it, sometimes we flipped and rolled and leaped like a pair of moonstruck dolphins. I fretted Gord couldn't help but notice us and feel embarrassment or disapproval, perhaps even a smidgen of jealousy. So much conversation, Gord forced, by times, to its fringes, you and I selfishly making verbal love, quoting a cherished song lyric, a vital passage of poetry or prose, sharing moments from movies or from our own lives, opinions and nuances that seemed to mirror one another, completing each other's sentences, all of it a demonstration of fate's flawless rhythm, two perfect strangers instantly aware, and growing more certain of it with each passing second, that they were made for one another.

I felt guilty about Gord. You and I were polite about bringing him into our conversation but politeness was all we could manage. A couple of times, when he left us to visit the bathroom—an errand we all ran more than once that afternoon because of the tea we continued to consume—I sensed you and I scarcely noticed his absence, so enthralled with one another had we become. The afternoon commenced with and maintained a sense of unreality that Gord could not penetrate. Not even when he and I were alone, could he break through the apparent spell I was under in this, our first meeting.

"What do you think of her?" he asked me when you took your turn in the john.

"I think I'm in love," I said, trying to be glib, trying to conceal the shocking realization I might actually be confessing the truth.

"I thought you were already in love."

"Jesus, man," I said more or less to keep him at bay, uncomfortable with the reminder, having no ready answer for his remark.

"That's a diamond on her left hand, you know. I'm beginning to think all the good ones are taken."

"Yeah, I noticed the ring," I said.

You'd mentioned your fiancé twice by then, the way women do when they're tempted by somebody else. I'd mentioned my girlfriend twice too, the way *men* do when *they're* tempted by somebody else. No names, of course. Like we hadn't brought them up as people so much as states of being, as items with a function, as characters in our own little play, as modest monuments to our roles, rituals or anticipated obligations in the lives we'd planned for ourselves to this point. Yet, while mentioning our romantic obligations to strangers back home in Canada seemed like the honest thing to do, it did not modify the chemistry crackling unmercifully between you and me at the café table. No, we continued to gaze at one another, smiling like insipid fools, so preoccupied with one another we had little regard for anything else.

You didn't mention you had a sister that afternoon. And I noticed no resemblance between you and Judy. The difference in height perhaps. Judy's more provocative figure. Your marvelous cheek bones. Your astounding blue eyes. It was impossible to think of Judy much that afternoon, with me believing over and over that you were the most beautiful woman I had ever seen. In fact I even concluded it was possible your beauty would haunt me for as long as I lived, and now, looking back on this conclusion, I am amazed at the accuracy of my observation. Since you, sweet Jan, I have believed much more fervently in my powers of intuition whether I have since ignored them or not.

You said your last name was Smith. "With a 'y' and an 'e,'" you added.

"Oh, Smythe," I said, pronouncing it as Judy did.

"I say, 'Smith,'" you countered. "Seems less pretentious to me somehow."

I nodded empathetically. Destiny let me get away with

ignoring the apparent coincidence in your last name and Judy's being spelled the same way. Besides, at this moment, I wasn't interested in such mundane machinations as the spelling of sir names. I had no interest for this brief time, here in our dark and intimate café setting, in the reality I had previously known. You and Judy as sisters, or even cousins, would have been too provocative a coincidence to be believable on a day like this.

I felt blissfully aware that I was living some kind of cliché. But, at the same time, I knew the cliché to be one I'd only heard about and never had the opportunity to enjoy. Love at first sight. There I was, up to my neck in it, in all the stereotypical delight in which most humans refuse to believe, yet for which, I am convinced, they secretly yearn. I enjoyed each and every aspect of this wonderful cliché as I sat there all afternoon, loving you at first sight. I felt spellbound when our eyes met—yes, yes, spellbound, stereotypically swept away by your gaze. I wanted to place each finger of each hand on what I thought were your perfect cheekbones. I wanted to clutch the back of your head tenderly in the palm of my hand. And I wanted, ever so delicately, perhaps without even touching them at all, to precisely, slowly and tenderly brush your lips with my own. I wanted to feel the sweet agony I knew would be created by everything I did to you, no matter how innocent, no matter how reckless, no matter how inevitable.

Cliché. All of it. I knew it even while I delighted in it. But what does a man do when, one shiny Christmas Eve, he encounters Santa Claus dusting off chimney and fireplace soot from his legendary red uniform? He embraces the myth displayed before him, does he not? He holds the clichéd, wonderful fantasy now presented to him close to his heart. Because it's merely a dream, you see. Because the myth simply cannot be, he hangs onto it for as long as he can, until his arms ache, until, when the moment of truth at last arrives—as it must, as it surely must—the myth is taken away, leaving him to stumble forlornly back to reality's inflexible region of endless compromise again.

That's what I did that Austrian afternoon, in the wake of my chair lift acrophobia , as I sat in the babble of the small café with you. I embraced your myth in Westendorf, with my friend Gord sitting on my right hand, serving as my tenuous link to reality. I dove into the cliché, the stereotype, the myth of romantic love with maniacal glee. In the end, what difference could it make? What would be the harm in letting myself enjoy this single three-hour moment I would cherish for the rest of my life? What difference could it possibly make, when normalcy would inevitably return?

For all I knew, you were thinking the same thoughts. Then again, maybe not. Certainly, I suspected there must be a contrast in the degree of feeling between us. Would it not be too perfect if you were choosing the same myth to observe and be a part of at the very moment I was? At the time, I couldn't be sure. Could anyone else—even you at this moment—feel with the clarity and intensity with which I was feeling now? Do we not perceive feelings like these alone, this solitude God's little joke on mankind? We know best what we know alone, do we not? And there really seems to be no one who can truly share what we feel on our own, right? Still, I sensed whatever was happening between you and me wasn't happening to me alone. You seemed to be suffering the emotional link connecting us nearly as much as me, which only enriched my sensation of it more.

In a perfect world at some point, perhaps when Gord went to have a leak, I would have told you how I felt. In a perfect world it would have been permissible. How wonderful it would have been, just for one incredible moment, to defy convention enough to tell someone something that was so fucking and briefly true I could happily subscribe afterwards to society's endlessly mediocre edicts the rest of my life. But it's not a perfect world and it wasn't perfect then. So I adhered to convention and didn't say anything. You didn't say anything either. We just embraced in a figurative sense inside this wonderfully unexpected mythical moment of love in an Austrian café, when even what was left unsaid seemed to say *everything*.

I too visited the café washroom to relieve myself, limping between the tables, carrying my cane, standing at the urinal, bemused by what was taking place. It occurred to me I'd never had a day like this one before. A glimpse into the face of death on the ride down the side of the mountain, more figurative than literal, granted, but a brush with death just the same. Then you, a presence so profoundly perfect, you seemed nearly imaginary, as if I'd ventured drunkenly into the confluence of life and death, and had only to swim another hundred yards to escape to some vacuous verisimilitude again.

When I got back to the table, you and Gord were standing. Seeing me returning, you smiled and reached for your ski jacket, a simple blue affair that I nonetheless noticed seemed to match your eyes.

"I must be going," you said. "I can't believe what time it is."

Gord and I both glanced at our watches. To argue that it wasn't yet late? To verify it was? I don't know. Humans are always looking at the time. To save a moment. Or regret one. Or pass it on like a relay race baton.

You shook hands with me. "Nice to have met you, Tom," you said.

"Nice to have met you too," I replied, our gazes lingering again, an excitement surging through me even though this afternoon of unexpected delight was now drawing to a close.

"*Auf Weiderzehn*," you said, brushing by me on your way out of the café.

Gord and I left shortly too.

"Our new friend, Jan, may join us this evening at the Keller Bar," Gord said when we were outside, preparing to make our way to our pension.

"That would be nice," I murmured, feigning as much disinterest as I could manage.

Gord only grunted reflectively.

And I limped along beside him in silence, not certain whether it was a good idea to encounter you again or not.

AS IT HAPPENED, YOU did show up in our favorite bar a few hours later. I realized in some nebulous way, that we were sunk from that moment on, that for the immediate future, for the few days remaining to us, we weren't done with one another and what seemed impossible to ignore between us. Two nights hence, when you and I succumbed to a brief few hours of truth and honesty, you would tell me how you nearly didn't show up at the Keller Bar that night. You knew it would only make worse the chemistry bubbling hotly between us.

But there you were. I saw you come in the door, scan the various tables, then spot us on the other side of the room. You caught my eye and smiled, then waved somewhat offhandedly, as if the wave could water down the pleasure in your smile, passing it off as meaningless when it actually wasn't. As you circumnavigated an empty dance floor near the *oompahpah* band, I watched you coming towards us and I felt again the same delight I'd enjoyed all afternoon.

You'd known Gord the longest, since yesterday at least, so he took proprietorship of you and introduced you to our other friends. I watched their various reactions and noticed, to a man, they were instantly charmed by you. Eventually I would realize, by the time we left Westendorf, that all of us, in varying degrees, were somewhat smitten by you.

You sat down opposite me at our table while the *oompahpah* band came back to play another set. I'd asked for more Strauss. *Blue Danube. Viennese Waltz. Tales From The Vienna Woods.* The music now felt deeply romantic to me. And we telepathed from one to another that same profound attraction we'd shared all afternoon in the café, letting it leap across the table and into each other's grateful, private perception. We were so polite with my friends, on the surface of it, at least. I was stunned that they didn't notice we were so taken with each other.

You even danced with each of my friends a couple of times, I noticed. I sat there at the table, my mountain climbing pick cane resting against my admonishing leg, the torn ligaments throbbing in pain and my stomach fluttering with lovesick angst. I watched you dance with the others and admired your magical beauty, something extra I could appreciate now that I could see the way you moved.

The way you move, sweet Jan, this has been, for me, a catalyst in my love for you. Over the years, a couple of times, David Cruickshank and I have discussed, in an abstract way, the correlation between love and the mystical way in which a person *moves*. David's opinions are speculative. Despite his trio of marriages, he claims never to have truly been in love.

"Are you sure?" I've asked him incredulously. "Why would you marry women you didn't love?"

"I said, 'in love,' Tom."

"Oh."

"What I'm saying here is I haven't met the woman who, when I watch her move, makes my mouth go dry until I can't swallow. You know what I mean?"

"I guess so," I replied, knowing *exactly* what he meant.

"I've seen other guys feel it, though," murmured David sadly.

"Yeah. Me too." I wanted to give him this concession, at least. I couldn't tell him about you, so I could only agree with him on general principle.

The way you moved, Jan. The way you *still* move. There's no defining it and this is just the point. It isn't about the aspects of how someone we love moves—no, it's about something metaphysical in how the way they move causes us to respond to them. Like the right person has a way of moving that signals to us that they are the right person. Walking towards us. Turning their head a certain way. The way they walk away from us, the way they climb stairs, the way they look at us when they're listening, the way they gesture when they speak.

David's view that the right person will announce herself to us in the way they move was based only on his observations. My view, Jan, confirms his because I remember how you moved back then, how you still move today. My throat went dry and I couldn't swallow at times that day. And it was because of the way you moved.

"Can you dance with that leg?" you asked me at last, done with my friends.

"I'm not sure," I said . . . .

There were hoots of derision from my companions.

". . . But I'm willing to give it a try."

Indeed, I wanted desperately to dance with you. Dancing for me has always been an essential fiber in the weave of true romance, me touching the woman in my arms while some melody acknowledges and favors us. I'd taken Judy dancing a couple of times by the time I met you, but although I'm an average dancer I felt Judy was critical of my ability. For me, because of the connection between dancing and love, a high rate of dancing skill was irrelevant. Judy, I'd discovered, viewed dancing in terms of varying degrees of excellence, dancing as an art to be adjudicated within some exacting standard, a juried practice where someone is the best and someone shouldn't bother, which is different from my own, more romantic view.

So I limped to the dance floor with you, my skill now moot because of the injury to my knee. I spun you as well as I could to the music of Johann Strauss, merely enjoying the luxury of holding a beautiful, fragile you in the loving safety of my arms. When at last the music ended and we turned to go back to the table, I know that we were flushed from even so innocent a physical connection. I wanted to take your hand on the way back to our table, perhaps pretending my injury needed the support. But I didn't. There was Judy, after all, and I didn't want my friends to recognize that I was now deeply enamored—tempted, in *their* minds, I would have suspected—by someone else.

I felt trapped between loyalty and this new and powerful temptation I recognized in you. Loyalty isn't as intellectually adept as temptation is. Loyalty is a kind of working class quality, admirable, yes, but a virtue with little imagination. It can't compete with true temptation where imagination is concerned. I should have known Judy would be a changed woman for me when I returned to Canada, but I didn't contemplate this for a second. Temptation knew Judy would seem different. Loyalty lacked the imagination to even consider the possibility. In combination, as far as loyalty and temptation were concerned, there would be this perfect now, then normalcy would fall into place behind me with the ease of a wake behind a speeding boat. Amazing what we tell ourselves when the two sides of our nature—the tamed and the untamed—are having an argument with one another.

Periodically that night in the Keller Bar, I glanced at the diamond ring you wore on your left hand. I overheard you mention to Gord or Fred, I'm not sure which one of my friends, that you were getting married in a little more than a year, that your fiancé back home in Canada would be at the airport in Toronto to meet your returning plane on the following Monday. These incidents should have dampened my spirits. They should have doused me with the cold wash of reality. Strangely enough, though, they had no impact on my ardor. I was puzzled by this that night in Westendorf. I couldn't understand why you and I were falling so carelessly in love when we both obviously believed we loved someone else back home.

I suppose I figured it out later, theoretically, at least. For us, having mere days to know one another, what made this love at first sight business so perfect was that it didn't have any future. In fact, it hadn't even germinated in any kind of past. Without those other two eras—past and future—to touch it, to intrude on it, to try to shape it, the present possesses no obligation or responsibility. It merely *is*. It has no capacity for cowardice; it is capable only of courage. The present, because it isn't going to end until it becomes the past, always displays valor. It can lose its nerve in the past, or turn away frightened from the future, but the present makes no commitment. It just *is*, in wonder, majesty and bravery. It just . . . *is*.

Even only vaguely sensing this proposition about time and love back then, I suppose I suspected you and I would go back to Canada, grateful to have been fortunate enough to enjoy the inexplicable freedom we'd had in Westendorf just to *be*, that brief moment in time when we know there is something else more real in life, that there *can be* something else, before we meekly embark on our commitment to society's conventional tepidness. In other words, while this day might reflect a falling in love for us, we both knew it wouldn't last beyond a matter of hours, that what we felt for one another was merely *a glimpse* of some more intense and potentially perfect kind of love. And a glimpse was all we should expect.

I understand now the rather cruel codicil we, as a society, affix to anything wondrous in human life: the reason it can never be, the reason it isn't *allowed*. You see, if this kind of love is real, it's no longer merely myth. If it fails to be myth and is real, then we must face the fact many of us cannot find it, or don't know how. But we *all* can enjoy the myth. Because damned few of us can have the real thing, we create the myth as a society and remind ourselves repeatedly that it is myth. In this way, we minimize an inevitable envy from our peers. In a way, as a society, we all work to maintain the lowest common denominator, thereby limiting our potential for success. Especially in love. Of course, I'd never be caught *saying* so.

I knew that much that night in Westendorf, as you sat across the table from me, your relatively modest engagement ring gleaming in the candlelight floating in liquid wax in the center of our table. I knew that night, without the means to explain it clearly, that life is a desert, after all, only to keep alive the myth of an oasis. If the oasis is actually real and not myth at all, well then we'd find ourselves refusing to accept the desert, wouldn't we? And as my maverick friend David Cruickshank has pointed out to me more than once, society cannot function if its myths are actually realities. No, when myth becomes reality, society's various human components begin to want things they believe they can actually have, items with substance, such as love, peace and freedom, goods no one yet has figured out how to sell.

But while I was approaching the truth of something philosophical that night in Westendorf, I was also falling in love. And fate's perfidious nature was setting a trap for me.

FOR THE NEXT FEW DAYS, you and I drew lines in the dirt between us, sweet Jan. We would promise ourselves that such lines could not be crossed. These were lines honoring our commitments to existing lovers, Judy in my case, Greg in yours. We would draw lines in the dirt and then, against all reason, cross them shortly afterwards.

Separately from one another, we agreed never to meet for coffee alone, or so we mentioned later when all the damage was done, yet the next morning we did. And the morning after that one. We would find ourselves mentioning coffee the previous evening—after all, I couldn't ski—and soon, without the knowledge of my friends, we would plan the café and the time. I know I drew a line in the dirt that I would not touch you in any way, not even on the dance floor again. But I did. I danced with you each night remaining to me. And I held your hand across the café table just for a moment one morning. And you reached up and touched me on the chest with the palm of your hand at one point, in one of the two cafés where we clandestinely met a couple of times each day. And, of course, we embraced to say so long, embraces that felt new to me in the way they left me breathless and aroused.

The touching, Jan. I had never known such innocent touches to be so provocative, to so lacerate my flesh. I even feared, soon, when I returned to Canada, touching would never be the same for me again. If so, what would I do then?

You and I nearly admitted to one another what was going on between us those first few days. Nearly, but not quite. Instead we clung to our own private excuses, variations on the lines we drew in the dirt. While our brains searched frantically for any reason for why we were so drawn to one another, I'm not sure we came up with anything concrete. It was enough, I guess, to believe at least we'd tried.

For instance, you blamed our exotic setting in Austria for our mutual attraction the second morning we had coffee together. Remember what you said?

"This place, Tom, makes everything magical," you said.

"Westendorf?"

"These mountains."

"Yes."

"It makes everything seem possible . . . ."

"Yes."

". . . Even when it probably isn't."

182

I thought your words were wise but I couldn't say so at that moment. Any agreement I contemplated only caught in my throat as some fierce sense of loss. I wanted to believe this mirage in the desert was actually the oasis it seemed to be. But I couldn't believe it because I was too terrified of being wrong. After all, do people prolong their mistaken choices in life only to convince themselves they were right?

"Magical places like this," you mused, "probably impair our judgment. Exaggerate everything. How we think we feel, how we view things. You know what I mean?"

"I guess so," I replied, although it continued to hurt me to agree with you. "A place like this is a holiday, you're saying. It's removed from reality, from responsibility."

Your beautiful eyes swallowed me in tragic hopelessness.

"I guess that's what I'm saying," you said.

"Maybe it's true," I disclaimed. "Maybe we just rationalize everything away in the wonder."

But you only looked at me. I think I would have killed at that moment to know and lose myself in whatever you were truly thinking, to know if, at that moment, there was any chance I could convince you of what I have since learned is the permanence of my love for you.

Still, with all of our doubts, with all of our reservations, with all of the caution that was so familiar to us, you and I inexorably drew closer and fell more and more in love. We either forgot we had barely more than a day remaining to us, or else we remembered this all too clearly. At the time I wasn't sure which.

THE LAST NIGHT OF OUR STAY in Westendorf—you had two more days remaining before *you* must leave the friends with whom you were staying—I danced with you again, stumbling around the dance floor with my protesting, injured leg. I was sitting beside you among my friends at our table on this, our last evening together—I'm not sure which one of us arranged to do so—and I ached with the knowledge that soon I would never see you again. When we returned from our dance to sit down again, I took your hand underneath the table and you held it for several minutes.

Although it was barely ten o'clock, you soon announced that you should be going.

My friends all groaned in response.

"I'm really tired," you said with a smile.

You still held my hand, and before you let go of it, you locked your fingers in mine and squeezed as hard as you could.

"I'm going too," I told my friends. "My knee is killing me."

"I'll see you guys tomorrow morning," you promised as we left the table. "I won't let you leave Westendorf without saying goodbye."

Then we made our escape. My friends, if they noticed our deceit, didn't say anything. By the time we reached the doors, they had turned back to their own conversation.

"Walk with me?" I said when we were outside.

"Yes."

It was chilly again. The cycle of Westendorf's warm days and cool nights continued.

"Where are we going?" you asked.

"I don't know," I said.

You took my hand again not long after we started down the village street. We strolled along quite slowly, me limping my way over the icy ruts, you staying close by my side, leaning tantalizingly close. We didn't say anything else for a time, but we stroked each other's gloved fingers as we walked along.

"I'm getting married in a year or so," you confessed again, so quietly it seemed you were actually speaking to yourself. "It makes sense to marry the man I'm going to marry."

"Yes," I replied. "And I'll probably marry the woman I've been seeing for three months. It's always seemed to make sense."

"This is totally crazy," you said. "You and me, I mean."

"But *wonderfully* totally crazy," I countered.

Silence.

"Even if it's insane, don't you think it's wonderful?" I asked.

"Yes. Yes, I do. The most wonderful insanity I've ever known."

"Yes," I said. "That's how it is for me."

"We're going to marry other people, though."

"Yes. That's what we keep saying."

"It's like it's some other reality back there. Something to go back to."

"Yes. Some other reality."

"So what are we doing *right now?*"

I thought about this a moment before I answered you. "Being crazy, I guess."

I heard you sigh in the near-darkness beside me.

"What?" I asked.

You said nothing.

"What?" I asked again.

"I'm crazy in love with you, Tom, you know. From the moment I laid eyes on you. It's insane."

"Yes, I know. It's been that way for me too. I can't sleep. I can't stop thinking about you. I'm in love with you too. At first sight."

We were near my pension by now and we stopped along the street a few yards from the square in front of it where, scant days ago—an eon—an epoch ago—I had been dropped with my luggage and friends into this different, exotic world. We turned and gazed at one another in a kind of delicious wonder. What we had just said to one another, so easily and so frantically. Was I dreaming? Were we in this dream together? Then, holding my stupid mountain climbing pick cane aloft in my right hand, I took you into my arms and kissed you with everything I'd been feeling for you for the past couple of days. Your mouth was sweet, your gentle, darting tongue exquisite, the kiss electric and addictive, unleashing a sensual appetite in me I had never before even imagined. It felt like the first kiss of my young life. Now, sweet Jan, two decades later, in a way that pain defines, I sometimes think of that kiss as my last.

We wore relatively bulky jackets. As we stood there kissing more and more deeply, more and more hungrily, frustrated by the bulkiness of our winter jackets, we began decoding the network of zippers, cords and belts that kept us separate from one another, forgetting, for the moment, that we were still outside.

"Jesus," I gasped, when I realized what we were doing outside the front doors of my pension, as I noticed I had all but removed your jacket to press myself inside, more closely against you. Realizing I had embarked on disrobing you right there in the street, I was astonished with myself. I was not normally such an incautious man.

"Time to go inside," you said.

"Yes."

My excitement as we approached the pension was tempered by fear. I don't know why exactly. It wasn't disloyalty to Judy. It wasn't sexual ambivalence. It was more a fear that in a moment or two I would suddenly wake up and discover I was dreaming. Still, hand-in-hand, we went inside and climbed the stairs to my room. The amorous moment we'd lost on the street came back instantly, as soon as we closed the door behind us. We tossed our jackets onto the floor and you returned to my embrace and I came back to yours.

We made love until nearly two am. While your body, your smell, your taste were new to me, there was something that felt ancient to me about your appropriateness, the way each corner of your flesh fit so perfectly against mine. There was no clumsiness, no awkwardness, the kind I'd come to expect in a first sexual encounter. We were, by turns, gentle with one another and then astonishingly impassioned. I felt we made love with every secret I'd ever known about myself, like we exchanged anxious mysteries with one another through the pores of our skin, perhaps in some quest for a simple, but elusive truth, or seeking, I think, some necessary redemption.

I had never known myself to be so insatiable. Yes, with Judy our first night. We'd made love for hours too that night, but this time my unappeased appetite was more than sexual. I felt like I was trying to break into your body, climb inside your flesh where, should I be successful, I would find I truly belonged. At home there, inside your being, I would keep myself safe and giving, married to you forever.

We wept together at some point that night. Then we laughed at the notion that we would cry. I had just come, you had just come.

"My God," you whispered. "My God."

"Yes, yes," was all I said.

We made more love, endless love, it seems, licking each other's flesh, our mouths, our fingers, probing, exploring, until we were exhausted. I guess we must have slept for an hour or so in the middle of the night. I remember your head against my shoulder, your soft flesh held in my arms. I heard you snore at one point, gently, a snort, but I drifted in the darkness, clinging to your body. We soon woke up simultaneously, as if by arrangement. We gazed at one another in the darkness, not seeing much, I guess, yet seeming to see *everything*.

I couldn't help myself. I started kissing you again. I trailed kisses over your small breasts and along your belly. I grabbed your buttocks and lifted your sweet cunt towards my mouth, then I made love to you with all the gentle joy you miraculously inspired in me.

You took me inside you again. We climbed the face of our wonder again, that ecstatic slope, that hill of joy again, gasping, murmuring and crying out at the delight, the perfect delight we had discovered in one another.

It was around four am. when you mentioned you should go, that you should sneak back to your own hotel.

"I'll walk you back," I said.

"No, your knee."

"Never mind my knee."

"No, Tom. I want to go back alone." You kissed me on the chest to ameliorate the sternness in your voice.

Then.

"It's perfect, isn't it?"

"Yes," I said. "It is."

"And you're wondering what to do with something this perfect."

"Yes. Are you?"

I felt you nod against my chest. You moved in closer and I embraced you more tightly. You laid your leg over mine. It felt so wondrous holding you in my arms this way, I felt tears again begin to trickle down my cheeks. I had never known myself to be so emotional. But it *was* perfect. It really *was*.

Several minutes passed before you said, "The trouble with this kind of perfection, Tom, is that it doesn't last."

"You think so?"

"How *can* it?"

"I don't know," I murmured.

"You and I are kind of a little gift to one another. That's

what this is."

I shuddered. I knew, now, you were pulling away from me and I didn't want you to go. I suppose I knew you were right. I suppose I doubted this kind of perfection lasts. Yet I wanted to keep it anyway, although I didn't know how I could.

"We'll look back on this in delight," you said, a tremor in your voice.

I felt wetness against my bare chest. Your tears, I realized.

"We'll look back on this and say thank you, when things are kind of tough and kind of average, when things are mundane and not very special. We'll look back on you and me, and say, thank you."

"You don't think it can work?"

"Maybe. But what if it didn't? How would you like to look back on a night like this, on the two and a half days we've had, only to discover it wasn't special over the long haul, that even a night of love like this can't sustain itself?"

I said nothing.

"Something as perfect as this is supposed to be temporary. Like being a princess for one day. Then you go back to real life and keep the memory. Right?"

"I don't know," I whispered sadly, puzzled that my heart was breaking so much, a little angry to learn you seemed even more cynical than I knew myself to be.

It occurred to me the imperfection we discussed had arrived already, even while you still lay naked in my arms. Already, to my dismay, it was apparent I probably loved you much more than you loved me. Or were you only wiser than me, much less the fool?

"Tom," you said, moving up to where it would be obvious in the darkness you were looking at me. "I've never felt or known such perfect love as I've known with you, since the moment we met. Everything. The talking, the dancing, the lovemaking."

"Me too," I whispered.

"That's just it," you said. "I want to keep it perfect."

"I know."

"I want you to leave tomorrow knowing that you're my one true love, my soul mate, and, knowing that, accepting that you'll never see me again."

What you said made so much sense to me. I don't know why. Because at this moment, I felt my heart was breaking and would remain broken for good, if I never saw you again. I sensed, if I never saw you again—my perfect lover—something in me would permanently die and I would not enter willingly life's new and obvious mediocrity.

"We could run away," I said weakly.

"We already have," you replied. "Now we have to go back. It's just the Alps and Austria, a warp in time and place."

"You mean we can't eat caviar every day."

"That's right. We can't eat caviar every day."

"I feel like we're throwing in the towel," I said.

"Yes. Me too."

"So don't you think what we have is worth fighting for?"
"It ends up in the same place, Tom."

"The same place?"

"Yes. Wondering why we failed. Wondering where perfect love went."

"Maybe, when it's perfect, it doesn't go away."

"Tom," you whispered.

And you abruptly pulled away and got out of bed. I heard you begin to dress, unable to see you well in the darkness.

"Listen to me, Jan. Maybe when it's perfect, it doesn't go away."

"Or," you argued, " if it's perfect, when it evaporates, it's perfectly awful, much more awful because it was perfect."

I said nothing else while you finished dressing. I just laid in my bed, the smell of you—and the smell of you and me together—wafting all around me. I just laid there aching for you and what I knew I would soon be missing.

"I love you, Jan," I said after you bent down and kissed me on the lips. "I love you so much."

"I love you too, Tom," you said.

I heard the zippers and clasps of your ski jacket. I watched you slip out the door. I caught a glimpse of you, caught you looking back at me—as if you had decided it was all right to turn to salt—in the light leaking into my room from the hallway just outside.

Then you were gone.

THE SUNDAY AFTERNOON my friends and I left Westendorf, I was dismayed that you actually showed up to say your final goodbyes where we sat waiting on board our idling bus. Dismayed and delighted, I grew newly hopeful, I guess, that you'd had a change of heart. After all, we hadn't promised anything. We hadn't sorted anything through. We'd loved it all out with wondrous bliss much of the night. Then we'd worked out a halfhearted accord based on a cynical respect for what we had learned to believe about the impossibility of fine, romantic love. You were going back to your fiancé. I was to go back to the other woman I had decided to love, to perhaps marry in the near future. Was this not what we had decided? Were we not donning the past and the future like black armbands, remembering, as a brief and wonderful spell, when we had found new life in the present? Were we not going to share the memory of a time when, ever so briefly, the present was all there was?

But there you were boarding our bus in the last few moments before our departure and it struck me suddenly that I wanted desperately more of the present. I wanted the present to never end. This wish, this possibility came over me violently. I actually shook. Could I stay here in Westendorf perhaps, at least until your plane left a couple of days from now? Was this not why you had boarded our bus, to keep the present going, because you'd found a way to make the spell endless after all? Were you not here because you'd found a way to lock the future in a closet where everything works out permanently? Were you not on this bus to tell me the mirage was no mirage, but an actual oasis after all?

You walked down the aisle of the idling vehicle. You sat on the edge of an empty seat. You remained too far away for me to touch. Just as well in view of the proximity of my friends. It was like the first afternoon we met: you and I gazing at one another in a state of longing my skiing friends could not seem to see. You shook hands with everyone. You even shook hands with me. I know you did because we both knew you had no choice in this but to treat me similarly. I felt the touch of your hand and my fingers ached afterwards. We were closing the door to the way we felt compelled to gaze at one another. I understood this now. When you left this bus and walked away, and when it pulled slowly out of the driveway to leave Westendorf behind, I knew this would be it. We would never see one another again. This was how we would preserve the perfection of the present. We would leave it perfect by exercising our choice, by knowing whatever lay ahead for us separately would never again resemble what we had known with one another during the past few days. Parting now, we wouldn't be able to make any mistakes. Parting now, we would keep our love flawless, an extraordinary love, a jewel we'd managed to extricate for ourselves from the deep mine our world contrives to make life conveniently mundane. Once you and I parted, our love would remain perfect, unblemished by the banal.

The rest of these few moments passed for me in a haze. You perched on the edge of the empty seat and we gazed at one another in what I now remember as a deep and provocative yearning. I remember you walking down the aisle. I remember you going down the steps, our driver stepping aside to let you pass. I remember you standing outside in the pension courtyard. I remember your astonishing blue eyes. I remember believing I would love you until I died, knowing it was true. And I remember nearly getting up to dash down the aisle, just before our bus pulled away, intent on disembarking, intent, I guess, on some decision of mine to convince you of the notion that perfect love at least had a chance with you and me living it in the way we apparently could.

Then, somehow, while I gazed helplessly out the window, it was absolutely too late. The bus pulled away with an aching grinding of gears, and you disappeared in its wake. After you were gone, as the bus rolled down the highway back the way it had come only eight days before, I found myself negotiating with God again, the way I had on my chair lift ride down to safety a few days before, those long minutes when I had traded promises for a chance to live again. This time I asked Him to save my life by having you change your mind and materialize before me back home in Canada. Then I would show Him how love can work in His world. I would do anything, I promised. But, again, I didn't really have anything to trade. Instead, in the end, I knew I spent the long bus ride only wishing, wishing you—or the idea of you—could go on a little longer as a delightful reality, putting off the inevitable moment when it turned itself into myth.

I was silent virtually the entire trip to the airport at Munich, gazing vacantly out the window at spring in Austria and Germany pushing winter back across the seasonally embattled landscape. It was all I could muster, lost the way I was in a deep and hurtful heartache.

I like to think on the plane back to Heathrow, then, as we crossed the Atlantic in the direction of Ottawa, that I gradually became comfortable with the inescapable notion I would never see you again. Still, for weeks and months afterwards, as I gradually tried to accept what would never happen to me, what would never belong to me, I would peer around street corners hoping to see you, sometimes even convinced I *would*. Or I might think I saw you waiting at the corner for a green light. Eventually, though, while I never lost hope, I began to believe the woman I saw in the distance would never ever be you.

We'd had our moment in the present few people get to enjoy, I soon decided. To want more was probably merely greed. I would know when I married Judy I was richer for the experience I'd had with you. I believed Judy would draw something beneficial from the residue of my secret, learning to enjoy some of my new capacity to love, perhaps, without me explaining you to her, without me having to confess what society calls everything wonderful when a man finds and loves his perfect woman. I would never have to admit my brief love affair with you was just another infidelity, just another fancy betrayal of what everyone insists should remain merely myth.

NINE

IT RAINS ON SATURDAY MORNING. I awake to the drizzle's patter on the roof, its whisper on the evergreens, on the dull and dancing autumn leaves still clinging, deprived of the sun's reflection, to the hardwoods outside the lodge's windows. It's more or less dawn, so gray in the rainfall it's hard to know how early it actually is. I dress at the foot of the bed, shivering at the chill clinging to my clothing, Judy snoring in whispers on her side of the bed, her arm up protectively covering the side of her face. I gaze at her as I dress and wonder what is wrong with me. Why do I think of *you* each morning when I awake, when it would have been much easier to think of Judy. Judy's okay. In some ways, Judy's probably wonderful. But . . . .

I slip carefully out of the room, listening to the rain, remembering you on the porch with me last night and recalling what I may have nearly said, still haunted by the notion that last night may have represented my perfect moment for a confession of continuing love, still haunted to remember I let the moment pass. What if the moment never returns? What then?

I prepare coffee in a percolator on the stove: there is no coffee maker here at Gladys Pinkster-Smythe's resort. Everyone groaned last night when the missing coffee maker was announced. It was me who found the dusty old percolator in a deep corner of one of the cupboards. I camp every year. Perking coffee is something I do with experience. And I have a taste for it; perked coffee is delicious.

"Whoever buys this place," reflected Greg last night, "is going to need a lot of money to buy the kitchen equipment. I mean, for a resort, it's pretty primitive."

"Not our problem," Judy said.

I just went ahead and prepared the coffee, silently musing that too much reliance on convenience takes the pleasure out of life.

This morning I put on a parka and take my mug of coffee out onto the porch. The rain is easing and, in the distance, I can see a jagged seam forming in the clouds, an opening of blue where a tepid autumn sun might yet find a hole it can leak through. But for now, it's cold and I can see my breath. October rains, like their November counterparts, can be miserable and relentless, but I like the sheen and the shine on the trees and leaves, on the grasses and the prolific weeds and shrubs loitering between me and the shoreline. I like the stillness of the lake, the way the raindrops invent their rippled selves across its face. And the smell of everything. I love the smell of this place, the woods, the plants, the earth, the water. It's like a gentle and endless orgasm. It reaches my nose and clings there, tirelessly stroking me, hoarsely whispering, coming and going in waves of artful pleasure. And I think about how this feeling of precious peace connects a man like me to what is too often elusive during his necessary exchanges with the conventional world: his own authentic version of himself.

David and I have discussed this topic on numerous occasions whenever we are camping.

"Whether we know it or not," he has said, "Mother Nature is our mistress."

I always know what he means and I say so. "Yes, that's true."

"Mostly, when we lie down to rest, we lie down with our elemental selves."

"Yes. Mother Nature."

"It's our elemental selves that truly fall in love, you know. The perfect woman for you and me is the one who seems to walk naked right out of the wilderness of whatever it is we are inside, the place in each of us where we are part of what's around us, where what's around us is part of us."

"You're a poet, Mr. Cruickshank."

"We have to reclaim our pagan selves, Tom. Being reasonable is fine, but we shouldn't lose touch with the primitive in our souls."

"Easier said than done, my friend."

He looked at me a moment, then sighed. "So where did my perfect woman go, the one with the pagan soul, the one I once believed would happily get on an ice flow with me?"

Thinking of you, Jan, I swallowed. "She's out there, David," I said, although my words sounded pretty lame to me once I heard them out in the open, on my own account as well as David's. I'm as left behind by true romantic love as David is. But I at least can glimpse the wondrous notion of you—and who you are to me—as you keep dancing away from my sanguine grasp.

I don't remember when David and I last had this kind of discussion. One gets tired of looking fruitlessly for a pagan soul-mate in a world where people walk down the sidewalk, crying into a cell phone about who said what to whom or the salvation and security, it is believed, that can be found in a visit to Home Depot. Besides, duty calls, and I leave the porch and its rainy October vista to go inside to the dishes.

Everything's still on the table the way we left it last night. But I change my mind about tackling the dishes first, opting instead to cautiously approach an old wood stove in the far corner of the room. I tap on the stove pipe, checking for creosote. There's a pile of ancient wood in a handmade rack by the side of the stove. I contemplate building a fire to take the chill out of this area of the lodge but I'm rusty with wood stoves, in fact practically a neophyte. What if I burn the place down?

I stand there a moment longer, thoughtfully sipping my coffee, feeling like a coward. Then, fuck it! I stuff the stove with Greg's *National Post*, gathering up the small bits of kindling the rack has collected over the years. I start the fire, opening the draft, then gradually feed ever larger logs into the stove's cavity. I wait for the explosion, the stench of too much smoke, then, when these catastrophes do not materialize, I silently congratulate myself.

Now the dishes. Alone at this hour of the morning, I happily set to work, wondering if Greg has already deducted the cost of a heavy duty dishwasher from the market value of this beautiful northern property.

Greg, as it turns out, is the first one up later this morning. By then I'm working on the big breakfast I promised everyone the previous night. Greg pokes his head into the kitchen and asks me what's cooking.

"Wilderness breakfast," I reply. "Home fries with onions, eggs, back bacon, regular bacon, ham, sausage, mushrooms, fried tomatoes, Texas toast."

"Christ," he says. "Cholesterol attack."

"One morning won't kill you."

My brother-in-law looks distracted and tense to me. I nearly ask him what is wrong, but decide against it in the end. Away from his work, Greg frets in a state of deep and endless angst. So I ask "Who else is up?" instead.

"Huh?"

"The women. Are they awake?"

"Passed Judy in the hall. She should be down any minute. Jan was still in bed. She's awake, though. Mentioned she had a bad night."

I say nothing to this, although I'm vaguely pleased at the possibility you may have suffered similarly to me during the rest of the night that followed our conversation.

"You can smell the grease up there in the bedrooms," Greg is telling me.

"Grease?" I say with a sniff. "That's the smell of good old-fashioned bacon."

Greg doesn't like the rain and uses this fact to switch gears. "Wet out, isn't it?"

"Fresh."

"That's one way of looking at it." Then he fidgets his way out of the kitchen, leaving me alone to conduct my noisy orchestra of happily frying food.

The oven is huge in this kitchen. It's no trouble at all keeping everything warm until I've set the table. Up goes the property value. Shit, I couldn't work in real estate. Money and enterprise, on today's modern scale, reduce human experience to the shabbily facile.

In the dining room, I find Judy taking a seat at the table and Greg pacing restlessly around the adjoining living room, caged by his self-imposed notion of the regular feedings he hopes exist in the corporate zoo to which he has always aspired. He's carrying his iPhone around with him again and it strikes me that I will not be surprised if he announces he and Jan must go back to Toronto early. I will be dashed if he does.

Ritually I kiss Judy on the top of the head just before I begin to set the table. "Good morning, Chef," she says, puckering up to kiss the air without taking her eyes off a magazine she's perusing.

"If you guys want coffee, it's on the wood stove. Coffee is

self-serve this morning."

"No grounds in it, I hope," mentions Judy.

"None I put there on purpose," I reply.

Jesus, save the modern world from the calamity of coffee grounds.

"How do you like the wood stove" I ask my wife and brother-in-law.

"I'll give you one thing," says Greg, almost accusingly. "You're good at this lodge/resort stuff."

"Thank you."

"Toasty," says Judy.

"Thank you."

I glance at Greg again.

"I have three deals closing this weekend," he says, as if I've asked for an explanation. "I just hope nothing is going wrong with me stuck way up here in the woods."

"You're a workaholic," Judy says pleasantly enough.

"Look who's talking," I reply over my shoulder, heading for the kitchen.

She sticks her tongue out at me, still without glancing up from her magazine.

Then, at last, you come down the stairs, puffy and bleary-eyed. My heart ignites again, the way it always does when I witness your approach, sending bolts of need up and down my arms and legs. I love you somehow for showing such powerful evidence of your sleeplessness, for not hiding it from me or the others. But you don't look at me. Perhaps, while not wanting to, I said too much last night. I will worry about this, I know, at least for part of the morning. Even a fragile, failed connection to you feels like *everything* to me, like it could represent what was once some avoidable disaster.

But my coffee is strong and recuperative. Eventually, after we've polished off my elaborate breakfast, we all sit around the table, dipping corners of wedges of toast into receptive jars of jam.

"It's going to clear up," I say, gesturing towards the window.

By now you're more awake. You glance at me, perhaps forgivingly. "I've always loved the sound of the rain on a cottage roof or in the woods. It's comforting somehow."

"Yes," I say. "It *is*, isn't it?"

Judy just shakes her head, like she would if she were exasperated by a pair of misguided children.

"It was the rain last night that finally lulled me to sleep," you are saying. "If not for the rain, I might have been up all night." And you look at me a moment with what I hope is a degree of intimacy.

Whatever your glance means, it's enough to cause me to feel an exquisite bolt of excitement.

"I've got sleeping pills," Judy says. "Let me know if you need one tonight."

"I'll be okay, I think," you reply.

Greg hasn't been listening to us. "I've got to go into Temagami," he says. "I really should make some phone-calls. I have deals closing this weekend."

"And the cell's not working?" you ask your husband.

"No," he replies dejectedly. "I might as well be on Mars."

Silence.

"Does anyone want to come along? Does anyone need anything?"

But we all decline.

"Well," says Greg. "I can go in alone, I guess."

Judy gazes at me. "Are you sure you don't want to go into town with your brother-in-law?"

"Yeah. It's going to clear up. I've got some exploring to do."

Judy frowns at me.

"Maybe tomorrow," I say.

THE RAIN HAS STOPPED. As expected, a large patch of blue sky has slowly begun to take shape directly overhead. While you and Judy attack our weekend's most recent batch of dishes, I go outside again with the companion of myself and stand on the veranda a moment, smelling the sweet scent of wet pine and spruce. Soon I stroll down to the dock and tiptoe gingerly over the broken boards to peer into the water. The sleeping, tranquil bottom of the lake displays yet again waterlogged tree branches and brown leaves from the moultings of autumns past. I stand there a long time, studying the shine of the developing day, the way it seems to relish its own sense of peace, not boastfully, but in a self-possessed, confident fashion. I believe people and their natural settings enjoy every potential to learn from one another. Self-possession. Confidence. Are these not qualities we learn from our environment? Harder in these times to accomplish being our elemental selves, I know. Our world will not relent in its apparent need to make each one of us the same as one another long enough to simply let us be ourselves.

Up here at Gladys Pinkster-Smythe's lodge, I can imagine a life less focused on explaining to my peers or some punitive arm of government why I want to be alone with what I believe is the wisdom of myself. Would I not be more wondrously *me*, if I didn't have to dedicate so much of my life to worrying about where to park, applying for this rewards program or that rewards program, explaining myself to various authorities who take my valuable time and commit it to the perpetual operation of society's machine? Would I not better thrive in a world less preoccupied with keeping me at home, imprisoning me with ever more complex and pointless minutiae designed to modify my ambitions so that they parallel those of my peers?

Thinking these things, I stand at the end of the dock a very long time. And somehow, in a way I can't quite define, I begin to sense something for me is changing. Something big. Something important. I don't recognize what it is at this moment, but I sense I've begun to cross some mysterious and vital bridge towards a more satisfactory personal destination. Even while this feeling remains nebulous, I feel buoyed by the sensation that I am in motion in some way, that I have begun the process of heading somewhere necessary to my private happiness. I begin to believe at this moment that I will do something important soon, be it conventionally wrong or right. I will take some important step that could possibly change my life forever. I suppose, without realizing it, I've reached the contemplative stage of some personal turning point. Some significant transformation for me is impending. One thing for certain, whatever I decide to do, I know I need desperately to do it.

At last the lake depths at the end of the dock mesmerize me no longer. I turn. I see you standing on the top steps of the veranda of the lodge. I catch you gazing down at me in much the same way I'm now gazing back at you. The moment is instantly charged with a palpable intensity. I embrace this electricity and hold it tightly to myself. Ritually, because what I feel about you is supposed to be wrong, I am tempted to wave carelessly at you to defuse this connective moment in time, making light of it in the propitious way I normally would. But I've begun crossing that barely defined bridge of transformation I recognized a few minutes ago, and I feel new value in myself and in my honesty. So I don't wave, I don't dismiss the moment by waving companionably at you. Instead I just keep staring at you until, in the face of the fierce onslaught of the love I hope is visible in my gaze, you turn away from me and retreat back inside the lodge.

Feeling a kind of sad triumph afterwards, I stand there on the dock a few more minutes, lonely now, but gleeful too. Looking at you the way I did reflects a moment of excellence to me among so many months and years of average grades, of not even showing up for class. So I truly appreciate myself at this moment, for my display of unexpected courage and honesty. But I must stand at the end of the dock for several minutes to keep this feeling alive. I have no idea, if ever, when I will feel such a wonderful sensation again.

ABOUT TWENTY MINUTES LATER you come down to the dock where I am crouched, surveying the bottom of the old aluminum canoe. I have turned the vessel over and carried it to the water at the edge of the dock, to see if it leaks.

"Want to go for a spin?" I ask you then, as you mosey up beside me. "I found two paddles on the ground underneath the old beast."

"Lead on Mac Duff," you say.

I hold the canoe steady while you climb inside. You wince as you sit on the cold, aluminum seat.

"Would you like me to go and find a cushion?" I ask.

"No. That's okay. It's just a shock at first."

"You're warm enough?"

You turn and smile at me. "Yes," you say. "I'm fine."

Even this minor exchange unleashes a belch of smoke and ash from the volcano of my love. Even this makes me wish that I could embrace or at least touch you in some way, just for a moment, just to feel again the exquisiteness of your touch.

Tom McNamara, I reflect, you really have it bad, don't you? You really have it bad.

"What're you grinning at?" you ask me so that I realize you've been watching me.

"Life," I reply with a shrug.

"At least you can grin about it."

And I wonder what you mean. I wonder if your words are

designed to convey some dissatisfaction to me, to provide me with a cause to dedicate myself to.

I climb in, taking my seat—it's too cold for me to kneel—and we begin to move along the shore away from the dock. It's so calm, I can hear the swish as the old canoe parts the surface of the lake. I hardly have to paddle; I hardly have to steer. You are infected by the calm as well. You stroke once or twice, then lift your paddle out of the water, positioning it across the gunnels before, a few minutes later, you resume stroking the lake again.

It's so quiet at this moment, I whisper when I speak. "God, it's beautiful here."

"It is, isn't it?"

I notice you whisper too, like whispering prevents the giving of offense to this place, or brings us into this setting in dignity and humility.

I realize at this moment, in a way I haven't truly acknowledged for twenty years, that my love for you is permanent and will never evaporate. I imagine I will die with my love for you confessing itself on my breath, whether there is someone there to hear my words or not. Strangely enough, until now, I've tended to believe my caring would go away somewhere some day. Or I would change somehow into a more respectable man, inexplicably able to get over what I have so far *never* gotten over about you, me, and love's desperate intensity.

We slip silently up the lake for fifteen minutes before someone remembers to speak.

"God, the stillness," you say.

"Yes."

A long pause. You turn and glance at me.

"Still thinking about you grinning," you tell me at last. "You know, at life, as you put it."

"It's grin or give in to the heartbreak," I reply.

"I suppose."

I steer us gently along the shoreline, saved by each period of silence between us. I want to tell you I still love you, but I can't find the courage or the means. How do you cut away twenty years of silent undergrowth with one well-aimed stroke of the scythe? What brilliant comment can I conceive of that will take us comfortably back over such a long stretch of time to revisit our decision in Westendorf to go our separate ways? I hardly know where to begin. Even still feeling on the verge of a personal transformation, I cannot find the magical formula to make you feel the kind of love for me that I feel for you, or to take you back in time so we can achieve a final closure. Closure, I know, would probably break my heart. So I wobble on the fence between yes or no—it's a familiar place for me. I cling to the way my indecision inspires at least a modicum of hope.

"I see what you mean about places having the potential to act as transformations," you say shortly, as we reach the end of the lake and begin to move west, still hugging the shoreline.

"I think it's true."

"But how temporary is it?" you ask.

"Temporary?"

"Yes. A place like this is a wonderful respite from living in

Toronto. It's peaceful, tranquil, so quiet. But does it stay this way? Can the attraction in the contrast last?"

"You mean after a weekend, a week maybe, you'd hate it and want to go back to the hustle and bustle?"

"More or less."

"Well, it's possible. It depends on who we really are. How well we know what we want."

"You'd stay here and be just fine, wouldn't you?" you ask, turning around to watch me answer.

"I like to think so," I reply.

"And you don't worry about how transitory the attraction of this place is?"

"Who decided it's transitory?"

You stroke the lake with your paddle and do not answer at first.

We are approaching a lagoon of lily pads. We whisper through and among them like a needle through a piece of luscious green-blue satin.

You place your paddle across the gunnels again.

"I guess I believe," you say at last, "the more powerfully something is felt, the less permanence it can have. Like this place. If you succumbed to its powerful attraction and moved here, the attraction would soon dissipate. The infatuation would quickly evaporate. You know?"

I take a deep, careful breath, then find the courage I seek. "If you don't mind me saying so, Jan, you and I had a similar conversation more than twenty years ago, when we were in Westendorf. It's amazing how little has changed in such a long time."

Silence.

Then, "I remember," you admit. "I was afraid you'd mention that."

"That's funny," I reply. "I was afraid I *wouldn't*."

You turn to glance at me, but in the end you resist the urge and turn away again. I am left to peer at the back of your head once more.

"Anyway," I say at last. "You think this place is so attractive, the attraction just can't last. Right? You think, for something to last, it has to be less intense. You know—what we're used to, the relatively mundane—has much more staying power."

"Oh, Tom," you reply almost irritably. "You make it sound so *awful*, so *underachieving*. I don't know *what* I think."

"Like I said, Jan. We had this conver . . . ."

"I know what you said," you whisper.

And I let it lie right there.

We are silent for many minutes until we pass the brilliant stand of maples I noticed yesterday from my place at the end of the dock now on the other side of the lake.

"Well," I say at last, "I don't care what anyone thinks. I love this place. I'd stay here in a minute."

"Just like that?" you ask.

"Just like that," I say.

"I don't know," you muse aloud.

"And the transitory thing? The impermanence of deep attraction?"

"Yes?"

"As far as I'm concerned, that's just a crock of shit."

You laugh gently.

"You know something, Jan? Harder to be a believer in life, than it is to disbelieve. Harder to live for a cause than die for one, they say."

More gentle laughter.

I shut up. I've said enough for now.

The lake opens itself up like a flower to us as we paddle for home.

SHORTLY, AFTER I'VE LEFT YOU to return to the lodge, I strike out along a path that follows the shoreline of the lake. Greg has revealed this resort property stretches south along the shore for another half a mile. The adjoining land beyond belongs to the Crown. As I hike the narrow path, clambering over exposed evergreen roots, entering, then leaving a series of clearings abutting the lake, I roughly count my paces to get a feel for the extent of Gladys Pinkster-Smythe's southern property line. The pathway, I discover, has no regard or consideration for the boundaries between private and public lands. It just crosses the border and continues on its way into the deeper woods owned by the Crown.

I wonder if I run the risk of wandering into some hunting season or other, now that I've left the resort property. But it's too early for moose hunting season. Deer? I really have no idea. I'd hate to walk innocently into the path of some speeding bullet that, a couple of miles away, missed its intended target.

In the end, though, I hike a little further. There's a large climb of rock at the southern extremity of the lake, and I want to gain the top of it to check out the view. It only takes ten minutes. Soon I am standing on the summit of a small cliff peering out over the lake. I can make out the lodge and its network of cottages in the distance.

It is not a spectacular view but the crest of the promontory presents a welcome panorama. As I stand there for an unmeasured length of time, I begin to feel a sense of proprietorship over all that I survey. It gets underway quietly, this sense of stewardship I feel, then it increases in intensity. Soon I am overwhelmed by the adventure, in the potential inherent to this place, and an undeniable sense of responsibility I feel for it. A raven *hronks* by overhead and I wave at it, as I would an old friend. Welcome back, the raven waggles, before it soars upwards in a majestic glide.

And, at this moment, I begin the process of deciding to purchase Gladys Pinkster-Smythe's unexpected treasure of a resort. I don't know why, exactly, except that I love this place and feel, in some strange way, that it loves me a little back. Or maybe, Jan, I want to shoot down in spectacular flames your theory—the one about love for places or people as transitory and shallow—so that you understand love—our best known example of the feeling of truth and the truth that resides in feeling—in the same way that I have learned to understand it.

Yes, standing here looking out from the precipice over the peaceful majesty of this lake, I am certain you are wrong and convinced that I am right: love is not necessarily shallow because it reveals itself at first sight. I stand here as proof of this. In twenty years my passion for and devotion to you have not waned, from the moment I first laid eyes on you in a small café in the Austrian Alps.

It's not just my endless love, though, that tells the tale for me. It's the way the conventionally mundane—the ritual of the life I have embarked upon as a way of resisting you—has not wholly captured me, has not been able to seduce me away from you. People tend to believe that love is maintained through duty and responsibility, that it is sustained by a kind of noble acceptance of its innate inadequacy. I have tried to embrace these conclusions myself, as a kind of catholic adherence to the anti-romance of determined and adequate love. But all of these pressures—societal, religious, moralistic—have failed to destroy or even injure the intensity of the love I felt for you at first sight. It would appear the conventional experts on the transitory nature of instant emotional love are actually more transitory than the love they enjoy decrying. And *they're* the ones spending most of their average day in an embrace with empty minutiae. Are these the people I would ask to judge the depth and permanence of my love? Should I respect *their* verdict?

I stand overlooking the lake, verifying the fundamental truth I find in my love for this place. I felt this love at first sight. I felt it loved me back as well. It is not a transitory love. A week here, a month, a year and I would not miss my suburban home in Ottawa.

Of course, for the moment, at least, I'd never be caught *saying* so.

BY THE TIME I GET BACK TO THE LODGE, I am a man with a mission. Greg remains in Temagami as he said he would this morning, until his business in Toronto is complete. You and Judy nap in your respective bedrooms. Alone, I am free to explore the secrets tucked away in the main lodge building. I have decided I want to own this place. It is my business to intimately explore this building for the secrets it now must give up to me.

Mostly, though, I find only what the average person would expect, a couple of closets upstairs. More bedrooms, of course. Another bathroom too filled with cartons of taped up goods to be of any use. I'm mildly curious about what might be inside them and, for a moment, I contemplate opening one or two. I even take out the Swiss army knife I carry in my left trousers pocket, extracting the larger blade. Then, recalling this place is yours and Judy's, I fold the blade up again and return the knife to my pocket. Another time perhaps, when I have been granted the right.

Downstairs seems to yield few secrets at first. There's the kitchen, the dining room, the living room, another large bathroom. In a way, Greg's right. To make this lodge functional again, there would have to be some significant renovations— another bathroom, a new dining room built on the side so that even the cottagers not staying in the lodge itself could enjoy communal meal times with the other guests. A ramp for the physically disabled. There is much that would have to be done.

I find a door bearing a sign announcing it bars the way to

the office. It's down a short hall beyond the living room. This area is deeper than the rest of the building and I descend four stairs to reach it. It's a room purposely hidden away from the anticipated bustle of the lodge building. And it's padlocked.

I stand there a moment in deep ambivalence. Greg, who carries all the keys, is still in Temagami. But I noticed a large screw driver in one of the kitchen drawers when I was cooking breakfast. It wouldn't take much prying to remove a padlock as flimsy as the one locking this door. Still, I waver for a few moments. On the one hand, this isn't my resort. On the other hand, I'm seriously considering trying to make it mine.

In my ambivalence, Jan, I think of you. I contemplate the courage I now require and this new need in me to have destiny reveal it does indeed have some kind of purpose specific to me. So I hurry to the kitchen to retrieve the large screw driver that announced itself to me this morning, as a potential partner in my modest little crime.

It doesn't take long to remove the padlock. A couple of ancient screws fall to the floor and I bend down to pick them up. I put them in my pocket. The door squeaks a little as I push it open.

Inside it's dusty, but there are few cobwebs. It smells a little like mothballs. I don't know why. There's a desk with a lamp on it, facing a pair of small windows peering into the dark shadows of the woods beginning immediately outside. There's a large leather chair against one wall and a built-in bookcase, although all the books have been removed. I reach for the lamp, pulling the chain. When the light actually goes on, I grunt in satisfied surprise.

Not much here, I decide, as I go through the drawers of the desk. A couple of paper clips, a runaway staple, an old ball-point pen. Then I find an envelope. "Photos," it says on the front. I sit down in the hard wooden chair behind the desk and open the envelope.

Most of the pictures—there's one of a golden retriever gazing into the camera—are of a younger Gladys Pinkster-Smythe with a man I do not recognize. I've seen pictures of your dad, Jan, and he was a short and portly man. The fellow posing with my recently departed mother-in-law is tall and fit. He's bearded and, in a rugged sort of way, rather handsome. He's wearing jeans and a blue plaid shirt. And it's obvious, in the way Gladys is looking up at him, in the way she has placed her hand on his chest, in the way he has his arm around her shoulder and is gazing lovingly back at her, that these two people are lovers.

And I feel something vibrate through me that I can only describe as respectful glee.

I go through the photographs at least a half dozen times, trying to understand what their discovery represents, what their discovery might eventually mean to me. At first I can't decipher when exactly Gladys and this man were lovers, although I suspect both you and Judy were alive, though much younger at the time. So, if my conjecture is accurate, your father would be alive when your mother was in love with someone else. I gaze at the photograph where Gladys smiles adoringly up at the profile of the much larger man. Love captured on film, it's there for anyone to see. I wonder who took these pictures, then imagine Gladys's lover positioning the camera on a stump and setting the timer expertly before hurrying to strike his pose beside the woman he loved.

I don't know why I feel so much redemption as I intrude on this intimate knowledge that Gladys Pinkster-Smythe at one time had a lover. Does it reinforce the power and joy of love for me? Or does it somehow rationalize the endless love I have felt for the wrong one of this woman's daughters? I don't suppose it matters what inspires my sense of redemption. But redeemed is what I feel and it goes down delightfully, giving me strength.

I go through the photographs once again, knowing they explain how Gladys Pinkster-Smythe happens to have owned a small resort in the vicinity of Temagami. The man with his arm around her shoulders probably left it to her. And the love she felt for him would have inspired her to keep it, even while she was persistently mortgaging the Rosedale family home to maintain herself in her accustomed style. What was it Judy asked me rhetorically yesterday? Whatever would possess her mother to buy this wilderness place? Well, the question now becomes why she kept it, once she'd inherited it. And the love displayed in some of these photographs makes the answer entirely clear: to honor the man she loved; to maintain her connection to him.

Soon I put the photographs into the envelope, then the envelope back into the drawer where I found it, but not before I study each photograph one more time. The pressing question now about what I suddenly know, the riddle I have solved, is:

what do I do with this newfound information? Do I tell Judy? Do I tell you? Do I tell both of you? Is it my job to clear up the mystery of how this isolated property came into the family's possession? Or should I keep Gladys's secret as best I can, the way she might want me to?

There's a side of me that wants to tell, I know, to prove to you that the permutations of who should be in love with whom have little regard for time or space or convenience or arrangement. And to prove, I think, that even transitory love has a value to human life, whether it is truly transitory or not.

But for the moment I've decided to keep silent. The news would anger Judy, in fact might anger *you* as well. And Gladys, for all her faults, despite her constant disapproval of me, perhaps deserves to have a man like me protect her secret for her, for the time being at least. Besides, if I decide to try to keep this place, I hope to find out more so that Gladys's story is complete.

Still, I wouldn't put it past myself to tell the story to *you*, sweet Jan, if I thought it would help win back your love. Yes, where you are concerned, the last vestiges of my scrupulousness are falling away like rotting shingles.

GREG STILL HAS NOT RETURNED from Temagami when I begin preparing dinner in the sprawling lodge kitchen of Gladys Pinkster-Smythe's not-so-whimsical secret resort. You and Judy continue to nap in your respective bedrooms, and I am left alone with the secret I share with Gladys. I have even re-screwed the padlock into the door of the resort office. I am a conspirator now. I skulk around this place, covering my tracks. I am part of the necessary cloak and dagger silence that love sometimes requires of us, when it finds its perfection outside the bonds of conventional marriage.

I pull out an old cutting board from a cupboard in the kitchen. This block of wood weighs a ton but it pulsates with tradition. I stand there preparing a salad, shaving, dicing, cutting carrots and celery into slivers, feeling really good about myself and my new friend Gladys, wondering if she prepared a meal or two here herself, or if her rugged boyfriend did the cooking. Somehow, Jan, in a way I cannot explain, your mother's affair several years ago has justified to me how deeply I love her daughter, the one now married to someone else. I find myself whistling some tune I haven't heard in years, the title of which I cannot remember. I nearly dance as I stand at the cutting board, gleefully preparing salad. My mood is celebratory. I feel some strange gratification at achievement, without even knowing what I've achieved.

Eventually I sense someone has entered the room behind me. I turn and smile at you, as if I knew it was you all along. You smile back at me.

"Good sleep?"

"Not bad, I guess. I'm . . . ." And you leave the rest of your sentence there to dangle like a string of summer kitchen garlic.

I go back to what I'm doing.

"Do you need any help?" you ask, moving closer until you are standing beside me.

"Nah. I'm kind of enjoying myself."

"Yes," you say. "I noticed."

You stand there a moment longer, then pull up a stool so that you can sit across the island from me.

"This place may be a little run down, but the kitchen is great. I'd cook here any time," I tell you.

"You *do* look comfortable here."

"A good kitchen is important. If you don't mind me saying so," and I smile to make what comes next as unpersuasive as possible, "I think you and Judy should consider the kitchen when you make your decision about what to do with this place."

"Well I think you and I concluded last night, when we were talking on the veranda, that the kitchen isn't the issue about this place. This resort has crossroads written all over it. I think that's what you were trying to tell me."

"Yes, I was."

You nod. "It's not entirely a real estate decision, this place. There's much more to decide."

"Yes."

And I start thinking about how this lodge, the moment Judy and I arrived, seemed perched on the hill waiting for someone to name it.

"What?" you ask, peering at me carefully, clearly aware I want to share some notion with you.

"The resort wants us to name it," I say. "I noticed it the moment Judy and I drove up."

"What did Judy say to that?"

I hesitate. I glance down at the baked potatoes I am

clumsily sealing in tinfoil. "I didn't mention it to her. It was a private observation. Judy doesn't look at these things the way I do."

"I see."

"Anyway," I say hastily. "I just thought this place came up to *me* rather than me driving up to *it*. And it said 'name me.' It whispered into my ear. 'Name me, Tom,' it said."

You are smiling. "And have you come up with a name?"

"Maybe," I say, feeling suddenly shy about what we have been saying to one another.

"C'mon, Tom, spill it."

"Well actually," I tell you, "I think *you* just gave me the name."

"Crossroads," you cry gleefully, clapping your hands together as soon as the answer dawns on you.

"Yeah. Crossroads Resort. Or Crossroads Resort and Cottages."

You don't say anything, but you keep smiling, not at me necessarily, but at something in your own thoughts that I would kill to spy upon.

"So whaddyuh think? Does 'crossroads' work?"

"It works. But, Tom, just because the naming works, just because we just gave this place a name, it doesn't mean we've solved what to do with it."

"Of course not."

We fall silent. I season the ribs I've boiled, making them ready for the barbecue. You rest your face in your hands, your elbows on the counter.

"We all get caught in the ritual of whatever we do, don't we?" you say at last.

"I'm not sure what you mean."

"I mean: we embark on what we think is right for us and eventually, even if it doesn't seem as right any more, we stick with it because it's too hard to break away from it."

"Yes. Most of us do, I guess. There's a lot of pressure to just keep going," I say. "Less chaos for the conventional world to have to deal with. And it's familiar too. We know what's wrong with what we're doing but it's the devil you know versus the devil you *don't* know."

"God," you say disconsolately. "Like life is some subtle headache you have to live yourself through, that you put up with until you die?"

I nod.

"This place aggravates your complacency, doesn't it?"

"Yup."

"Me too, I guess."

"Not just us, Jan. Others before us, I think."

"My mother?"

I shrug.

"You think this place was a crossroads for my mother?"

"Could have been," I say.

You consider this idea in silence a moment. Then, "you don't suppose it's haunted, do you? You know, some ghost of restlessness, some tragic character who wasted her life and died here unfulfilled, who walks the hallways now, haunting people like you and me who . . . ." You fall silent and look at me, alarmed.

"Yes?"

"Sorry," you say. "This place *is* haunted, Tom. I'm not normally so careless in my thoughts and words. It's the ghost. She's just picking on my overactive imagination."

"That's not true," I say. "I remember . . . ."

"Tom. Please."

"Sorry," I say. "Sometimes I think it would help if we talked about it a bit."

"It?"

"Westendorf."

"Oh. This place *is* haunted."

I want to push this conversation. I want to tell you what I have learned about your mother and her lover. I want to demonstrate the redemption you and I probably need and share in your mother's romantic choice a number of years ago.

"Jan," I begin.

"Oh, Tom," you interrupt. "I don't know if I'll ever be ready to talk to you about back then."

"No?"

Your face is flushed. "I'm afraid I'll get mesmerized again. You make life seem less difficult than it really is. I don't mean to be unkind, Tom, but your view is just smoke and mirrors to me. I mean being truly happy isn't very realistic, is it?"

"Huh? Did you hear what you just said?" I gaze at you with all the intensity I can muster. "Maybe life isn't supposed to be so difficult, that's all. Maybe we make it difficult so we can hide inside its *difficulty*."

But you sigh and turn away from me. You slip off the stool and move around the island towards me, in the direction of the door back into the dining room.

"Jan?"

I don't even know what I'm going to say, if you let me say it. Plead my case I guess. Change the world with a few deft words or sentences, I suppose. Contrive, then convey that pot of gold magical sentence that makes lovers forever lovers, calling birds out of the sanctuary of the trees, waking Cinderellas from their slumbers, uniting at last the star-crossed deviants, Jan and Tom, in the bonds of undying love. But I don't get the chance. As you walk by me, you raise a gentle finger to my lips to silence me. Then, as you pass, you lean up and kiss my cheek, before vanishing ethereally out the door.

And in a way, I know then that this place *is* haunted. By you and me and Gladys and the man in the blue plaid shirt, by the atomic implosion of the people we are required to be, versus the people we really are or really want to be. I can feel it coming, my important telling to you of all these thoughts and ideas. Then again, maybe I don't feel it coming at all. Maybe I will never find the courage.

I ASK GREG, as we sit around the dining room table, hungrily devouring my spare rib dinner—Judy has already complained about the increase in her appetite here in the wilderness and about how she would get fat if she lived up here for any extended length of time—if he knows the name of the man who owned this place before Gladys.

"How do you know it was a man?" Judy asks me with a satirical arch of an eyebrow.

"Just a hunch," I reply. "Greg?"

"Don't know," my brother-in-law replies.

"You mean it passes to Jan and Judy without that information?"

"We'll find out when it's sold, if you want. The new owner will know. At least his lawyer will. There's a title search when a property is sold."

"So, let's say if I were the guy who bought it, I could find out who owned it before Gladys. Right?"

"Sure."

I feel you watching me. "Tom and I have decided this place might be haunted," you announce.

"You and Tommy *would*," your sister remarks.

"A benevolent ghost," I put in.

"Not *entirely* benevolent," you counter.

"Oh, I don't know about that," I say, fixing you with a fierce stare. "I'd say completely, shamelessly benevolent."

"Why?" you ask.

"Existential ghosts are *always* benevolent. And they have no patience with artificial shame."

I become aware that Greg and Judy are staring at you and me, bemused.

"Any time you two are through," Judy remarks when I catch her eye.

"Sorry," I say with a shrug. "You see? It's just the ghost. I had a moment there when I felt its haunting."

"You're crazy," says Greg amiably enough.

"I just like mysteries," I say.

"Huh!" Judy snorts.

"You ever notice all those shoes along the shoulder of the highway?" I ask everyone as soon as the thought pops into my mind.

"Shoes?"

"Yeah. Empty shoes. You see them along the sides of the roads. Sneakers mostly. But sandals too and oxfords and deck shoes, slippers sometimes."

"*I* don't see them along the side of the road," says Judy.

"Me neither," adds Greg.

"Jan?"

You sigh and shrug helplessly. "I've seen them."

"Shoes," says Judy, clearly exasperated. "Just sitting there on the side of the road?"

"Yes," I reply. "I do a lot of highway driving by times. You know that. And there are shoes on the shoulders sometimes. You see them often enough to notice it. Right?"

"Right," you say with a smile.

"My point is," I explain, "how do they get there? Empty shoes. Do they blow out windows? Do they fall off trucks? Or are the people wearing them snatched into space and only a shoe is left behind?"

Smiling, you gaze at me. "He's got a point," you say.

"So what's this got to do with this lodge and it's ghost?" asks Judy. "Or who owned it before our mother did? I call this place, 'Gladys's Folly,' you know. What does Gladys's Folly have to do with empty shoes on the side of the road?"

"I'm just desperately curious, that's all."

"Where people go," you muse. "Why they go there? Do they disappear sometimes into some other truth?"

I nod. "A truth that's more truthful than the one that appears to be so truthful when we're racing through life, essentially spinning our wheels."

There is a long silence in which I find myself gazing at you and loving you to death, wanting you beyond all comprehension. I swallow. I believe fervently that this moment in my love for you must be clearly visible to our respective spouses. I tear my eyes away to prevent any further damage.

"What's for dessert?" asks Judy.

Almost disappointed, I realize I've escaped again. And I wonder, just for a moment, if I have imagined every moment of love I have ever felt, or if love takes place in another dimension each one of us must happen upon or perceive entirely on his own.

I STAY UP LATE ALL BY MYSELF, well beyond midnight, deciding what to do. Not about you, so much, but about this place I love and would name "Crossroads Resort and Cottages," if it belonged to me. I try to imagine what my best friend David Cruickshank would say. He would love this place too, I know. He would visit often if I was ever able to purchase it from you and Judy. And if he knew Gladys's story with the man in the blue plaid shirt, he would want to tell it in a novel, using the tale as he always does to call all of us to arms to embark on some necessary existential rebellion.

And if he knew the me that endlessly quivers with love for you, he would insist that I tell you clearly so that at least you knew, so that at least I'd tell a powerful truth in a life of seemingly necessary lies dedicated to little else than our seemingly necessary conventional arrangements. It is late at night and, the way one always does in the darkness immediately before sleep, I feel very brave at this moment. I feel mesmerized by faith and something in myself I like, something that has crawled out of the shell of the other man I frequently must be, the one I have come to rarely like at all.

It is lucky for you, sweet Jan, that you do not descend the lodge stairs to sit with me tonight where I rattle my saber not far from the old lodge wood stove. If you did, I would confess to you everything I feel about you before sleep and dawn teamed up to caution me, before sleep and dawn convinced me it is unwise to be caught *saying* so.

TEN

AFTER WESTENDORF, it took me some time to recover from everything that had happened to me there. The pain seemed profound and felt endless at times. The torn ligaments in my knee. The heartache of losing you to what amounted to some ideal of perfection, and its antecedent, the purportedly necessary reality of *imperfection*. What was it you'd said? *Something as perfect as this is supposed to be temporary. Like being a princess for a day.* On good days I caught a glimpse of the sense your words seemed to make, but it was only a glimpse. On bad days I thought we'd shot off our right foot to prevent ourselves from ever suffering corns.

I tried to love Judy in exactly the same way I had before I'd left for Westendorf and what I angrily thought of as fate's nasty treachery there. Treachery was how I viewed the way *you* had been cast into my life when I'd assumed it was taking place happily enough without you. In the aftermath I tried at times to pretend you had never happened to me at all. But I ached over losing you the way I had. It lay heavy on my chest before I fell asleep each night and returned again in the morning when I awoke, some leaden tumor in the pit of my stomach. This period of suffering lasted weeks, then stretched gradually into months. Time bleeds slowly when you're getting over so much loss. Second by second. Drip, drip, drip.

My objective, of course, was clear: go back to exactly whom and what I was before I'd ever met you. While I knew it would require commitment and resolve, I had no doubt I would succeed in resuming the life that I had considered pleasant enough before you and an inexplicable grave passion had intruded on it, dangling the carrot of some larger, mystical happiness in front of my nose.

I appreciated the slow process of healing in my knee. I saw my doctor within days of my return to Ottawa, and he had the injury x-rayed. It was a relatively serious case of torn ligaments, he said, but I would recover over time with the help of some physiotherapy. It appealed to me to have to endure a physical ailment as chronic as the ache in my heart over never seeing *you* again. I even enjoyed the notion that recovery from both injuries would have to be achieved in tandem. As my leg gradually healed I became convinced the damage to my broken heart was curing itself at the same rate.

I went back to work, walking stick and all. I got through my first working day and then the first week, and finally the first month. I nearly told David Cruickshank about you and me, about what had truly happened in Westendorf, but David's marriage was on the rocks at that point and what I'd been through with you seemed insignificant by comparison. I was convinced he needed my support during this period more than I needed his. So I kept you all to myself. I carried our brief affair in Austria around like my secret, dysfunctional Siamese twin, waiting for it to die so it could be cut away from me and I could get on with my life.

I didn't make love with Judy until nearly two weeks after I returned from Westendorf, blaming my leg for my vanished libido.

"It hurts," I gasped in her bed the first night she invited me to sleep over after my return.

"I can see that," she replied, her hand on my flaccid penis.

"You'd be astonished at how much it hurts."

"Poor baby."

"Sorry, Jude."

"Teach you to be more careful," she said, kissing me chastely on the cheek, removing her hand from my uninspired cock.

I had the strange notion that night that making love with Judy would have reflected infidelity to *you*, a feeling I hadn't so much as glimpsed on your last night with me in Westendorf. In a rational sense, this moral ethic seemed backwards to me: I'd known Judy longer, she had a right to my faithfulness. But emotionally, feeling unfaithful to *you* made perfect sense to me because I loved you so powerfully. Eventually I determined infidelity had nothing to do with either of you. No, it had everything to do with being unfaithful to myself, the way I'd betrayed my certainty that the woman I'd met in Austria had been presented to me as—and actually was—my true romantic fate.

What made me crazy at first, Jan, was the way I ceaselessly looked for you. I would find myself on an Ottawa street corner, scanning the faces of all the people bustling by in emerging spring, believing fervently that I would suddenly see you among them. And when I did, I imagined myself limping in your direction, calling your name. And you would turn and recognize me, and there would be a wondrous reunion on the street as you and I rushed into each other's arms to take our chances with the oasis of passionate love we'd discovered in the middle of society's envious, finger-wagging desert.

I would despise myself after I emerged from these not infrequent fancies. I felt they were stupid and hopelessly sanguine. Childish. Silly. Pointless. Fortunately, as the months passed and I began to heal, these fantasies occurred less often. Over time, I knew, my three-day passion for you would compress itself in my life into a small, infrequently remembered experience I would appreciate now and then for its brief and pleasant beauty. This seemed a respectable way to file away my short-lived experience with perfect romantic love.

Still, I suffered regularly. After I resumed making love with Judy, I could not escape the sensation of feeling lonely during sex in a way I never had before. Like Judy was Judy and I was me, and the kind of *usness* I'd felt with you was now beyond my capacity to replicate. For months, after technically satisfactory sex with Judy, I would feel a tightness in my chest and an emptiness in my belly that nearly brought tears to my eyes. But I persisted in my commitment to love Judy in the way I had before my vacation in Westendorf. For the most part, I was able to endure this curious feeling of emptiness after we made love, hoping it would eventually disappear. As far as I was concerned, all I needed was more time.

During this period with Judy, I realized our lovemaking had been growing disconcertingly inadequate even before my trip to Westendorf. While Judy and I had begun our tradition of sex in a tireless fashion—making love our first night together for hours—we had quickly evolved into sex that was embarked upon and concluded in less than half an hour, without buildup of any kind. Like lovemaking now held a purely functional purpose and was something to be considered only whenever one of us felt a practical physical need that should be abruptly satisfied. We even ritualized *when* we had sex, after retiring for the night or occasionally in the morning, if we had been too tired the night before. This eliminated any spontaneity we might have garnered by, say, making love on the couch, in the car, or in some deliciously risky, nearly public place. Immediately after ritualized sex, Judy would roll over onto her side, her back to me. Soon she would murmur a sleepy goodnight and gently begin to snore. But I would lie there beside her, feeling restless and incomplete. I needed more touching and more love. I may have even needed more sex. I felt abandoned and lonely. And, at times like these, I would long for you anew—and the idea of you with an astonishingly deep yearning.

Yet I resolved to accept my disappointment in the devolving passion of my love life with Judy. I blamed my own unrealistic expectations for my disappointment. I decided the conventional world was probably right and I was probably wrong. About sex. About love. About *everything*. I would simply have to accept this fact, adjust and move on.

Despite the various sufferings I had no choice but to keep secret, Judy and I began to talk about marriage with increasing frequency during the weeks after my return from Westendorf. I even formally proposed one night—with roses and an engagement ring we eventually took back and replaced with one she liked better—me down on one knee at the side of her sofa, both of us grinning at the intentional parody in my speech proposing marriage. These talks about joining our lives together weren't cold or matter of fact, but they were often practical in tone. We were like a pair of engineers, making lists, tossing around laws of applied physics as we planned out the process that would transform us into a successful marital mechanism. And I kept telling myself that I was not only romantically healing myself, I was also growing up.

We set the date for September. We would marry in Toronto.

"You have to meet my mother," Judy said.

"Yes, I should."

"And you should meet my sister."

"Of course I should," I said.

I asked David Cruickshank to serve as my best man. He

shook my hand and told me it would be an honor

"Ironic," David said. "You're getting married and I'm headed down the rocky road to divorce."

"I'm sorry, David," I told him, not knowing what else to say.

"No wonder little old ladies cry at weddings."

"Whaddyuh mean?"

"They're old enough to have seen the beating faith takes at the hands of conventional life."

"Shit, David, it isn't as bad as all that, is it?"

He gazed at me a moment, then found a way to grin. "You'll be okay, Tom. I think you and Judy will be okay."

I OFTEN WONDER, JAN, what would have happened between you and me if I had seen you again a few months before Judy's and my wedding, instead of just a couple of days, as it ultimately worked out. Would learning earlier that you and Judy were sisters have altered the course of our respective fates? Would we have had time to recognize that destiny intended us to be together? Would we have found the strength to stop the steamroller of our impending marriages to our respective *other* potential partners, to take a chance on our perfect love? Or would we have come to the same conclusion we arrived at in Westendorf: that passionate, emotional love is just a mystifying iron pyrite amid the duller, nobler gold of conventional love?

It doesn't matter now, two decades later. What matters is that Judy's intention to have me meet her family some time that spring—then summer—simply didn't work out. We were too caught up in our jobs, in taking a vacation together, in planning where we would live, in whether or not we could afford to buy a modest house as we began our lives together. And each time Judy and I canceled a visit to meet you and your mother in Toronto, I was secretly relieved. Judy, after all, was already making adjustments to my habits—and even to my personality—so that I could survive my meeting with Gladys Pinkster-Smythe.

In a modest, but persistent way, I know I resented that Judy wanted me to conform to such an extent to some more acceptable model of her fiancé, changing myself to meet her mother's expectations. One night we nearly quarreled about this because, while it was apparent Judy loved me in her way, I was beginning to wonder if she approved of me. I fretted there were significant pieces of me that Judy didn't like, that there were aspects of me she merely tolerated or even felt superior to.

"What's wrong with me anyway?" I wanted to know.

"Whaddyuh mean, Tommy?"

"Well, are you ashamed of me? Are you afraid I won't measure up to Rosedale's high standards?"

"It's got nothing to do with Rosedale," Judy snapped. "My mother is very critical. The less she has to legitimately criticize about you, the less anxiety I'll have to put up with. That's all."

"But I'm beginning to feel there's something fundamentally wrong with me, as far as you're concerned."

"Tommy, don't be ridiculous. I'm marrying you, aren't I? Would I marry you if there was something fundamentally wrong with you? Why do you have to be so sensitive all the time?"

"I thought you liked me sensitive."

"Well, there's sensitivity and then there's *sensitivity*. You know what I mean?"

"I'm afraid I do," I said.

I gave in on virtually every issue, whenever we argued this way, despite my unrelenting suspicion that Judy did not entirely appreciate the real me. She insisted I cut my hair shorter than I had at the time she met me. She began to help me buy my clothes because, as she put it, "your color coordinates leave much to be desired." These intrusions were minor considerations that I felt I loved Judy enough to ignore. I even enjoyed learning some of these fashion nuances from her. What troubled me more, though, was the coaching I received about my conversation and interests.

"Don't go off on any philosophical tangents when you meet my mother."

"Philosophical tangents?"

"You know what I mean."

"No, I *don't* know what you mean."

"Oh, Tommy, you do *so* know. When you get going on and on about things."

"You mean politics?"

"Yes. Politics."

Politics was a bone of contention for Judy and me as a topic. Not that she and I lived at different political poles, but that I was sometimes outspoken about my views and this embarrassed her.

"Jesus, Tommy," she'd say. "I feel the same way you do about these things. But at least I have enough sense to know when my opinions are going to upset people, when they might not be welcome. I know when to go along, when to tolerate the status quo."

"Okay," I said in some annoyance. "But you know what you're asking? You're asking me to behave like a clergyman on a Sunday morning in July: when I start complaining about the people who haven't shown up for services because they're out golfing or something, I'll be haranguing the ones who are sitting there, about their missing brethren. You see what I mean? Let's preach to the converted; it's safer. It's more polite."

"See?" said Judy. "That's what I mean. My mother—and most people, for that matter—don't want to hear something like that. It just loses them and they feel stupid and you look like a smart ass. And, besides, it doesn't make any sense."

"Sure it does. Of course it makes sense. I'm saying there's no point in me arguing politics with people who agree with me. I have to take on the status quo because they're the ones who've slipped off the rails."

"Tommy, I'm just saying give it a rest with my mother. Okay?"

I sighed. I shrugged. I shook my head.

She kissed me lightly. "Thank you, Tommy."

"God, Judy," I said. "What does a person do when the man he really is becomes unpalatable to the median of society?"

"I guess he stops being so stubborn about it. I guess he lets himself change. He lets himself compromise or improve."

I winced at times like these. Improve? I wanted to feel at least a modicum of authenticity in who I was supposed to be. How much change could I endure before losing my personal views and beliefs, my authenticity? While I was willing to grant that all of us should be aware of areas of improvement in our behavior, I feared the standard to which I was to aspire was flawed and even wrong. When someone sets out to improve themselves, where do they draw the line and what is the criteria defining where the line should be drawn? I still don't truly believe conventional society knows. It just *thinks* it knows, which isn't the same thing at all.

No wonder the trip to Toronto to meet Gladys Pinkster-Smythe was delayed until the last minute. For my part, I wanted to get it over with. It both frightened and appalled me that I was going to marry one of the daughters of a woman who held court in a large home in Rosedale. Judy had a point politically, I suppose. I was a committed social democrat. Her mother was a Tory. I had good reason to be apprehensive. It was more than likely, unless I obeyed the instructions I had been given to the letter, the moment I opened my mouth, Gladys would begin to contemplate disowning her daughter. Besides, I knew I would behave. For Judy. For the sake of our anticipated life together. What bothered me was the restless something in my nature that didn't *want* to behave.

"But you'll like my sister, Janice," Judy said more than once. "My sister will approve of you."

"Well, that's something anyway."

You'd think I would have figured out by this time that fate has a treacherous side, that coincidence can and will exist if fate determines it should. But, of course, I didn't figure it out. I didn't recognize that there was any chance the Jan, the *you* I'd once loved as perfectly and completely as I had ever loved anyone, could be the sister, the Jan, the Janice of the woman I was soon to marry. This failure to perceive a powerful possibility seemed connected somehow to the brief time I had actually known you, so much so that, as September approached, I occasionally wondered if I'd imagined the entire Austrian incident. My relationship with you had taken place over a mere three days. Three perfect days, granted. But months ago now. Had I invented the intensity of my feelings, the pain of my broken heart? Was it possible I had mostly invented *you*?

Whatever the reason, I didn't make the connection between you as Judy's sister and the you I had loved briefly in Europe. To be fair, there is not a strong resemblance between you and Judy, especially when you are separate from one another. It's only when you are together that one can see enough similarity to conclude the two of you are sisters.

I suppose I suffer from a love struck bias in matters such as these. It's true I cannot stop myself from continually loving you with a blind subjectivity. Still, I have often wondered over time what powerful happenstance closed my eyes to the possibility back then that you and Judy were sisters. And I've never been able to answer this question. It just never occurred to me, not even for a moment, that my three-day perfect love affair had pierced the sanctity of your family, the apparent arrangement of all our lives, as skillfully and ruthlessly as a needle pierces an ear drum.

MORE OR LESS TO SPITE HER MOTHER and to demonstrate some benign assertion of our independence, Judy booked us into a Ramada Inn some distance from Rosedale, when we finally made it to Toronto less than a week before the wedding.

"There's no way I'm staying in that house with my mother before the wedding," Judy said. "She'll make us sleep in separate rooms and she'll drive me crazy with her constant nagging about what's appropriate and what isn't."

I nodded. "Only one drawback," I said. "It makes it feel like we're starting the honeymoon before we even have the wedding."

"Huh!" she replied. "No one in their right mind would ever confuse the five days immediately before their wedding with any kind of honeymoon."

"I was hoping I could, Jude."

"Could what?"

"Confuse our stay here with a honeymoon of some kind, you know, before the wedding."

But she was barely listening to me. "That's because you're a man. Men get to escape knowing how horrific weddings can be, especially when too many people stick their noses into the works. The plain truth of it is: weddings aren't important to men the way they are to women."

"Well it was just a notion," I said. "I just wanted to speak up for the romantic component of the wedding."

"The romantic component?" Judy gazed at me, perplexed. "Weddings are too stressful to be *romantic.*"

Granted, some of Judy's mood of pragmatic anxiety reflected the ongoing annoyance between mother and daughter as the wedding grew imminent. Judy had been roundly chastised for leaving so late my meeting the rest of the family. On the telephone they'd argued bitterly about this recently, and Judy was furious when she reported her version of the debate to me.

Nonetheless, we settled on the night before the wedding rehearsal to attend a dinner at Gladys's home. It was not to be a large gathering, a widowed aunt or two—all men seem to die young somehow in your family—a couple who were family friends, and your sister and her fiancé (their wedding would take place the following June). Judy said the matriarch herself would conduct events from her ritual place at the head of the table. There would even be an all-purpose servant. She and a temporary helper would be serving the six-course dinner.

"Jesus," I said. "Six courses? This isn't black tie, is it?"

"No. But you should wear a sports jacket, good pants, that wool tie I like so much. Wear the striped shirt, the conservative one. My mother will appreciate your taste, even if she recognizes that *I* picked it out."

"You know, Jude, this is all pretty old-fashioned and pretentious, don't you think?"

"Just something we have to go through," my fiancée said.

I did as Judy asked. I wore the outfit she suggested. To the tune of *Streets Of Laredo*: *Get yourself an outfit and be a Rosdaler too.*

Although we were nearly on time, we were last to arrive. Not my fault. Judy's fault. I knew better than to be tardy when I was meeting the matriarch. But Judy was grumpy and she felt anxious about the evening. She changed outfits three times before we dashed out of the hotel, careening as best we could along Yonge Street in the direction of Rosedale, the minutes we were late *bonging* by second by second.

It's strange how, as humans, we never see our disasters coming. I remember so clearly how I did not expect what was about to happen to me. It was a fine September evening, around six-thirty, the sun getting ready to go down. Quiet. No kids playing ball hockey in *this* section of Toronto. Judy had rung the doorbell. I remember wondering if Gladys employed a butler and I imagined the stereotype good social democrats like me inevitably conjure up when we contemplate a butler, someone stiff and affected, unaware of his victimization at the hands of class structure. I remember standing there amid the chirping of birds, thinking these things while Judy lifted a hand to brush a bit of fluff from my lapel.

"You look nice," she said, as if in gentle surprise.

The door abruptly burst open. No butler, I was relieved to see. No butler, just a relatively eager sister with a lanky, blonde real estate salesman fiancé in tow. Oh, God . . . .

I recognized you instantly. I saw you recognize me as well.

I literally grew faint. Everything spun. I felt I'd stumbled into the middle of some kind of explosion, except that the concussion was strangely silent, as if, as it erupted, it gobbled up its own sound. I felt the air rush out of my lungs in a stampede of panicky molecules. My feeble attempt to replace it barely succeeded; for a moment, I could not breathe. Beads of sweat formed on my forehead and abruptly trickled down the middle of my back. I split into two people at that moment: a gasping, startled fool who seemed on the verge of fainting, and a meticulous observer of the drama unfolding here on Gladys Pinkster-Smythe's front stoop.

You were staggeringly adept at minimizing your shock and astonishment. I noticed this, of course, even while my own dismay exploded like a small thermonuclear device. The observer in me noticed that you inhaled sharply, with a bit of a wheeze. It saw your eyes widen before you could prevent it, then noticed how, a second later, you lowered them demurely as you shook my hand, saying with painful clarity, "You must be Tommy."

I didn't fare so well. I was still gasping and someone—I think it was Judy—kept asking me what was wrong, repeating her observation that I was white as a ghost.

"Tommy? Are you all right?"

"Sorry," I managed to say, holding onto the door for support. My legs had gone rubbery and I staggered. "I just came over weak there for a second. Strange," I added for good measure, for your benefit, now that it was clear you and I would be pretending we had never previously met.

"You don't look so well," Greg said after I was introduced

to him. He seemed afraid to shake my hand, in case the effort on my part would lead to my collapse right there in the doorway, or my condition might be communicable, a kind of premarital anxiety leprosy.

"It's okay," I said. "It's passing. I just don't know what came over me." I took a deep breath, then gradually exhaled.

"He's okay," you said calmly, distanced from the astonishment only you could truly understand had nearly felled me. "I've had reactions like this. I think it's just nerves. Wedding jitters."

"Thanks," I said to you. "I'm okay now. You just never know what's going to happen, do you?"

God, you were cool, Jan. I'd given you an opening to at least cryptically acknowledge you and me, and what fate had done to us, an opportunity to at least say something subtle in return that made our three days together real. But you didn't take the bait. No comment with private meaning, no remark in code, not a word to me to acknowledge you and I knew one another, not even a glance to convey to me that we had been lovers a few months ago in Europe. Nothing. You were as impenetrable as rock. You turned away from me to hug your sister. It was clear my assignment was to do my part to respect the collective amnesia dictated by our circumstances. You and I would rewrite history; I was trapped into serving as your co-author.

I don't recall clearly how I felt about our collusion at that moment, as we all stepped into the front vestibule. I might have been a little relieved, but I don't remember it. Instead I remember feeling angry—at you for so easily burying what had happened to us in Westendorf—but mostly at myself because, as I glanced at you, I realized I *couldn't* bury the incident at all. No, here I was, newly in love with you, and newly destined to be brokenhearted. Here I was, alone in my role of blissfully romantic fool. It was brutally clear you had decided to leave me behind so that you could adhere to normalcy.

I don't know how I got through dinner and a few drinks afterwards. In a daze, I entered the living room and stood off by myself a few moments while Judy hugged her mother and her widowed aunts. At last I was introduced formally to everyone there. Then we all sat down for conversation so precise and cautious it seemed as starched as an old, white shirt. I remained two people for the longest time, half of me politely conversing with the assembly, the other half dazed and in shock, watching proceedings around me in a benumbed state of fascination.

"I hear you and Judy have bought a house," Greg asked me at one point.

"Yes."

"Who was the agent?"

"Guy named Boisvert."

"No, no. The company."

"Oh. ReMax, I think."

"Hmmm," said Greg, my future brother-in-law, no doubt wondering what kind of idiot I was.

I would glance in your direction by times that evening, hoping to discover you weren't who you were at all. But of course you always were. You were indeed the woman from

Westendorf with whom I'd fallen in love. I'd made wondrous love with you one night. I'd sat on an idling bus six months ago and gazed at you in a state of love so profound and deep that I nearly followed you off the bus to offer myself to you for the rest of my life. And since then, I'd been looking for you on every street corner, in every crowd, because I yearned to see you again. Now here you were across the room from me, so tantalizingly close, so coldly out of reach. It was awful. I had no idea what I could do, what I was *supposed* to do.

There were a couple of moments when a part of me wanted to stand up here in Gladys's living room, suddenly making the announcement that you and I had been lovers, explaining how we hadn't known who each other was at the time, selling an appropriate coincidence to the family members and fiancés who were here. Just to tell the truth, I guess. Just to be freed of the burden of secrecy our circumstances seemed to require. Just to make it possible for you and me and love to win the day. But we don't make announcements like these in conventional society. We don't stand up and confess the truth, anticipating a celebratory appreciation for our candor. No, we not only protect the people who feel they possess us in some way—our fiancés, our parents, our friends and relatives, our spouses—but we protect their cabal of conventionality as well, by keeping our silence. Who do we protect them from? *Us.* We protect them from from *us*, their misguided, idealistic progeny, the lovers and desperadoes some of us secretly remain inside, despite our frequent attempts to conform, to deny ourselves through guilty purgings of our hopes.

So, of course, for all the conventionally appropriate reasons, I didn't say anything. And you didn't say anything either. And I found the force of will I required to avoid looking at you most of the way through dinner. By this time I felt like an actor who hadn't yet learned his lines. There was a play going on all around me, but I barely participated. I was a minor character. It was safer for the outcome of the play to keep me relatively silent, to cut back on my dialogue. In case I botched a scene. In case I bemusedly tore the drape of convention in this act into permanent shreds.

I suppose, at times, I couldn't help myself and I took a few liberties, glancing at you in shock and dismay, and, to be expected, in admiration and love. I say, liberties, because I feared *you* would notice. Never mind your mother, Greg or Judy. I was aware, after all, in the midst of our mutual astonishment at the front door, we had arrived at some kind of silent agreement never to acknowledge our three days of perfect love in Westendorf. The liberty I took in glancing at you was that I wanted you to know I still cared for you, that I was still in love with you. I wanted you to see this fact written on my face, if only for a second, conveyed in my anxious, adoring glance, the truth that I would give up—as soon as you wanted me to—everything that was happening to me now, that was scheduled to happen to me in the next few days, so that I could willingly embark on a life with you instead, the woman all of my senses told me had been selected for me by fate.

But you did not respond to my glances. You acted with perfect propriety. You have always, I fear, honored the agreement you forced me to accept that day, and to which, grudgingly, I continue to adhere. Yet I feel no shame that I have regretted our arrangement ever since. For twenty years I have known something important, something undeniable took place in Westendorf between you and me and the condition of love itself. I have also learned and now know that it takes a courageously foolish man who can live the perfect delight of what I felt for you back then, then, upon meeting you again, indeed upon becoming part of your family, can walk away believing he will not wish for such delight again. Over time, I have learned I do not understand how I ever believed I would eventually forget my love for you. I wonder at my foolishness, the naiveté I employed when I decided I would be able to put you into a place somewhere with parameters specifically designed to minimize your impact on me.

Since that night, I have concluded with deep regret that it would have been better if I had gotten off the bus in the pension courtyard that spring day in Westendorf, to proclaim my love for you. Even if you had rejected me, we would have at least found a way to achieve some kind of closure. And I would have known myself, at least, my needs in love, my expectations of love, the kind of love it was necessary for me to find. So it is that day I left Westendorf with my friends and the evening in Gladys's living room loom large in my life as potential turning points when I have demonstrated my cowardice. I don't know for sure what is or isn't cowardice. I only know my failures to tell you how I feel have continued to pile up on one another in twenty years of dissipating time, like a wall of concrete blocks.

And now this structure has nearly walled me inside a closet of futility I find impossible to escape. I am a different kind of Amontillado, imprisoned by the villain of my own fears.

Judy asked me why I had been so quiet all evening, as we drove back to the Ramada Inn where we were staying, after Gladys's dinner party that night.

"I was nervous," I said.

"You seemed elsewhere a lot of the time. Distracted."

"Yeah. Sorry. Like I said, I was nervous. But your mum was less fierce than I expected."

"Yes," said Judy after a thoughtful moment. "I think it worked out for the best. Quiet or not, everyone seemed to like you."

"That's good," I replied.

I imagined saying, in a tastelessly chaotic moment of near delirium at this point, "Oh, by the way, I met your sister in Austria last March and I'm deeply in love with her. I'd love the chance to explain before it's too late. If you don't mind, that is."

But I managed to contain myself. Ours is not a world that thrives on these kinds of truths. No, ours is a world that succeeds as a hotbed of necessary myths. What else could I conclude? What other lesson could I derive from your failure to take me aside and acknowledge privately and clearly, in the wake of Westendorf, that I was who I was back then, and you had loved me a little as the man I really was? I felt new and bitter wisdom about the inherent tragedy of life, now that I was newly convinced the world prefers polite lies to its awkward, inconvenient truths. I should know; I perpetrate the same status quo. While I've come to this conclusion about the world's preference for lies a hundred times over the years, I've never found the guts to be caught *saying* so.

I DON'T REMEMBER MUCH about my wedding. Nerves, shock, dismay, some of them typical of a man's wedding day, others exaggerated fiercely by my discovery that after I gave my half of the vows, you would then be condemned to be merely my sister-in-law instead of my romantic destination. I've since asked David Cruickshank—he's been married three times and in several capacities can be arguably construed to be an expert about marriage—if he remembers any of his weddings. And he doesn't, at least not very well.

"I know," he has said thoughtfully. "It's odd, isn't it? I only have glimpses of memories about getting married. Maybe we're too nervous. Maybe the ceremony overwhelms the reason for the ceremony."

"Maybe it isn't like that if you marry the perfect person for you," I said before I could help myself. "Maybe if you want to marry them desperately, you know, feel you'll *die* if you don't marry them, well, not *die* literally, but, well, you know what I mean, maybe then you remember each moment of the wedding because of the passionate achievement it represents."

David was grinning broadly. "I'm beginning to wonder about you," he said.

"Why?"

"This incredible new romanticism."

"Oh, don't take me too seriously," I said. "I was just

wondering out loud, just speaking philosophically."

"Yeah, yeah," my best friend said.

And I swiftly changed the topic.

But David remembers *my* wedding much better than I do, for the most part anyway. For me, it's a vague event, shimmering with small shards of clarity, like pieces of glass on the shoulder of the highway after a motor vehicle accident.

Standing in the chapel, Judy beside me, stunning and beaming, me stammering over part of my vows, unable to overcome my curious dread that any "I do" I uttered would end my romantic life with you. Going on with it anyway, though, the way I'm sure I would to keep an appointment with the gallows, giving in to what has been *decreed*, making the walk to my fate without resistance, whether the reasons are just or unjust, simply *because* it's been decreed. Because my personal view of truth can't help but fail to be true when it is contrasted with society's view of truth. Because society is large and I am small, too small to ever be right.

The hubbub out on the chapel steps, the day hazy for September, a bit gray, photographs, supernova camera flashes and shutter clicks, standing there with Judy, dazedly following instructions to turn this way or that, standing beside you, Judy's maid of honor, confused by your proximity and the strange, dreadful feeling of too-lateness in which this day now found itself, because I had married Judy and could never marry you.

Strangely enough, Judy didn't notice my endless distraction, or, if she did, she never mentioned it. Her own nervousness perhaps. I don't know. Not even during the reception. I guess I was able to function, if not reasonably well, at least well enough that my fading memory of my wedding has exaggerated itself in the twenty years since it took place.

As my best man, David bought me the traditional drink from the bar.

"Are you okay, Tom?" he asked me as we stood in line, waiting our turn.

"Dazed and confused," I said.

"Yeah. Wedding's are weird that way."

"Is it showing?" I wanted to know.

"That you're dazed and confused?"

"Yeah."

"Not really," he replied. "No more than it does on anyone else, at least. But I thought I should ask, just the same. It's my job as best man."

"Shaky groom syndrome," some other me outside of myself commented calmly.

"Yeah. Shaky groom syndrome."

I remember wondering how you would handle meeting my friends again, the ones who'd accompanied me on the skiing trip to Westendorf. I saw you talking with them at one point during the reception. And Gord remarked to me what a tremendous coincidence it was that I'd met you in Westendorf and here we all were at her sister's and my bride's wedding.

"Yeah," I said. "Life's crazy sometimes, isn't it?"

To this day, I have no idea what you told your sister about meeting me in Westendorf, committed the way you were to the secrecy we'd embarked upon the night of Gladys's dinner party.

Maybe you didn't say anything at all and maybe you didn't have to. I avoided you most of the evening, especially when one of my skiing buddies was nearby. And it was clear none of them even remotely suspected you and I had fallen in love and spent a night in bed together when we were in Austria. As humans, most of us are really quite self-absorbed. To put two and two together, one must really have to have a deep interest in doing so. I think the wedding reception was too gala by nature for anyone to feel the need to connect the dots. There was too much going on for someone to take the time to try to construct a plot as fantastic as what coincidence had actually contrived around you and me.

Certainly, in our entire twenty years of marriage, Judy has never mentioned anything about you and me meeting in Westendorf. And she would, I know, if she knew. I must assume from this that it simply never came up. And you and I certainly don't mention that time in the Austrian Alps when we accidentally met, accidentally fell in love and then, by cynical design, decided never to see one another again.

OVER THE YEARS of our respective *inlawship*, you and I have pretended not to be—or that we ever were—in love with one another. We are aided by the distance between Ottawa and Toronto, not vast by Canadian standards, but large enough to restrict visits back and forth to once or twice or three times a year. Certainly six times a year is pushing it. On the surface of it, we behave as if Westendorf never happened. On the surface of it, I treat you like my sister-in-law and you treat me like your brother-in-law.

But inside, my love for you festers like an endless sore, a *Promethean* abscess that is daily picked at by conventional life and then grows back romantically to be picked at once again. The strange aspect of this love that will not wane is that nothing ever happens to make it grow or last. Nothing waters it or feeds it, nothing empowers its smoldering passion so that it can burst into larger flames. It lives as powerfully as it does without sustenance of any kind, apparently not needing the encouragement of your touch or the stimulation of your glance to thrive. Like my love for you is and will always be a being that lives endlessly, despite the fact nothing actually happens to feed or encourage it.

Then again, I sense you and I are close, sharing a secret intimacy which no one—including you and me—ever admits to. We don't touch improperly, nothing flirtatious is ever said. Yet, often, I imagine a state between you and me that implies its own special magic of comfortable intimacy, an intimacy that is, on the one hand, not nearly enough for me but, on the other hand, reflects the certainty in the love I feel for you.

There have been little moments, of course, when you and I approached the border separating us from what we pretend to deny and what we cannot deny. I store these incidents in the locker of my heart, collecting evidence, I guess, building the case that you and I are still in love and will figure out soon how to admit it and how to be together. I examine these incidents as much as I examine our three days of love in Westendorf.

An afternoon one late spring or early summer north of

Toronto a few years ago, for instance, me and Judy and you and Greg merely out on some small outing, walking beside a pond, the sun warm and pleasant, Judy and Greg hurrying ahead of us, always in a bit of rush, talking animatedly about something, you and I lagging accidentally behind, two swans going by like the most romantic of couples a few yards from us, leaving behind magnetic wakes on the water that soon dissolved into one another.

"Oh look, Tom," you said, pointing out the two swans.

"I see them," I replied.

We stood there in silence a time, watching the swans drift by in some kind of perfect, mated unison.

"Shit," you muttered at last.

"I know," I murmured back, wanting to take you into my arms.

"Shit," you said again, followed by a long sigh. Then you moved away from me before I could contemplate anything further, before I could do something important it would have been improper to do.

Or that New Year's Eve you and Greg came down for a visit, attending a dance sponsored by a ski club to which Judy and I belonged. You stayed at our house in Kanata, as you always did. I felt the same agonies and ridiculous hopes of romantic fusion I always felt when you were visiting us. It was merely the typical incidence of you being too close for my sensibilities and me struggling desperately not to let you see that this was so.

The dance in an Ottawa club was just a dance. Judy and I

dancing, you and Greg dancing. Judy and I dancing with some of our Ottawa friends. But someone in the crowd that night requested a Strauss waltz, of all things.

I glanced at you and you smiled at me. You spun your index finger as a way to suggest we might dance—perhaps for old time's sake—to the music and the setting we'd known in Austria. I nodded and we got up, walking out to the dance floor and, for the first time since Westendorf, for the first time in a number of years, I took you into my arms and shared a dance with you. I held you relatively tightly, but not *too* tightly. You tucked your cheek into my shoulder, but not *too* closely. And I skated for three precious minutes or so into a kind of bliss with you one more time. It was the first acknowledgment we had made since Westendorf that we had danced this way back then, that we had been in love and that the love we'd felt had seemed extraordinarily perfect.

And later, a couple of hours into the new year, sitting in our living room, Greg excused himself because he was tired. Then Judy excused herself. She was tired too. But you and I seemed wide awake, supercharged somehow. That one dance? Was that it? Maybe you and I were on the verge of resolution of some kind. If so, would it be the resolution for which I yearned? Or would it be something else, some reproach, some terrible denouement that I would find painful for as long as I lived?

You and I sat alone and talked deep into the morning hours. I learned you might have wanted children, but Greg was adamant he did not. I traded my version about children, Judy and me with you. We commiserated over each other's gentle disappointment and sadness.

"I wonder sometimes," you said, "why we make the choices we do."

"I think we think too much, Jan. When our instincts speak to us, we don't listen to them. We don't trust their opinion."

You gazed at me in silence.

I yearned to tell you at that moment how much, how deeply I still loved you, but I couldn't find the courage.

I think it was around four am. when we went through the motions of preparing to retire ourselves. We rose and went into the kitchen, taking some empty glasses with us to set them on the kitchen counter. I felt opportunity slipping away from me, but I still couldn't find the way to tell you the love I'd felt for you in Westendorf, so instantly and powerfully, continued unabated more than half a decade later.

We walked down the hall together from the kitchen towards the stairs. You stopped and turned to me. We embraced. I kissed you on the forehead.

"Jan," I whispered, hoping I was beginning to say something revelatory.

"We should go up," you said.

I don't know what else I might have said, although there was something blindingly truthful I wanted to confess at that moment. But you'd said *we should go up* and I assumed, I suppose, that this was gentle rejection, a reproach indicating you loved me much less than I loved you, even though in Westendorf we had been and felt the same as one another. Feeling rejected, I didn't say anything. I didn't proclaim my love for you and I didn't question our decision in Westendorf to sentence to only three days what I felt was wondrous love. I didn't say anything about love or Westendorf or the you I am crazy about. Because you said, *we should go up.*

"Yes," was all I said as we stepped away from one another, out of our embrace in the hall at the bottom of the stairs. And I felt empty and hollow and drained that night of much of my endless hope.

Still, on the verge of my despair, you did something odd to me, something I would never have anticipated, that perhaps was designed to convey to me your own particular ambivalence. You took my hand, as you turned away to climb the stairs. You took my hand, just for a second, and pressed it to your lips. And then you hurried up the stairs towards the room in which your husband slept.

Dismayed, I stood at the bottom of the stairs for a moment or two, bemused by new bliss and hope and love. I stood there at the bottom of the stairs, trying to figure out what your kiss on my hand had meant. Then, feeling that I should, not trusting in my own faith, I decided somewhat resignedly it hadn't meant anything much at all. Just *your* resignation, *your* giving in to the despair in our mutual self-denial.

ELEVEN

"IF YOU DECIDE TO SELL the lodge, I think I'd like to buy it," I nervously tell Judy Sunday morning.

I sit on the edge of our bed, holding her mug of coffee in my hands, trying to hand it to her like an offering. An ingratiation? My ritual placation? Or is this just how it seems to me at this moment?

Still stunned from sleep, she takes the mug in silence.

I've been preoccupied with the idea of purchasing the lodge all morning. It surprises me that I am as enthralled by the scheme as I was last night when I sat in the darkness not far from the wood stove, listening to the October creaking of this homely, wooden building and imagining ahead the delightful snap of its resistance each January when the temperature drops to minus thirty. Last night—and my accompanying certainty that I want to own this place—both seem long ago now; to know I still want to buy the resort as clearly this morning as I did last night is a powerful incentive for me.

I give a great deal of credence to a plan that survives the arrival of morning. Sometimes ideas conceived in the evening—passionate schemes born during the night—vanish like leprechauns with daybreak's arrival. It's as if they cannot withstand the glare, the interrogation inherent to dawn's pragmatic personality.

But not this notion of mine to buy this rustic lodge, which I will name "Crossroads" in honor of you and the persistence of my love, and as a dedication to anyone else who lodges here in future, hoping to define his or her own reality. No, my enthusiasm and commitment to owning this place have withstood entirely the cynical light of dawn, and so I confront Judy, empowered because my idea retains its lucidity even here at the beginning of a new day.

I plan to cook pancakes this morning. I plan to stand in the kitchen, a spatula in my hand, watching the buttermilk batter bubble in the large cast iron frying pan that hangs at this moment on the wall to the right of the stove. I plan to continue feeling at home, at peace within myself. And I plan to acknowledge I will always suffer from an old and fruitless love for you, even while I try to accept that this love can never work out. Perhaps this wilderness place where I feel so at home with myself is an acceptable alternative to the life with you I have relentlessly dreamed of, yet know will not transpire. I can't say for sure. Certainly I don't want to give you up, not even the *idea* of you. Nor do I want to give *up* on you. But perhaps my surrender of hope about you is something to think about when I stand in front of the stove a few minutes from now, after this important conversation with my wife. Perhaps, at last, I've reached the point where I should contemplate getting on with my life, whether you can ever be part of it or not.

"What did you just say?" Judy asks me now, catching me gazing off into space.

"I said I want to buy this place."

Judy laughs. Her laughter has a brittle, forced sound to it, and that edge of grudging tolerance I find so familiar.

While she finishes chortling, I get up and go to the window, trying to convey a self-assurance I do not feel, waiting for her to realize I mean business, waiting for her to consider the option of taking the authentic me seriously, something I now fear she has *never* done.

But she doesn't say anything.

I clear my throat and begin again. "Judy, I want you to know I mean it."

"Mean what?"

"That I want to buy this place."

"Oh, c'mon," she says. "You can't be serious. I thought you were pulling my leg."

"No, I'm not pulling your leg. And you know I'm not. I'm as serious about this as I've ever been about anything."

"Tommy, for Christ's sake. Buy it with what? Way up here

in the boonies?"

"I like this place," I say. "I feel like I've lived here forever. I feel this place is my destination."

"Oh, Christ, Tommy, don't be so fucking melodramatic. 'I feel like I've lived here forever.' That's laying it on a little thick, isn't it? This place a 'destination?' Jesus."

I sigh. "I'm trying to say it feels like home. I recognize it. It's familiar to me. You know what I mean by that? It feels like home? I can't explain it any better than that. If feeling mysteriously connected to a place is melodramatic, well . . . ."

". . . We don't have the money."

"We could get it. We could get the money. You *know* we could work out the money."

She says nothing to this.

"Look," I say then. "Let's not talk about money for the moment. Money's not the point."

"All right," she says, drawing her legs up under the covers, setting the coffee on her knees, tilting it with one hand to take her sips. "Money's not the point. So maybe you can tell me what *is* the point."

I hesitate. I wish I wasn't so shaky. I am aware that I have kowtowed to this woman for much of my married life. My own fault, I think. She didn't ask me to subordinate myself to her as much as I decided to do so myself. Consciously? Unconsciously? I don't know. Because Judy seemed more conventionally right? More adult? More realistic? Whatever the reason, I suspect I concealed the authentic Tom McNamara from her, not only for reasons regarding my true nature, but to hide you and me from her, to hide and live this secret, mostly imaginary life with you I would prefer to the one I live with her. Now I feel myself emerging from my peculiar closet of secrecy—not the one about you, Jan, but the one about me, the me who doesn't actually believe conventionality is any more adult than its alternative—and it frightens me. Judy will be astonished. What I say to her, as I explain, will feel like an ambush. She will not only despise this new truth I confess, she will despise it for being new, as she despises me for uttering it without at least some respectable period of warning. That's the trouble with kowtowing to people—we deceive them into believing we prefer our subservience when actually we don't. They believe their preference is *our* preference, when in truth it never was.

So I hesitate.

"Are you going to answer my question?" Judy says.

"Yes." My voice is a phlegmy whisper. It sounds timid to me. I clear my throat.

She sips her coffee and I hear the tiny slurp in the silence.

"I want to change the way we live, Jude, the way *I* live. I'm tired of what we've been doing. This place, this lodge feels *right*. Kanata feels wrong to me now. But this feels *right*. You know suburbia is killing me." I feel I've begun to babble, that I'm repeating myself too much, but I keep talking anyway. "I've been complaining for a long time now. Mall culture. You've heard me whining for years, griping about how much a stranger it makes me feel. You know I want out of there. You know I've had enough. I think we could make a go of it in this place. Or *I* could, if you didn't want to."

She either doesn't hear or chooses to ignore the implications of separation in my final remarks. "And what do you do for a job? The nearest town is miles from here and it probably has zero employment. Jesus, Tommy, are you losing your mind?"

Reluctantly I move away from the window and its view of the lake to sit down on the edge of the bed again. "This place becomes my job," I say. "I want to operate it as a business. All year round."

"Jesus, Tommy. It needs too much work. And it's too far away from Toronto. Without clients or customers from Toronto, it'd just stay empty."

"Oh, fuck Toronto," I say with a bitterness that surprises me. "Fuck, fuck Toronto. Ideas work without fucking Toronto being involved. Okay?"

After this outburst we fall silent. We are both surprised at me, although probably for different reasons.

"Look, Tommy," Judy says at last, "I'm trying to be understanding about this. But you're starting to piss me off. You bring me coffee in bed, then spring some crazy scheme on me that would turn our lives upside down. This whole idea is so incredibly naive and stupid."

"And authentic."

"Oh, Jesus."

"Something wrong with authentic?"

"Grow up, Tommy."

"Shit, Judy, do you have to talk to me like that? Why can't you discuss something like this seriously? Why can't we at least talk about this like it's a serious idea? Without the judgments, without the insults, without treating me like I'm inferior in some way."

"Because it's childish. You're like some little boy who refuses to grow up. Waiting for you to grow up makes me angry sometimes."

"Wanting to change my life is childish, is failing to grow up?"

"In this case, yes. It's like something inside you won't accept reality. It's like you resist responsibility, Tommy. You just can't let go of the fantastic. You're always looking out the window, as if something better is going to come marching over the hill at any moment. How do you think that makes me feel?"

I consider her question a moment and feel a fist of guilt punch me in the belly. But it's the kind of guilt Judy would never feel herself, I know, if our positions were reversed. And guilt is like walking through glue; it can turn a man back when he really should keep going.

I sigh. "Listen, Jude, I want to do something else with my life, something I find more meaningful to me personally. That's all I'm talking about. What's childish or irresponsible about that?"

"You have a job. I have a job. We have responsibilities to one another. Things are going well the way they are. You just don't give it all up on whim. It's self-destructive. Why do you want to tear down everything we've worked for?"

I gaze at this woman society calls my wife, feeling I understand so much more about how we differ from one another than I understood only a few moments ago. I realize, somewhere along the way, our marriage has become mostly business. David Cruickshank has talked often about this topic, complaining at length about the way this process of falling into business reflects the conventional decline of marriage. Business. Role. Ritual. Function. What needs to be done next. What duty can or cannot wait until tomorrow. What has to be *shopped for* next. What has to be achieved and planned for to give the relationship apparent value in the eyes of our equally married-as-business peers.

"It takes all the adventure out of love," David says. "You know why we stop making love in the morning, Tom? Because we'll get caught in traffic and be late for fucking work. You know why we don't prolong that embrace on a Saturday morning? Because the lawn needs cutting, we have to get to Canadian Tire, and the Jones's are hosting a barbecue down the street and everyone will be pissed off if we're late. Or the children need attention because they've done without it for five fucking minutes. And after a while all of this shit becomes ritual. We embrace the familiarity of it. We make it important when it's not. We even hide behind it. We forget about love. We fear to trust the intimacy we might have had. We turn our marriage into a crowd we can get lost in. You know what I mean? And love works better when we do more of what *we* want as a couple. It stops working when we do what everyone *else* wants. Somewhere in there, right in the middle, is a beautiful, love-sustaining balance between the two extremes. Here we find the necessary and exclusive intimacy love needs to survive. I keep looking for it. I keep hoping someday I find it. I keep hoping someone will love me enough to want the same goal, to go to that balanced place where love and obligation hold hands with one another. If I was to define what a couple needs in marriage, I'd say compatibility and intimacy, a compatible, intimate need to please one another that far outstrips the need to please everyone else."

This morning, as I contemplate Judy and her anger, David's words ring in my memory with new clarity.

But I'm not going to mention any of this to Judy. Not because it's difficult, or because I'll never be articulate enough to explain it. No, I'm not going to explain it because I am beginning to believe she should see the conundrum for what it is herself. If she was the right woman for me, if we were truly compatible, she would be as appalled as I am by what marriage can do to love. She should want something clearer and simpler herself, in her own right, not merely as a concession to me. If she's truly happy with where we are now—and I am convinced she is, regardless of the reason—it just means we're different from one another and someone should make a choice between compromising for the sake of the partnership or going his own way.

I'm the one who needs to be doing something else; I'm the one who must make the choice. Judy doesn't want to make a change. *I'm* the one who must bite the bullet here. With me being the one who has to choose, I see no point in explaining the concept of balance in love or marriage to someone who may not require this balance in the same way I do. Besides, I'm not quite ready yet to explain myself to her. Because of *you*, Jan. Because you have a part in this, you, my personal quandary. It's so ironic: I haven't touched you for more than twenty years, beyond a sisterly embrace, yet, for twenty years, I've been lying every day to conceal my ongoing affair with you. For twenty years I've been a liar purely to hide the *idea* of you from people. And, damn, why didn't I get off the bus in Westendorf that last morning more than twenty years ago, when I needed and wanted to? What was I afraid of? Embarrassing myself? Exposing my feelings of love to someone cruel or vicious? Or did I not know who I am, what it is that makes me authentic, an apparent component of which is *you* and my need for love?

"Well, Jesus, Tommy," Judy says. "Aren't you going to say anything?"

Her words jar me back to this moment where I sit on the edge of our bed. I gaze into my empty coffee mug and know only that I must change what's wrong with my life, with *me*, with love and peace and time and space and sex and love and smell and touch. Or else! Or else I will decay, my obligatory compromise eating away at my personal authenticity, pushing me ever closer to needless private tragedy. Then, when I eventually die, at the moment of my dying, I will know I am leaving this life an altogether too familiar impostor I did not want to be. How can we approach death without shame if we lack the courage to embrace our authentic selves?

"Tommy?"

"This isn't the right time to talk about this," I say with a deep sigh. "I wanted you to know what I was contemplating so you could think about it. I wanted to share my idea with you and I wanted you to take it seriously. I hoped you would be understanding."

Judy is watching me. I now detect a glimmer of compassion in her expression but I recognize the professional distance in her caring too. "You know, Tommy, I really do think it would help if you saw someone about this business of your missing authenticity. I think you need to talk things out with a professional. You know what I mean? And, at the hospital, I could get you in. It would all be through our insurance. Tommy, I think you're more troubled than we realize. You're not so hung up that you'd refuse to see a shrink, are you?"

I drift towards the door, then turn to look at her. "I should let you get dressed," I say before making my escape.

DOWNSTAIRS, BEFORE I HEAD for the kitchen, I throw on my parka and step outside onto the porch. It's rained again at some point earlier this morning—as it did yesterday morning—but, like yesterday, it has begun to clear up. While the sunshine prying apart the cracks in the clouds is weak, the day is unexpectedly warm. I unzip my jacket. A couple of hundred yards away the lake is calm; there is hardly a ripple on its pristine surface. And across the way the stand of hardwoods I've been admiring all weekend glows golden, red and yellow in the hesitant October sunshine.

I breathe deeply and try to calm myself. My stomach endures an all too familiar sensation of nervousness. Even here, outside alone on the veranda, I feel I still walk on the same eggshells my life with Judy has strewn along my path for so long.

I would be a fool to be surprised at Judy's reaction to my proposal that we—or I—purchase this lodge, then live here, operating it as a business. What disconcerts me is the scorn with which she received the idea. And it strikes me, as I stand here in the morning sunshine, that Judy suggests psychiatric sessions only for people who perceive life in a different fashion than she does. Judy has always believed she is right about everything. To a person so implacable, someone like me who has little interest in being right is inevitably perceived as wrong. That's just the way life goes. I know Judy will not live with me in this place. And, in truth, I suspect I would prefer living here without her. I suppose, in finding myself in this wilderness place—rediscovering a long lost, authentic me—I have decided in some way to leave Judy behind. So she can pursue *her* life and I can pursue *mine*. Not because of you, Sweet Jan. Not *for* you. Not even for the *idea* of you. But because I can no longer live a life that does not belong to me, that irritates and disappoints me, that fails to give me satisfaction.

These conclusions are a heady concoction for me. But shortly I feel calmer, renewed where I linger alone here on the lodge veranda I've moved to stake out my personal territory at last. I feel, in some wondrous way, that I have finally arrived. I take a deep breath of wilderness air, then turn away from the view of the lake, to go inside.

WHILE I COOK everyone their pancakes and sausages, I search the bank of kitchen cupboards for an enamel plate. I know Gladys's lover was the kind of man who would have owned an enamel plate and, sure enough, at last I find one in a stack of blue enamel ware buried at the back of a deep, dark cupboard. I have determined I will take my breakfast in the canoe in the middle of the lake, on my way towards the hardwoods I enjoyed seeing on the horizon earlier. If not normally antisocial, I'm at least feeling the need for some privacy in the wake of my discussion with Judy.

Soon, as I am getting ready to take the stack of pancakes to the table, you peek your head inside the kitchen. "Good morning, Tom," you say.

I think you want your greeting to sound cheerful but in this it fails abysmally. It draws attention to the exhaustion I notice on your haggard face. Your eyes are red and your skin is pale.

"Jesus, Jan," I say in obvious surprise, "You look exhausted."

"I'm not sleeping well," you admit with a nod.

I want to ask you why but, instead, I just tell you I'm sorry. Then, "You don't miss the noise of the city, do you?"

"No. That's not it."

You shrug and hold the door for me as I pass by with the platter of pancakes. I catch a welcome scent of you, even above the aroma of the food I carry, and I feel a tremor of the familiar love your scent never fails to inspire in me. My love for you remains pagan—it has always been this way—sight, taste, scent, as if my senses once blended with yours and can no longer separate themselves from you. At times I feel I love and want to live inside your skin as much as my own. I am grateful for whatever force inspires this paganism, this gift of sensual heresy, the same gift I have too often wished in the past would simply go away. I feel new about myself. It crackles in me.

Everyone is gathering for their breakfast as I set the food in place on the dining room table. Judy is at the top of the stairs, just beginning to descend. You have moved to the window to gaze out at the lake, but you are restless and don't stand there long, soon turning towards the table, visibly preoccupied by some consideration exclusively your own. Greg is in the living room, rifling through old magazines on an end table, looking for something he's misplaced.

"Have you seen my *National Post*?" he asks me as I arrive with the pancakes.

"It's been starting the morning fires," I reply.

"Well, shit, Tom!"

"Exactly," I remark as I turn away. We've argued about the merits of the Toronto daily newspapers before. No one intends to say uncle.

I put on my parka, then head back into the kitchen. I open the oven door and, with gloved hands, retrieve the pancakes and sausages I have kept for myself in their enamel dish. I have already serviced them with syrup so I can quickly make my escape. Carrying the plate, I return to the dining room, then stroll towards the main door.

"Where are *you* going?" Judy asks.

"I'm taking my breakfast out on the lake."

"Tommy, the mountain man," my wife retorts angrily.

I don't say anything to this. I merely slip outside, closing the door behind me.

IT IS A WONDROUSLY BEAUTIFUL October morning in the middle of the lake. I have paddled out here quickly, the water as smooth as satin, but my haste and the moderate temperatures have not prevented my breakfast from getting cold. Not that I truly mind, as I sit out here, devouring it. The tranquility and solitude are worth the gastronomical compromise. And I'm drinking my coffee black. It remains hot against my tongue.

I still feel impatient with everyone. Even you, Jan. All of you seem so far outside my view of life. It's as if I have now successfully separated from all of you in a way that clears my vision, my view of what lies ahead. Judy is not going to understand what drives me to run away to this place where I now feel I must reside. Not her fault. But not *my fault* either. If I can be faulted, it is in the way I have let so much time pass before deciding to make my stand. I plead guilty here, but with the qualification that knowing oneself can take time. I mean, who wouldn't prefer a generous amount of self knowledge at some earlier age? Self-knowledge may be the foundation of our personal wisdom but wisdom is rare when we are young, when, instead of becoming wise, we are trying to transform ourselves into something we believe our world is willing to accept or applaud.

And Greg? Greg may be the most satisfied of us all within the network of facile definitions linking the conventional world to itself. For him, all conventional conclusions make a linear sense. Towing the conventional line will never inspire in him the same regret I tend to feel so deeply. All of society's rationalizations, its motivation to conform, its simplistic definitions of experience, and its reductive need to materialize ambition will never trouble him. It's why he and I have never been able to be friends.

As for you, Jan, you share my cowardice, a cowardice we demonstrated two decades ago after we met in the Austrian Alps. We could have taken a chance on one another, on the love we felt for one another, but we opted to be afraid of its intensity and immediacy. Now, while I continue to love you as much as I did then, it is probably too late for us. Because you have stuck by your decision way back then to be cynical about what we felt for one another. Now, you and I will continue to merely flirt with what otherwise might have been.

Thinking these things and watching the sun establishing itself at the edge of a dissolving bank of clouds, I eat my pancake breakfast in the middle of the canoe drifting delicately on the surface of the middle of this lake. Here I think I have found the kind of middle ground I believe I can now embrace, that place of balance David has talked about, where we must do *with* and do *without*, to pay for our self-accommodation. Out here, at peace with myself, I can see the days are approaching when I will often be caught proudly *saying* so. And remembering all those times when I would *never* have been caught saying so, well, such occasions will dissolve in the fluid of a forgiving past.

Pleased with myself and my conclusions, I pick up my paddle and begin to cross the rest of the lake in the direction of the colorful hardwoods now reflecting themselves coquettishly on the mirror of the lake. I slip over the water's surface in near silence, my progress a whisper I share with the tranquility of the day. When the canoe scrapes over the stones on the shallow bottom at the edge of a small clearing in these breathtakingly beautiful hardwoods, I leap ashore, pulling the canoe up behind me. Soon I vanish into the trees, following what was once obviously a path deep into the wilderness autumn. The overgrown path—making it clear I am not the only person who has been attracted by the beauty of this section of shoreline—leads me deeper into the woods, easing what remains of my anger at Judy. Feeling at home again, I make my way up and down rocky hills, discovering along the way tiny clearings that dot this section of the shore as subtly as smudges on a window.

Gradually I begin to feel a trace of sadness for Judy—and for me as well, of course. At some point, during this extended weekend here in this wilderness setting, I have managed to arrive at a decision I might never have seriously considered back in Ottawa. It has nothing to do with you, beyond the fact one element of this "nothing" has *everything* to do with you. I think I realize, even if I had never met you back in Westendorf, even then I feel I would have reached this point I have now reached with Judy in some other way or time. The bottom line remains the same: she wants to stay where she is; she likes the fabric of her life. While I suspect she would happily move back to Toronto and find something that comforts her there as well, the substance of her choices reflects the way she lives her life right now. She likes the urban busyness of her life. She feels no need to radically change it.

But I have reached the kind of crossroads for which I will name the lodge. And I have decided to embark on my own path instead of tagging along with Judy's. You are not the factor in this I once thought you were, Jan. Judy and I are significantly incompatible, without you to underscore the contrasts. This incompatibility has nothing to do with you, save for those perfect three days in Westendorf and what they revealed to me about love: namely that the kind of love that is merely acceptable simply will not do when one has known the kind of love that takes its breaths in magic. I do not expect to enjoy this kind of magical love again. I suppose, if I feel any regret in this, it is only because beautiful, even awesome love is virtually worth dying for; and each time I encounter you, a frequency entirely due to the perfidious nature of fate, I am forced again to long for exotic love, wishing it could return and wishing you would share it with me.

But for the most part my decision to buy this lodge, to live and work here from now on, is based on the incompatibility between Judy and me. She wants to stay where she is. I want to go somewhere else. I cannot erase those three days in Westendorf and the endless longing they continue to inspire. But at least I can change what feels wrong about the way I live my life in Ottawa into something I believe ends up feeling *right*.

So I walk in the woods for a couple of hours, pondering how to go about what I must do. And by the time I return to the canoe to paddle back to what I am convinced will soon be my new home, I am a committed man. I am gently elated too to be somewhat freer of you and what happened to us in Westendorf. If I can never know the sweet joy of your love again, at least I can know what I really want to do to be authentic with what remains of my life.

WHEN I GET BACK TO THE LODGE I find all of you on the veranda, enjoying the warmth of the day. But as I draw closer, I realize you aren't actually enjoying yourselves at all. Up close the tension among you is palpable. I wonder what Judy has told you and if she has infected everyone's mood with her annoyance and frustration.

"The prodigal husband returns," she mutters as I begin to climb the steps to where the rest of you are hanging out.

"It's a fine day," I say.

No one answers me. Not even you, Jan. You look even more haggard than when I saw you last, as I was leaving for the canoe and my appointment in the middle of the lake. Judy is clearly still angry at me over what I told her this morning. And Greg? Greg is standing on the edges of everything, using the toe of his sneaker to fidget with some idea we can't see on the floor at his feet.

I wonder whether I should ask if everything is all right, but Judy preempts the question.

"I've told Jan and Greg about your cockamamie idea to buy this lodge," she says.

"And?"

"You're upsetting everyone."

"Upsetting everyone?" I glance at each face, trying to figure out why everyone would be upset. Judy? Sure. But what's the difference to you and Greg?

Your eyes meet mine for a long second, then slip away unscathed.

"What it gets down to, Tommy, is why the hell should Jan and I sell you this resort? Why would we want to do that?"

"Because you intend to sell it," I reply. I stand there blinking. I don't really want to go through this in front of everyone. But if I must, I will.

"But why should we sell it to *you*?"

"Just a minute, Judy," you say. "Don't speak for both of us. If we decide to sell it, who's to say Tom couldn't be the one to buy it? What's wrong with that?"

"Because *I* don't want to buy it," Judy snaps. "*I* want to *sell* it. Jesus, Jan. In case you've forgotten for a second, this idiot on the stairs and I are still married."

"Shit, Judy," you whisper. "Wanting to buy this cottage doesn't make him an idiot."

"Thank you," I put in.

"It does if I don't want to buy it *too.*"

"Okay," says Greg, holding up his hands as if to ward off an attack. "Let's not get aggravated with one another."

"Too late," says Judy.

"It is *not* too late," you counter.

"Maybe," I suggest, "we shouldn't talk about this right now."

"Yeah," says Greg. "Maybe the decision of whether to sell the place or not needs to be talked about first. In an isolated way, you know? I mean, I think you should sell it. But there are . . ."

". . . I just don't see why Tom can't buy it," I hear you say.

"Jesus!" cries Judy.

"Well wait a minute," says Greg. "Does all of this mean you two girls have decided to sell the place for sure?"

"No, it does *not*!" you cry. "Maybe we *all* should keep it. Or sell it to Tom and Judy. I don't know."

"But I don't want the fucking place," cries Judy.

"But I do," I say.

Everyone looks at me.

"There's a lot more to this than just a property sale," I add.

Judy glares at me, then glances at you and Greg. "Tommy wants to be authentic. Tommy wants to be authentic our here in the boonies. I'm just lucky he doesn't want to be authentic on Mars."

You glance at me and I think I detect a delicate smile playing along your lips. This worries me a bit. Are you stifling mirth at my foolishness or are you understanding my frustration?

"Authentic," echoes Greg, like he's never heard the word before.

"Look," I say at last. "If you two are going to sell this place, I just want you to know I'd like to buy it. What's so difficult about that?"

"Well, we're married and I don't want to buy it," cries Judy.

"How many times do I have to say the same fucking thing? How much clearer can I be?"

"But it's two different topics, Jude. Whether you and Jan are selling it is one topic. The other is, well, between you and me. I can buy it without you, for that matter. I'm just saying I want to buy it."

"Why?" asks Greg.

"To run as a business," I reply after I have gotten over the apparent stupidity of his question.

"Here?"

I look at him, bemused. "Yeah. Here."

Pale and tired, you struggle to your feet. "Maybe I want to keep it," you say. "Maybe I want to keep it and sell it to Tom." Then, while we try to decode what you just said, you disappear inside the lodge.

"Shit," says Greg in evident frustration. "Now you got Jan being all crazy too. In a way, we're back to where we were a couple of days ago."

"Well," I say at last. "I'm thinking about lunch. I'm going to see what kind of food I can scare up for lunch."

Greg doesn't answer me. Judy is silent too.

I go inside and head for the kitchen, suspecting you've gone upstairs. But I hope you're puzzling through your own conflicts on this issue. Did the glimpse I thought I saw of your sympathy for me reflect your view that this place might be an opportunity for both of us? Nah, I decide by the time I get to the kitchen. It's time I got over this proclivity I have for wishful thinking. Especially where *you're* concerned. After twenty years, it's time I faced the facts: whatever I decide to do, I'm going to be doing it on my own.

AFTER LUNCH, GREG ANNOUNCES he's going into town. "To get a fucking newspaper," he says, fixing me with a fierce stare.

"Sorry," I say. "I thought you were through with it. I really did."

"Yeah, yeah," he mutters.

"Can I go?" Judy asks.

"Sure."

"This place is beginning to get to me. I wouldn't mind looking through a few shops, if that's okay with you, Greg."

"Yeah. Fine. Jan?"

"No," you say. "I'm tired."

"Suit yourself."

"Tommy?"

"No thanks. Nothing I need in town. I think I'll do some more exploring."

"And the dishes?" Judy asks.

"You and Greg go ahead," I say magnanimously. "I'll look after the dishes. Not many here."

"I'm not sure I deserve you," Judy says.

I merely gaze at her, unable, as she intended, to confirm the sarcasm in her remark.

We disperse.

Judy and Greg have gone by the time you come into the kitchen where I am wearing rubber gloves and beginning to stack the dishes I have washed. You grab a tea towel and begin to dry and put away.

"You'll need an industrial strength dishwasher, if you buy this place," you say.

"Yeah. I imagine so." I glance at you, feeling the same passionate compassion I always feel about you. "I thought you might be wanting a nap. I can handle this."

"No. I had one before lunch. I'm fine."

"Your color's better."

"Thank you."

I fall silent. God, I love you. I can hardly bear to look at you, my caring is so deep. It just never goes away. I will take this love to my grave, regardless of what happens the rest of my life.

"Judy's really pissed," you say shortly.

"Yeah. I know."

"Do you mean it? Do you really want to buy this place?"

"Absolutely."

"And you want to live here and run it?"

"Yup."

"Wow. That's a pretty radical change in direction, Tom."

"Yup."

Thoughtfully you keep drying the same plate over and over. Eventually you notice this and wince, putting it into the proper cupboard. "But Judy will never do it."

"I know."

"I mean, are you guys okay?"

"I guess *not*," I reply.

"Look, sorry. This is none of my business."

"Yes, it is, Jan."

"Tom . . . ."

I turn away from you, let the water begin to drain out of the sink, mopping around the stainless steel with the cloth. There is a powerful gurgling sound. I consider life and its extraordinary contrasts, the mechanical reality of gurgling sinks, for instance, versus a feeling of love so powerful it makes me want to weep. What kind of world is this anyway? How do the lofty and the mundane coexist so easily this way? I take a deep breath.

"Jan, I know why your mum kept this place. I even know why she kept it secret until after she passed away."

"How?"

"Doesn't matter. I just made use of some long neglected investigative journalism skills."

"Okay. Are you going to spill the beans?"

"I don't know. I'm not sure how you'd take it."

"C'mon, Tom, take *what*?"

We have finished the dishes. Both of us now lean against the kitchen cupboards, perhaps a yard apart. Despite this distance, I want to confess everything at this moment: what I have learned about your mum, how I continue to feel about you. Still, even wanting deeply to unleash these powerful truths, I hesitate.

"I'm going exploring," I say at last. "Wanna come?"

"Yes," you say. "I do."

WE VEER LEFT ALONG THE PATH at the edge of the lake, the one I took yesterday when I came this way alone. Until the path narrows, you and I manage to walk side by side. Our hands brush one another a couple of times and I am painfully aware of this touch. I would love someday to hold your hand again, like I did that night before we made love in Westendorf. But soon our route narrows and you fall in behind me because you know I've walked this path before.

"So what did you find out about my mother?" you ask me as soon as you can.

"I'm sorry I mentioned it, Jan. It just came out unexpectedly, when we were alone there in the kitchen."

"Well, the cat's out of the bag. I want to know what you're talking about."

"You may not like it."

"What was she? An ax murderer?"

I chuckle unconvincingly.

"C'mon, Tom, don't do this."

I turn and glance at you. "Sorry, Jan. I'm not playing games. I really don't know whether to say anything or not."

"Well, I'm asking for the truth."

"Okay."

I hold back a branch until you've safely passed it. We continue along the path. I'm heading for the cliff that promises the splendid view of the lake I discovered yesterday. I even hope the raven that greeted me then is there today for you to meet him.

"Tom?"

"I found the resort office yesterday while Greg was in town and you and Judy were sleeping. Greg had the keys but I was curious. So I pried off the padlock and broke in."

You laugh. "Hardly a break-in, Tom."

"I know, in view of how much I want to buy this place, at least."

"Go on," you say.

"There wasn't anything in there really, until I looked through the desk. Then I found some photographs. No way of telling when they were taken, but your mum was much younger, much younger than when I first met her."

"Shit," you say. "And?"

"Well, she was with a man . . . ."

" . . . Who wasn't my father, right?"

"Right."

"And you think he was her lover."

"Yes, I do. You'd have to see the pictures yourself, of course."

"But that's your theory?"

"They sure look like lovers to me."

"Maybe it was before she married Dad."

"I wouldn't want to say, but I don't think so," I reply.

"Are you *sure*?"

"Positive."

"And the pictures were taken where exactly?"

I turn and gaze at you. "Here, Jan. The pictures were taken here."

"Shit."

"Which explains," I say, continuing down the path again, "why you and Judy own a lodge-slash-resort."

"My mother had a lover who left it to her."

"Bulls eye."

We turn to the right, following the shoreline. Gradually we begin to climb towards the cliff and its panoramic view. We trudge along a while in silence.

Then you ask me, "So how come these pictures just show up in the desk?"

"Well," I reply. "I suspect that's what your mother intended. I think the last time she was here, whenever that was, she put the pictures in the desk."

"To be found by Judy or me."

"Yeah."

"We can't be sure about that, Tom."

"I know. Maybe I just want fate or oversight to stay out of this for some reason. I'm tired of fate and oversight, to tell you the truth. Look what fate and oversight did to you and me."

I hear your intake of breath as you consider a reply, but in the end you remain silent.

"Anyway," I say as we gain the top of the cliff, "that's the story so far."

"I'm glad you told me, Tom." You come and stand beside me to gaze out over the lake. "Of course, I want to see these pictures for myself."

"Yeah. I'll bet you do. Maybe when Greg and Judy get back. I don't want to have to do another break and enter."

You are smiling. "No longer a virgin. What's the difference?"

"I suppose," I say. "I'd still like the others to be here."

We stand there in silence now, taking in the view.

"Beautiful, isn't it?" I say.

"Stunning," you reply. "You've been here before?"

"Yesterday."

"What do you think of my mother now that you think she had a lover?"

I turn to you and notice your cheeks are flushed. I know you're aware I'm looking at you, but you continue to study the panorama of the wooded lake.

For a moment I am silent, carefully choosing my words. Then, "It makes me feel closer to her, Jan. I understand her now. You'd have to see the pictures, the guy in question. You can actually see how much she loves him and how much he loves her. So I felt close to them."

"You're very forgiving," you say.

I look at you and fail to keep incredulity out of my voice. "Jeez, Jan, it's love. What's to forgive?"

For a moment it appears you're about to argue with me, but in the end you glance at your feet and gently nod. "Yes, of course," you say. "Then again, it wasn't *your* mother."

"Fair enough."

I stand there thinking my moment has arrived, my moment of truth is upon me, but you change topics on me and the opportunity slips away.

"You really want this place, don't you?"

"Yes."

"Are you and Judy in trouble?"

"I guess so."

"Why?"

I move to stand between you and your view of the lake. "A couple of reasons. She wants to be urban. I want to be wilderness."

"And?"

"I've been in love with someone else for my entire marriage."

You gaze at me defiantly. "So?"

"I can't stand it any longer. I can't stand not admitting it."

"To whom?"

"To myself. To the object of my affections."

You study me a moment more, then glance away, shaking your head slowly back and forth. "Oh Tom," you whisper. "It was just bad luck we turned out to be the people we are. You and I were never supposed to see one another again after Westendorf."

"I know," I murmur, reaching to take you into my arms.

You don't resist the embrace, but I feel your discomfort in my arms. I kiss you on the forehead, hoping it comforts you a little.

"God, Tom," you say, now moving more tightly against me.

And I kiss you gently on the lips, feeling a million joyful sensations cascading along my flesh.

You begin to kiss me back, but then you pull away from me, turning your back on me.

"I've never stopped loving you, Jan," I tell you then. "Not for one second since Westendorf."

"Tom? Please."

"It's true," I say. "I'm sorry."

You say nothing.

"You believe me, don't you?"

I wish you'd turn and look at me so I could see your face. But you don't.

"Jan? You believe me, don't you?"

"Yes. I believe you, Tom."

"Jan?"

Now you turn and you're angry. "You're married to my sister, Tom. You married my sister."

"We fucked it up," I say. "Back then, in Rosedale, just before the wedding. We fucked it up."

"Yes, I suppose we did," you say.

"We underestimated what we had, Jan. And you didn't say *anything* then. I thought you didn't care."

"Tom, I'm going back to the lodge now. I don't want to talk about this anymore right now. Okay?"

"When then?"

"Maybe never. Okay?"

I feel my heart breaking. I feel it shriveling up. I feel my heart forming into fists and punching itself in self-recrimination. Stupid, stupid, stupid, it cries. But I take a deep, slow breath and manage to look at you and nod. "I'm sorry about this," I whisper. "Not sorry for loving you. I don't seem able to help that. But sorry for telling you."

"I'm going back," you say, turning away from me, heading down over the rocks the way we've come.

"I'll be along later," I reply, my voice sounding a little like a cracked window. "I'm sorry, Jan," I call.

You turn once and glance at me, then disappear into the embrace of the trees, an embrace, it now strikes me, that must be much less sinister than mine.

I DON'T SEE YOU AGAIN until much later that afternoon, after I return to the lodge. At one point, as I glance out the window, I glimpse you down on the dock, gazing out over the lake. You look so lonely and fragile at this moment, I want to go to you. But I resist this need with sheer force of will. I've said my piece. I should leave you alone to deal in your own way with what I've confessed today.

As for me, I'm torn between sadness and jubilation because I have at last told you the truth. I'm sad, of course, because it is now obvious you are lost to me. I'm jubilant, I've determined, because I'm released from a distressing secret I've carried around for twenty years. Without this burden of secret, unrequited love, I can approach the rest of my life with a new sense of personal freedom. In a way, I finally got off that bus in Westendorf. I view today's confession as a metaphorical triumph over my cowardice when I sat frozen in the vehicle idling in the pension courtyard my last day in Austria. You've rejected me, I know, but at least you know the truth: my love for you has not faltered in more than two decades.

ALL OF YOU COME FOR ME about the pictures later that day. I have lit charcoal again in the old stone barbecue and I gaze into the flames, mesmerized by their gentle dance and the turmoil of my incessant concoction of melancholy and resolve. At this moment, I feel a new wave of sadness that I have been loving you for so long while you *haven't* been loving me. It's a feeling I am glad all of you interrupt.

"You didn't tell me about these this morning," Judy says accusingly, the photographs in her hand.

"No," I reply. "I didn't know whether to say anything or not. Out of respect for Gladys, I guess."

You and Greg stand a yard or two away from Judy like unhappy support staff. I glance at you two and shrug.

"But you told Jan," Judy says, handing you the pictures as if they belong to *you* now, as if you have demanded she give them up.

I shrug again. "Yes. It seemed right at the time. Just impulse, Jude. I didn't want to make you even angrier."

Judy glares at me. Her jaw is tight.

But Greg innocently saves the moment. "The pictures explain a lot," he says. "Now we know why you girls own a lodge, at least."

"Do you think I'm right about them being lovers?" I ask.

No one answers me. In this way you all convey some kind of disapproval.

"Any idea when the photos were taken?" I ask.

"She was married, Tommy," Judy snaps, "if *that's* what you want to know."

You glance at me, pursing your lips. This time it is me who must look away.

"It doesn't matter now," I remark lamely.

"But it *does*," Judy insists.

"Mum's dead," you whisper. "Tom's right. It's all water under the bridge."

"But I didn't need to *know* this, Jan."

We are all silent.

Judy glares at me. "You could have protected us from this," she says to me. "You could have kept it secret. You could have left us with our childhood illusions, for Christ's sake."

"Judy, it doesn't matter," you say.

But she ignores you. "Why'd you spill the beans, Tommy? Why didn't you spare us this?"

"I'm just the messenger," I say. "I think Gladys intended for you to know. Whatever, I'm tired of keeping secrets, like secrets are my *job*."

Shaking her head, Judy turns away and makes her way to the steps. They creak as she climbs towards the lodge.

Shortly you and Greg turn to follow her. Gently, though, you place your hand on my arm as you depart, just for one exotic moment. The sensation of your touch infects my entire body and I feel the virus spreading along my flesh. I watch you and Greg go inside before I turn back to the flames and my plate of waiting hamburger patties.

SOMEHOW I AND EVERYONE ELSE crawls or staggers through the rest of the waning afternoon and early evening. We are like the living dead, by times voracious, by times manic, then dazed and distracted, each of us residing in this state of unreality for his or her own peculiar reasons. I have not brought up my purchase of this property again, but I remain more committed than ever to buying it. My befuddlement now concerns the love I confessed to you today on the cliff overlooking the lake. I remain torn between the satisfaction of having been truthful and the deep pain I feel because I have squandered the last of my hope.

In truth, I miss hoping for your love as much as I miss your love itself. Because my hope has lasted twenty years and is now gone. The love remains—there is no need to miss it. But my hope? I now realize that even when I thought it was extinguished, it continued still to thrive. My hope you would love me again in the way that I love you. Yes, this particular hope did not relent. I had no idea it continued to live so hardily in me. Now that it is dashed, I wish I had not confessed my love for you. I never *had* your love, but in remaining silent, I would have been able to keep my hope intact.

Which is why *I* am distracted all through dinner. Greg is the chatty one by times, trying to interest us in what is wrong with Temagami, his chief complaint being how far away it is from Toronto. But even *he* gives up eventually and I notice at some point all that can be heard for long stretches during dinner is the clatter of tableware on porcelain as we eat our salad and nibble at our hamburgers, too tired and perturbed to attempt conversation.

For her part, Judy has progressed from anger with me to puzzlement. She glances at me now and then almost clinically, as if trying to remember if she married me way back then or not. But at least she's being pleasant when she asks someone to pass the salad.

And you, Sweet Jan, I guess, are preoccupied with how best to ignore what I told you this afternoon about my love for you, and how I got you to admit you knew that it was true. In conventionally social terms, you and I now face an awkward future. If and when we encounter one another, you will squirm uncomfortably, knowing how much I love you. I will squirm uncomfortably, knowing you do not love me back. Perhaps, after Judy and I split up so that she can live in the city and I can own this lodge, it won't be necessary for me to see you again. I will have bought your lodge. Beyond this, I will have little importance in your life or in your sister's life.

"I wonder," Judy says while we are having coffee, "how mother met the man in the photographs."

"I've been wondering about that too," you say.

"I mean, what would she have been doing way up here?"

We all shrug.

"As a child, I hardly remember her ever being away."

"I know," you say. "Yet she must have seen this man on occasion."

"Maybe he wasn't a lover at all," I suggest at last, although I don't believe it. "Maybe he was just a dear friend or a close cousin or something."

All of you look at me.

I am encouraged by this. "Yeah, what if he wasn't a lover at all? Maybe all the pictures were taken during one weekend or something, as part of some kind of reunion."

"No cousins like him in *our* family," you say.

"A friend then."

"No, Tommy," Judy says. "Pandora's Box is open. We saw the pictures. You can see on their faces that they were fucking one another."

"Jesus, Judy," you say. "What a way to put it. This was our mother, remember."

Judy shrugs in half apology.

"Although," you add, "I could see they were lovers too."

"Well," says Greg, pouring himself more wine. "Look at the bright side. You girls own a lodge you can sell."

Even Judy does not remark on this.

"In my defense," I say, "I really do think the photographs were left in the desk to be found when you inherited the place."

"How did she know they'd be found?" you ask.

"It's a calculated risk, I suppose."

We all fall silent again. We retreat. We slip back into our living dead personae.

While the rest of you head to the kitchen to wash the dishes—I am excused because I did lunch dishes and cooked the dinner again—I go outside and stand in the darkness on the veranda The night is starburst and balmy. If there is a moon, it has not risen yet, or it lurks somewhere behind the trees where I cannot see it. I stand here for five minutes or so, then descend the stairs, headed for the dock. As I pass, I glance into the lap of the stone barbecue and notice that the coals still glow weakly against the contrast of the darkness.

I have no flashlight, but I stride confidently into the night on my way to the lake. I seem to glide over the rough, weed-strewn ground, instinctively certain that I will not hurt myself here in the dark. I realize this confidence has nothing to do with an illusion of uncanny night vision, but because this property is my place, the home where I'm supposed to be. I have at last arrived, I know; I cannot be injured here. Here, I cannot be lost. Not tonight. Not now that I am a man who, while losing the woman he loves, has managed to find *himself*.

I walk out onto the dock where I can hear the gentlest of ripples whispering against the ancient planks and boulders forming the crib of this structure. I stand here a long time and feel comfortable with this place. I hear the scream of a lynx and this does not startle me. I hear it scream again and know instinctively that it will now fall silent. Because I know things now. I know this place. I know what will and will not happen. I stand on the dock a long time and feel comfortable with myself, knowing I am authentic, knowing my authenticity will see me through.

There is something that will always be missing for me, of course. That something is you, Jan. But here, in this place I know will belong to me, I can learn to live with the loss. Here, I believe, my preoccupation with you and what will likely never be can find a place of quiet repose, a place to give up on itself in return for tranquility. I can live reasonably happily up here without you. In a way, I am nearly as in love with his place as I am in love with *you*.

So I stand on the dock in the darkness for a very long time. I stand on the dock in the night of this wonderful place and increasingly derive that special comfort a person can enjoy when he or she recognizes whom they really are.

BY THE TIME I GO BACK INSIDE, all of you have gone to bed. It is chillier now and I start another fire in the wood stove. I sit down in the nearest chair, an objecting assembly of wicker I overpower. Feeling exposed in the glow of a nearby lamp, I flick the switch to sit by myself in darkness. The building creaks now and then and occasionally the burning wood snaps or crackles, but all else is silent.

I'm okay. I will *be* okay. I have questions about the nature of love that will probably go unanswered for the remainder of my life: why would you be presented to me as such a perfect partner only to resist the partnership, for instance? But I fight the urge to wallow in the sadness of this question. I remain glad I confessed my true feelings to you. My apparent loss of you as a lover, well, I suppose I have already begun to live with it.

At first, when you whisper my name from some point halfway down the stairs, I wonder if I have imagined or dreamed it. I sense a great deal of time has gone by and it is now the middle of the night, but I cannot be certain of this. I have no idea how long I have been sitting by the fire, thinking my private thoughts. I feel fresh and alert, certain I have not been dozing. Knowing this, I begin to realize it is not as late as I first thought it was.

"Tom?" And there it is again, the whispering of my name, more hoarsely than before.

"Jan?" I whisper back. I reach for the light, fumbling to find the switch.

"Leave it off," you say, hearing my clumsy fingers.

"Can you see?"

"Leave it off." Your voice is much closer.

And I can see you now. You wear the same man's shirt you wore the other night when we encountered one another in the chill outside on the veranda

"Are you all right?" I ask.

Fearing you are going to stumble in the darkness, I get up out of the chair. You glide like a butterfly into my arms.

"Oh Tom," you say. "What's the point of it all?"

I would try to answer you, although I don't actually know if there's ever a point. But you kiss me hard on the mouth, a sweet and hungry kiss that interrupts anything I might have been preparing to say.

"Jan?" I gasp after the kiss.

"Oh shut up, Tom," you say. "Just stop talking for a while."

I hold you so tightly in my arms, I fear I will crush you. But you fit perfectly against me, standing on your tiptoes, your head against my shoulder.

"I love you, Jan," I say a couple of times.

"I know," you say. "I know."

I wait for more but there is silence. Then, an eternity later, "I need a lot more time, Tom. Back then, now, it's so large a gap. Judy is my sister."

I nod. I understand.

"I'm tired of fighting," you whisper. "I'm tired of pushing it away. I do love you, Tom, but Judy is my sister." You sigh. "I hope you'll give me enough time to deal with this."

"Of course I will," I say

"I lay in bed up there, trying to sleep. I couldn't sleep knowing you loved me so much. This has been a terrible weekend."

"I'm sorry."

"Oh shut up. Don't be sorry. I haven't slept well since we got here. Judy's my sister, Tom. We're different from one another—we know that—but once upon a time we were innocent children together."

"I know," I say.

You just kiss me again, gently. We hold each other tightly and rock back and forth in the embrace like some ancient, windblown tree.

Eventually we sit down on the couch. There is a blanket there I wrap around your shoulders.

WE REMAIN AWAKE for much of the night deciding what to do with each other and with ourselves. Talking at times. Or just touching one another delicately on the hand or the arm in the compulsively delicate silence.

"Maybe this way was best," you comment at one point.

"You mean waiting this long to reconnect with Westendorf?"

"Yes."

"But we wasted twenty years. We lost twenty years."

"Maybe without the twenty years, it would never have had a chance to possibly work out."

But I don't think I can accept your theory. "Why do we

think perfection must be tested?" I wonder aloud.

"We didn't know it was perfect, Tom."

"Yes, we did," I say. "That's what frightened us."

In the end, though, it doesn't matter. What's done is done. Of more importance, we know, is what lies ahead, the tough, imminent moments we must go through if we are ever to belong to one another at some vague point in the future when you can be comfortable with it.

"Do you think you could be happy here?" I ask you at one point.

"Time will tell, I guess," you say. "I have to deal with what has happened here, with my guilt. I have to deal with my sister first. Beyond that, I don't know. I love her, you know, Judy, I mean. We're not close in so many ways, but she's still my sister."

"I love this place, Jan." I say this because this place is not Judy, for you *or* for me.

"I know. Maybe someday I'll love it too, as much as you do. Because I love *you* so much."

I swallow. I touch your cheek with my fingertips. I kiss you. I mention to you that Greg or Judy could wander downstairs at any moment and find us here, sitting on the couch, touching one another.

"I know," is all you say.

We do not move. We have already decided to tell the truth when Greg and Judy awake. We both believe none of us can move on in any way without the truth about Westendorf being revealed.

"I'm glad you came down the stairs earlier tonight, Jan," I tell the woman I love.

"Me too," you say. "There have been other times I nearly came to you."

"When?" I ask, unable to prevent myself from asking the question.

"It doesn't matter now," you say. "I'll tell you later, when this has all been worked out."

At some point a few hours before dawn we doze where we sit on the couch, you resting your head on my shoulder.

"Crossroads," you whisper.

"Yes."

"Perfect," you reply.

WITH HARDLY ANY SLEEP at all next morning, we gather our spouses around the table to tell them what happened two decades ago in Westendorf. As newly defined duos, we are a striking contrast. Greg and Judy, having slept alone all night, look fresh as daisies to me. You and I apparently do not.

"Jesus," Judy says. "You two look like shit." Then she turns exclusively to me. "Maybe you don't love this place as much as you think you do. If you can't sleep . . . ."

"That isn't it," I say.

You and I woke shortly after dawn and you climbed up the stairs to change. I made coffee for all of us. Then you and I sat at the table, surreptitiously holding hands, drinking coffee, waiting for Greg and Judy to arrive for our confession. I told you then in detail how I wanted to get off the bus in Westendorf.

"To stay behind with you," I said.

"I remember that," you admit. "I wanted you to."

"What would we have done if I had?"

"I don't know," you said. "It sure would have made things easier."

"That's for sure," I said.

Now Judy's voice, "Tommy? You really look like shit and you're drifting away again. What's going on?" She is aware something important is up.

"We have to talk," I say.

"You and me?"

"All of us."

"Before breakfast?" asks Greg.

"Before breakfast," I reply.

Judy and Greg take seats at the table. They seem impatient with this moment. Judy sighs. Greg wants breakfast. Another awkward quarrel about me wanting to own this lodge, they suspect.

"There's another skeleton in the family closet," I begin.

And as concisely as possible, with as little hyperbole as we can manage, you and I tell Greg and Judy that we met in Westendorf more than twenty years ago, not knowing we had Judy in common, not guessing after we fell in love that we would see one another again. We spill it all, how we met, how we admitted we were attached to other people, how, despite this, we fell in love anyway. We tell how we agreed it was best to part as strangers, how shocking it was to meet in Rosedale just before my wedding, to discover life was going to put in place the mechanism which would force us to see one another from time to time as brother and sister-in-law.

We tell it all, without shame, without pride. And Greg and Judy sit there the way people do when they encounter news that is too fantastic to be immediately absorbed: bemused, stupidly, refusing to grasp what they are actually being told. There is a long silence when you and I finish telling our story. I actually have time to get up and offer everyone more coffee while Greg and Judy take the time they need to grasp the implications of what they've been told.

"I don't get it," Greg says at last. "What are you telling us?"

"Your wife and my husband," Judy explains with menacing calm, "had a love affair in Austria before they married us."

"Oh," says Greg, sounding strangely relieved. "That's what I thought they were saying."

"If you can believe it," Judy adds.

"It's true," I say. "I didn't know Jan was your sister. She didn't know I was seeing you, Jude, her sister."

Judy glances at you. "I didn't even know you'd gone skiing in Europe. You've never mentioned it. You didn't mention it back then."

"Of course not," you reply, fatigue in your voice. "At first it just didn't come up. It was an incredible coincidence that I would meet Tom in Europe. After I realized who he was, well I thought it best to skip it."

I can feel Judy trying to control her anger. I suspect, soon, she will give in to it. "And so, when you met at Mother's dinner just before our wedding, you and Tommy already knew one another?"

"Yes," you admit.

"Intimately," adds Judy.

"Yes," I reply.

"Gee, that meeting must have been difficult for you."

"Yes," I say again, ignoring my wife's sarcasm.

"So," says Judy, turning her attention to Greg. "On top of everything else this weekend—our mother's affair, this stupid, fucking lodge as Tommy's stupid, fucking, authentic destination—you and I, Greg, are now being told our spouses have fucked one another more than twenty years ago!"

"Judy . . . ."

"Well that's it, isn't it?"

Neither you nor I reply.

"Jesus," Judy says. "What's going on this weekend? Truth serum in the food? Sodium pentothal in the wine? Can't anyone here this weekend keep a fucking secret?"

"Secrets are a heavy burden, Jude," I say.

"Are they? What about the truth? Maybe you've just transferred the burden onto Greg and me."

Out of the corner of my eye, I can see Greg nodding vaguely. I have the curious sensation he isn't quite certain what he's agreeing with exactly.

"Fuck," Judy is saying. "I'm dealing with idiots."

"I don't get it," Greg says at last.

"What don't you get, Greg?" you say.

"Why are you two suddenly telling us this? What does this have to do with us now?" He glances at Judy. "Judy, I think, after twenty years, you and I can live with this. It's not like it was just last night. Or does this have something to do with the lodge?"

"We were coming to that," I say, relieved that I can ignore his remark about last night. "Jan and I are going to buy this property from Judy. We're going to buy the other half. We just wanted you two to know why."

"You and Jan," says Greg, still failing to understand.

"Yes."

"Buying this place?"

"Yes."

"I still don't see the connection," he begins. Then, at last, it dawns on him. "Wait a minute! You mean you and Jan are going to buy this place together? Run it together?"

"No," I say, "not together. For now, I'm going to run it on my and Jan's behalf."

If there are galaxies anywhere in this universe where silence is all there is, where silence is as large as space itself, I am aware we have entered one. The silence here among us now is so severe, a napkin dropped to the floor would explode like dynamite.

No one breathes for a very long time. A stolen breath would represent cacophony.

"What?" says Greg.

"What?" says Judy.

"I'm going to open this place as a business," I say

"Like fuck you are," says Judy, slamming her hand down on the table.

I am very calm with her. I gaze at her a moment. "Yes, Judy. Jan and I discussed it last night. It's what we want to do. It's what we *have* to do."

She flicks her gaze to her sister, fury in her eyes. "Jan, tell me my fucking husband has lost his mind."

You shake your head. "Tom's right. We both think it's what should be done."

"You traitorous, fucking bitch!"

And Judy rises from the table, knocking over her chair, then rushing out the door, opening it so violently it crashes against its hinges. I hear her receding footsteps as she hurries down the veranda steps.

"I'm not sure exactly why, but I feel I should punch your lights out, McNamara," Greg says then. But he can't muster up the anger his words require. Instead he sounds tired and bemused.

"I'm sorry, Greg," I say. "Jan and I know this is a bit of a shock."

He doesn't say anything to this. Instead he too gets up from the table. Calmly he throws on a jacket, remembering to take Judy's off its hook and fold it over his arm. Then he follows her out the door. Shortly, when the moment presents itself, I turn and glance out the window. I see my wife and your husband standing down on the dock, staring at their feet, talking, moving their toes, their hands in the pockets of their jackets where they are no doubt making fists.

I take your hand in mine and raise it to my lips. You bring my hand to your lips too and I remember that time at my home in Ottawa when you mysteriously kissed my hand. I understand now why you did it. We sit here a long time in silence amid the ruins from which, unfairly or not, you and I know we must emerge.

You decide, if I have time to get this place ready enough by Christmas, that by then, perhaps, you can come here during your school break to take some kind of next step—with us and with this place. It seems a long way into the future. Then again it's not at all like twenty years.

"I've got a lot to deal with," you say, "when I get back to Toronto with Greg. And my sister's going to need me, whether *she* thinks so or not.

"I know," I say. And I *do*. "I have to deal with Judy too, in a week or two, I guess."

AT MID-MORNING, I WAVE POLITELY when all of you depart in Greg's SUV. Only you, sweet Jan, wave back. All of this *will* take time, the way you said it will. Being sisters is not a casual thing. That's what will take the time. But I believe in you and me, sweet Jan. And I feel a stronger hope that in this place I will call The Crossroads, you and I can work out as the lovers I feel we were meant to be. Once Judy is over her anger and hurt. Once everyone has moved on.

Hours later, I've called my office from Temagami. I've called David Cruickshank and told him everything. He wants to see the place. And he knows I need a friend before I go back to Ottawa to deal with Judy.

Now I stand on the dock, thinking these thoughts, and turn

to look at our lodge, yours and mine, Jan. Crossroads. It's a few months into the future and there could be struggles ahead, but I stand here in the sunshine and cling to my unshakable hope. One thing I know for certain. Whatever comes up in my life, whatever needs to be said, I will be *caught* saying so. As far as I can see, when the truth is there and needs to escape, the best thing to do is open the gate to let it out.

ABOUT THE AUTHOR

Barry Grills is a former chair of The Writers' Union of Canada and the Book and Periodical Council. His short stories have appeared in various literary magazines and anthologies over the years, including Best Canadian Stories. His critically acclaimed memoir, *Every Wolf's Howl* won an Alberta Book Award for its publisher, Freehand Books. He is also the author of three musical biographies on the lives and careers of Anne Murray, Alanis Morissette and Celine Dion. His work on an updated version of Dion's life, co-authored with Jim Brown, was the source for a CBC television movie. He currently lives and works in North Bay, Ontario, Canada.